ALSO BY JOHN WILSON

Young Adult Fiction
Lost in Spain
Germania
The Alchemist's Dream
Where Soldiers Lie
Red Goodwin
Four Steps to Death
Battle Scars
Flags of War
Flames of the Tiger
Adrift in Time
Ghosts of James Bay
Across Frozen Seas
Weet Alone
Weet's Quest
Weet

Young Adult Non-fiction
Desperate Glory: The Story of WWI
Discovering the Arctic: The Story of John Rae
John Franklin: Traveller on Undiscovered Seas
Righting Wrongs: The Story of Norman Bethune
Norman Bethune: A Life of Passionate Conviction

Adult Non-Fiction
Ghost Mountains and Vanished Oceans:
North America from Birth to Middle Age (with Ron Clowes)

CRUSADE

The Heretic's Secret, Book I

John Wilson

KEY PORTER BOOKS

Library and Archives Canada Cataloguing in Publication

Wilson, John (John Alexander), 1951-
        Crusade / John Wilson.

(The heretic's secret ; bk. 1)
ISBN 978-1-55470-096-7

        1. Crusades—Juvenile fiction. I. Title. II. Series: Wilson, John
(John Alexander), 1951- . Heretic's secret ; bk. 1.

PS8595.I5834C78 2009   jC813'.54   C2009-902107-2

ONTARIO ARTS COUNCIL
CONSEIL DES ARTS DE L'ONTARIO

The publisher gratefully acknowledges the support of the Canada Council for the Arts and the Ontario Arts Council for its publishing program. We acknowledge the support of the Government of Ontario through the Ontario Media Development Corporation's Ontario Book Initiative.

We acknowledge the financial support of the Government of Canada through the Book Publishing Industry Development Program (BPIDP) for our publishing activities.

Key Porter Books Limited
Six Adelaide Street East, Tenth Floor
Toronto, Ontario
Canada M5C 1H6

www.keyporter.com

Map: Carl Pelletier for Polygone Studios
Text design: Sonya V. Thursby

Printed and bound in Canada

09 10 11 12 13 5 4 3 2 1

For all those who suffer
in the name of unproven beliefs.

*"Such are the heights of wickedness
to which men are driven by religion."*
—Lucretius, 99–55 BC

A Word from the Author

Lucretius knew what he was talking about. In the two thousand years since he lived, millions of people have died or suffered in religious wars—and there is still no shortage of hatred and fanaticism around the world today.

It is difficult, sitting comfortably in a chair reading a book, to understand what drives an individual to kill in the name of his or her God. How much more difficult is it to understand what motivates entire nations to go to war for their beliefs? Yet, historically, it is not an uncommon occurrence.

Eight hundred years ago, religion dominated most people's lives and guided their actions on a daily basis. People in the thirteenth century weren't scared of cancer or climate change. Instead, they worried about what would happen to their souls after they died. To them, the soul was as real as the body, and they were concerned with it in the same way we might be concerned about what would happen to our bodies after a car crash. The difference is that damage to our bodies lasts only until we can be fixed up in a hospital. Damage to the soul lasted for eternity.

To save an eternal soul, you were entitled to do almost anything to the temporary body. Monks whipped their backs to a bloody pulp to purify their souls. Anyone who put their own, or someone else's, soul in danger could be tortured in unspeakable ways, and then burned alive. The people who supported and took part in these punishments truly felt they were acting for the best.

The soul was so much more important than the body that anything was justifiable to save it, and many Christians fervently believed that it was their duty to go out into the world and forcibly convert non-Christians, or kill them in the process. Time and again, European kings and lords led armies into the Holy Land and to Al-Andalus—the part of what we now call Spain that was ruled by the Muslim Moors—to do battle with people who believed in a different God. The crusades were popular, and people—from kings and emperors to holy men and children—flocked to them. But not all crusades were fought in far away places.

In this strange world where belief was all important, thousands of people in Languedoc, a separate country in what is now the southwest corner of France, believed differently. They were Cathars—Christians whose beliefs did not match those of the Catholic Church. In the eyes of the Church, the Cathars were heretics, endangering their own souls and those of all to whom they preached. They had to be got rid of, even if it meant building human bonfires.

In 1208, Pope Innocent III called for a crusade against the heretics of Languedoc. In doing so, he triggered a brutal war, not in some far off corner of the heathen world, but in the heart of Christendom. It was called the Albigensian Crusade, and it resulted in tens of thousands of deaths and the destruction of a unique culture and language. The war lasted from 1209 to 1244, although the Inquisition's search for individual heretics lasted much longer. The last known Cathar—William Bélibaste—was burned at the stake in 1321 in the courtyard of the castle at Villerouge-Termenès, long after the crusaders had gone home. There is no evidence that any souls were saved.

List of Characters

Adam*	*One of John and Peter's friends.*
Adso*	*Soldier and John's friend.*
Albrecht*	*Expert in siege engines.*
Arnaud Aumery	*Abbot of the Cistercian Monastery of Citeaux and spiritual leader of the crusade.*
Beatrice of Albi*	*Cathar Perfect and John's teacher.*
Bertrand*	*Brigand leader.*
Dominic Guzman	*Travelling priest and preacher. Now known as St. Dominic, founder of the Dominicans and the formal Inquisition. The first nunnery he founded was a copy of a Cathar Perfect House.*
Eudes III	*Duke of Burgundy, Knight of the Crusade.*
Foulques	*Bishop of Toulouse.*
Herodotus	*Roman historian.*
Hervé de Donzy	*Count of Nevers, Knight of the Crusade.*
Innocent III	*Pope who called for the crusade against the Cathar heretics.*
Isabella*	*Friend of Peter and John in Toulouse.*
John*	*Boy who gets caught up in the war.*
Lucius*	*Ancient Roman author.*
Marie*	*One of John and Peter's friends.*

* denotes fictitious character

Mother Marie*   *Abbess of the Priory of St. Anne
                      in Toulouse. She taught John and
                      Peter to read and write.*

Oddo of Saxony*   *Mercenary soldier in the Crusader
                      army and leader of a band called the
                      Falcons.*

Origen   *Early church father whose ideas
                      were later rejected.*

Peter*   *John's childhood friend.*

Pierre of Castelnau   *Papal legate to Languedoc.*

Raymond of Toulouse   *Count of Languedoc and, before the
                      crusade, the equal in standing to the
                      King of France.*

Roger Trenceval   *Viscount of Carcassonne and Béziers.
                      Liege to Raymond of Toulouse.*

Stephen*   *Boy who grew up in Minerve.*

Simon de Montfort   *Landless lord who took over the
                      crusade in exchange for the lands
                      he could conquer. His youngest son,
                      also called Simon, is credited with
                      calling the first parliament in
                      England.*

Umar of Cordova*   *Half Moorish Cathar Perfect.*

William of Arles*   *Troubadour*

William Bélibaste   *The last known Cathar Perfect.*

William of Minerve   *Lord of Minerve.*

CRUSADE

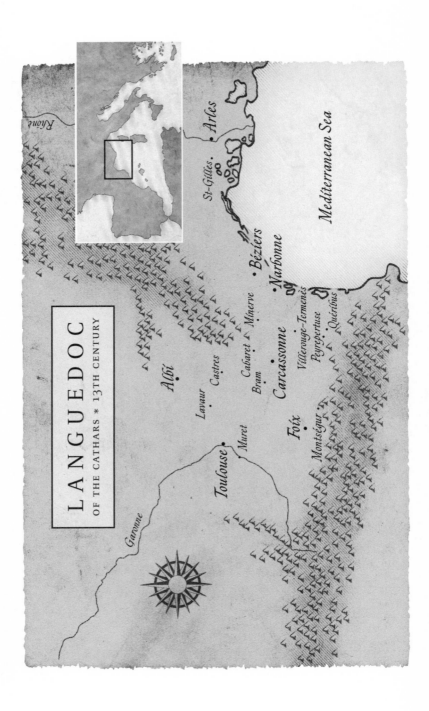

Fire

The Last Heretic

Villerouge-Termenès

AUGUST 24, 1321

"You will be the last to die," the black-clad priest said almost gleefully. "There are no more. Once you are dust, this land will be free from your foul heresy."

William Bélibaste forced his shattered mouth into a parody of a smile. "What you say, Master Inquisitor, may be true," he slurred, "but it has taken all the might of the Catholic Church more than one hundred years to kill a few thousand of us. Does that not show you the power of our ideas? When you examine your mind, is there not a tiny piece that says, 'Perhaps they were right?'"

The priest shook his head. "A hundred years is but a blink in God's eternity."

"And the momentary pain I face is nothing compared to the paradise to which I go. It is you I pity, facing endless repetitions of an ignorant life in the cesspit of this material world."

"We shall see what your pity is worth on the bonfire," the priest responded, angrily pushing Bélibaste forward through the archway into the bright courtyard of the castle at Villerouge-Termenès.

Bélibaste squinted in the sharp light, closed his eyes and

raised his head to feel the sun's warmth on his face. He drew in a deep draft of air and caught a faint smell of lavender. It reminded him of his childhood, tending his father's flock of sheep among the limestone hills around his village. They had been happy days, before a life of loneliness, running and hiding. But he was content now, too.

If William had one regret, it was that he had not lived one hundred and fifteen years ago, before the armoured knights of the crusade and their compassionless inquisitor priests had thundered down on his people. It was difficult to imagine those wonderful days when men and women of the Elect could walk openly, meet and minister to their congregations; when they were welcomed everywhere, from the simplest village hearth to the court of the most powerful lord. It must have been as close as this evil, corrupt world had ever come to paradise. But it was a vanished world. The priest was right: William Bélibaste was the last of the Elect.

A push in the small of his back brought William back to the present. He opened his eyes to see the stake in front of him, surrounded by neatly tied bundles of dry logs, straw and vine cuttings. To one side, a hooded executioner stood holding a burning torch.

William stumbled on the rough cobbles, not through fear, but because his crushed left foot was twisted in at an awkward angle. Every hobbling step sent needles of pain shooting up his leg, but he would not give the priest or the watching crowd the satisfaction of showing it. He wore a coarse woollen tunic that stretched from his neck to his ankles and hid the livid scars where red-hot irons had seared his flesh. His arms were tied behind his back, but there was no need—both his shoulders had been so seriously dislocated that, even had his arms been free, he would not have had the strength to lift a spoon and feed himself. William also suspected that several of his fingers were broken.

As William approached the pyre, he was intrigued to see that the builders had thoughtfully shaped the bundles of sticks into a short staircase up to the stake.

"Do you renounce Satan and all his ways?" the priest intoned.

"Of course I do," William said, through his broken teeth. "I renounce Satan and all this worldly filth. And I renounce Satan's minion in Rome—the Pope and his corrupt Church."

A gasp ran through the watching crowd.

"So you admit, as you face an eternity of the torments of hell, that you are a Cathar Perfect, and that you have led others into this abominable heresy?"

"You call us 'Cathars' and the Elect 'Perfects', but to ourselves we are simply Good Men and Good Women, struggling to bring light into this darkness."

William found strength as he spoke. He forced himself to stand taller and look his inquisitor in the eye. "Together, we are Good Christians, preserving the old ways and offering hope. Your degenerate Church is putrid at the heart. It offers nothing but suffering and damnation."

William raised his gaze to address the men and women gathered behind his questioner. "You think you eat the body of Christ at Communion? How big was this Christ that his body can feed so many?"

The crowd shifted uncomfortably, but William heard a choked laugh and saw a few heads nod in agreement.

"You bow and scrape to priests and cardinals who drown in the filth of the material world. How can they lead you to anything but depravity? You worship idols and—"

"Enough!" The inquisitor's voice cut William off. "Enough of this evil! The Holy Inquisition is done with this verminous devil. I place him in the hands of the secular authorities to do with as they see fit."

The Mayor of Villerouge-Termenès stepped forward nervously. He would rather not do this, but he had no choice. The Inquisition could investigate, but it could not condemn. Although that decision was left to the secular authorities, it would be a brave man who refused to do the Inquisition's bidding.

"For the crimes of heresy, denying the divinity of Christ, consorting with devils and seducing others into your evil ways, I sentence you, William Bélibaste, to death by burning."

Two men stepped forward and half led, half carried William up the pyre to the stake. There they bound him around the waist and chest so that he remained upright. The men hurried down, leaving William alone.

"I shall pray for your misguided soul," the inquisitor intoned.

"And I yours," William replied.

The mayor nodded to the executioner, who walked around the pyre, thrusting his torch in among the dry kindling. Tiny yellow flames grasped eagerly at the straw and grew. They turned orange as they began to eat at the sticks.

William shivered. He began to recite the only prayer the Elect recognized.

Our Father Who art in Heaven,

The flames gathered strength and moved toward William's feet.

Hallowed be Thy name.

His feet were burning, the skin blistering, the pain shooting up his legs.

Thy kingdom come,

The inquisitor's mouth was moving in prayer, but William heard only his own voice and the crackling of the hungry flames.

thy will be done on earth as it is in Heaven.

The pain moved higher as his robe burned. Searing, blinding pain.

Give us this day our supplementary bread,

William concentrated with all his might. The pain was transitory. It would pass. It *would* pass.

and remit our debts as we forgive our debtors.

William knew what he had to do. It had been drummed into every member of the Elect. He must wait and endure the agony as long as possible. And then, when the pain became too great, he had to breathe in the fire as deeply as he could. That would hasten the end.

And keep us from temptation

The bright flames raced hungrily up William's body.

and free us from evil.

His hair was alight.

Thine is the kingdom,

He closed his eyes and threw his head back.

the power and glory

Wait! he told himself.
William's heart was racing.
Wait!
He had stopped sweating and felt oddly cold.
Wait!
The agony engulfed him.

for ever and ever.

Wait!

Amen.

William thrust his head forward into the flames and drew them into his body with a single deep breath. The shock stopped his heart and he slumped forward. The charred ropes holding him upright gave way and his body collapsed into the roaring heart of the fire. The crusaders and the Inquisition had won—the last of the Elect was dead.

PART ONE
Old Friends

Debate
Toulouse
AUGUST 15, 1206

"That was as much fun as watching a group of travelling players," John said with a laugh. "Bishop Foulques is such a fool, it's not surprising that the Cathars won."

John and Peter stood in the square in front of the imposing bulk of St. Sernin Cathedral in Toulouse. It was August 15, the Feast of the Assumption of the Virgin Mary, the day when Christ's mother ascended, body and soul, into heaven, and there was a party atmosphere in the air. It had been a hot day, and although the sun had already dipped behind the surrounding buildings, heat still radiated uncomfortably from the uneven cobbles underfoot. People stood in small knots, animatedly discussing the debate that had just finished in the cathedral. Pairs of black-robed Cathar Perfects, both men and women, strolled through the crowds, stopping to talk to those who hailed them.

"The point is not to have fun," Peter replied, staring seriously at the cathedral, "and it's not a question of winning or losing. Only God can win."

John looked hard at his friend. Lately, it had become almost impossible to have a light-hearted conversation with him. Peter took everything John said so seriously, and he seemed to have suddenly developed a certainty that he knew better than John what God wanted.

John shrugged. He wasn't going to let Peter's new-found pomposity spoil his fun on his favourite feast day. "All right," John conceded, "the debate was a serious matter, but even you must admit that the Cathars were a lot more popular with the audience."

"Popularity is fleeting. Souls are eternal, and it is *their* well-being that the Church must address."

"Of course the Church must look after our souls," said John, stifling a sigh of frustration, "but must it not also win over the mass of the people to convince them that it *can* save their souls?"

"You think too much of what happens in this world, John." Peter turned and looked gravely at his friend. "It's the next world that's important. Look at all the time you spend on your drawing. Where does it get you?"

"What's wrong with my drawing?" John asked indignantly.

"Art is only important as a way to glorify God," Peter said, his voice taking on a lecturing tone. "Look at the magnificent golden paintings of the saints in the cathedral."

"But they're not real! They have no depth, no life." John could feel himself growing angry. It was one thing to disagree over the debate, quite another for Peter to criticize the thing John loved more than anything. Peter opened his mouth to object, but John held up his hand and continued. "I agree that art in the great cathedrals should glorify God, but why can't that be done with realistic paintings?"

"Because God does not wish it," Peter said, his eyes

gleaming with conviction. "He does not want us to dwell on this world, but to give our minds over to contemplation of the next."

John shook his head in annoyance.

"Look at all the hours you have wasted trying to draw things," Peter went on, oblivious to the irritation he was causing. "You've learned nothing! Your sketches of animals, people and buildings are just the same as they were when you began years ago. And why? Because God does not wish you to draw these things. If you want to be an artist, then accept the way things are done and work to glorify God."

John took a deep breath. Losing his temper wasn't going to help, and he did want Peter to grasp what was important to him about his drawing. "I don't understand why God does not wish me to draw more realistically. Surely I can glorify Him that way, too! Imagine—paintings that showed the Crucifixion, the Annunciation, or the lives of the saints realistically, as they actually were. Would that not amaze people and draw them even closer to God?"

"It's the same as these Cathars trying to make themselves popular with the people," Peter said, ignoring the rising excitement in John's voice. "Only God matters and, obviously, He does not want you, or anyone else, to draw the way you imagine must be possible."

"Then why did God give us the power to think and the free will to try new things?" John asked, struggling to make Peter see. "Surely it is partly to find new and better ways to glorify Him. Look at the cathedral." John waved his hand to indicate the west front of St. Sernin. The wall that loomed over the square was plain and unornamented except for a round window and two doors, deeply set into the thick walls. "It looks like a fortress. The walls are plain and must be the thickness of a man lying down."

"The inside is painted to glorify God," Peter objected.

"Exactly," John agreed, "and you can barely see the art because the windows are so small."

"You know it has to be that way," Peter said. "The walls must be thick to support the roof and to put in more windows would weaken the walls. Do you want the roof to crash down on our heads as we pray?"

"Of course not," John said, forcing himself to stay calm and develop his argument, "but I hear stories of churches that are being built to the north—churches where impossibly thin columns soar upward with nothing more substantial between them than coloured glass. Surely God must be happier with all His light flooding in to illuminate the paintings that glorify Him?"

"Indeed," Peter said in a puzzled tone, "but what does any of this have to do with your scribbling?"

"Things change," John explained patiently. "One day, someone, somewhere, decided that the old way of building churches wasn't good enough. He thought and worked and planned until he came up with this new way of building churches and glorifying God. A way that allowed more light in to illuminate the paintings inside. That's exactly what I want to do—find a new way of doing things, a better way to draw and paint."

The two boys fell silent. John wondered how they had grown so far apart. For thirteen years, they had been as inseparable as twins. Neither had known his parents and both had been abandoned as infants, only weeks apart, on the steps of the Priory of St. Anne. Whether their parents had died in one of the typhus epidemics that regularly swept through the overcrowded streets of St. Cyprian, beneath the towering walls of Toulouse, or whether they had given their child up because it was simply one mouth too many to feed, no one knew.

The boys had grown up together, playing, studying and dreaming, under the care of the old abbess, Mother Marie. She had taken to the pair and decided to teach them both the rudiments of reading and writing in hopes that they might seek a life of devotion in the church. It had worked well enough with Peter—who saw knowledge only as a tool, a way to advance in the world—but with John, her teaching had unexpected results.

The more John learned, the more he wanted to learn. He craved knowledge for its own sake. For him, knowledge brought one closer to truth and, therefore, to God. John didn't think the Church should limit knowledge. It should be available to everyone.

In the days when the friends could discuss things without annoying each other, John had been fond of quoting Peter Abelard, who had written that doubting was good because it encouraged enquiry and enquiry led to truth. Peter would counter with Anselm of Canterbury, who said that belief was more important than doubting because only through belief could someone understand. They had laughed about it and joked that one day Peter would be Pope in Rome, and John would be his advisor on all matters complex and arcane. But now, with Peter's growing certainty that he knew God's wishes, John doubted if his friend would need any advisors at all.

"If God is stopping me from learning how to draw realistically," John said, breaking the silence, "why didn't He also give the bishop and the priest arguments this afternoon that would have convinced the people? Then the Cathar Perfects would have been defeated, and everyone would now be standing out here glorifying God."

"I don't know," Peter said with a frown. "God does, sometimes, work in mysterious ways. Perhaps he is testing us. Perhaps—"

The boys' discussion was interrupted by a commotion at the cathedral doors—the Church delegation was leaving. They were led by Foulques, bishop of Toulouse, surrounded by fawning priests and lay brothers. Foulques was a fat man and beads of sweat glistened on his plump cheeks and forehead in the late afternoon heat. His large body was completely covered in sumptuous robes, richly embroidered with silver and gold thread. His jewel-encrusted mitre sparkled in the dying light.

As Foulques appeared on the steps, a ragged cheer rose from a crowd of rough-looking men standing to one side. A few of them were dressed in dirty white robes with black crosses crudely drawn on the front. Foulques acknowledged them with a half smile and a nod.

"That must be one of God's more mysterious ways," John said, looking at the men. "For a bishop of the Church to control a bunch of thugs who wander the streets robbing and beating up whom they choose—and call them Angels— is a disgrace."

"His intention, to control heresy, is commendable," Peter said, "but I agree his lack of control over them *is* a disgrace."

Foulques had been appalling in the debate. The fat man had blustered mightily all afternoon, but had not said anything intelligent. He'd misunderstood what the quieter, thoughtful Cathars had said and had had no reply to their reasoned arguments.

Much more effective had been the short, scrawny, olive-skinned priest who stood on the cathedral steps in Foulques's shadow. He was dressed, like the Perfects, in a simple black robe that was travel-worn and stained. He was bare-headed, wore practical walking sandals, and held a knotted staff in his left hand. He was surrounded by a small group of similarly dressed priests.

The man's name was Dominic Guzman and, in a voice heavily accented with his native Castillian, he had held his own against the Perfects. Foulques' rants were always made against a murmur of background conversation, but when Guzman spoke, silence fell over the audience. He had argued for a return to the uncomplicated life of the early Church and for orders of itinerant priests who would own nothing and wander the land, as he did, preaching to the people.

It was similar to what the Perfects did, and John could see that the idea resonated with the people much more strongly than Foulques's overblown bluster and rich life.

The debate, like the many others that were being held all over Languedoc these days, had been inconclusive. Neither side had convinced the other of its point of view. In the end, though, John knew that the Catholic Church would view it as a defeat. It was they, after all, who were trying to eradicate the Cathar religion. The Perfects were happy to merely carry on the way they always had.

Foulques waved to the crowd, which largely ignored him, and swept down the steps toward his ornate litter as Dominic Guzman quietly disappeared into the gathering gloom of the narrow streets surrounding the cathedral.

John noticed that Peter's eyes had been following Guzman, not Foulques.

"He's quite an extraordinary man," John said. "It must be very hard to live the life of itinerant poverty that he is sworn to. And he has a power when he speaks that makes people listen."

Peter absently nodded agreement.

"In fact," John continued, "Guzman lives his life much like the Cathar Perfects."

Peter turned to John, ready to argue, but stopped when he saw his friend's mischievous smile.

"You say these things just to annoy me," he said, his expression softening.

"I do," John admitted. "There's so much we don't know in this world—how can we take it too seriously? I know you don't think fun is important in God's grand scheme of things, but let's not argue about it. We've been friends all our lives. Let's not lose that just because we have different ideas."

"You're right," Peter said with a weak smile. "Our friendship's important to me, too."

"Good," John said, clapping his friend on the back. "Now let's go over to the Château Narbonnaise. Count Raymond and Countess Eleanor have invited the troubadour from

Arles to perform tonight in the square."

Peter didn't answer right away, and John could see the doubt written on his face. Peter didn't like troubadours. He thought their love songs frivolous, and the jokes they sometimes made about the Church annoyed him. But John didn't want to end the evening with their argument still fresh in their minds.

"It will be one of the last times we will all be together," John encouraged. "Adam leaves in a few days for the court at Foix and Marie is betrothed to that dolt down in Carcassonne. We are all at an age when the world beckons and life will allow few enough opportunities to continue the carefree days of this summer."

Peter looked uncertain.

"And Isabella will be there," John added, teasingly. "You know she never misses a troubadour."

A smile flashed across Peter's face, and John knew that his words had hit their mark. Isabella was one of Countess Eleanor's attendants. She was the same age as the boys and often spent time with them and their friends, singing or playing games. Like Dominic Guzman, she was from across the mountains and had the dark eyes and olive skin of her people. Peter was totally smitten. Whenever the crowd of friends got together, Peter gravitated toward Isabella and engaged her in conversation. He always tried to partner her in the board games they played.

John thought it a very odd match. Isabella was high-spirited—always laughing at some joke or clever song or listening with interest to the stories John told—and she was very beautiful, with a high forehead and long dark hair that she wore in elaborate styles or simply tumbling down over her shoulders.

In contrast, Peter was serious and often missed the point of jokes—and no one had ever called him handsome. He was tall and gangly, like a tree that has sprouted too fast, all angles and sharp corners. His face was long and thin and his pale skin seemed to be drawn too tightly over his skull; his high cheekbones made his eyes appear deep-set and worried. John used to tease his friend that God had run out of flesh and bone when he made Peter and had to fall back on sticks and string. But whatever the reason, John was pleased at the feelings his friend had for Isabella. Perhaps her sense of humour and exuberance might act as a balance against Peter's increasing religious certainty.

The mention of Isabella had the desired effect. "All right," Peter said, "I'll come with you, but I'm not going to stay late."

John laughed at his friend's transparency as they set off through the darkening streets.

The huge square was a riot of sights, sounds and smells. Everyone seemed to be dressed in their brightest clothes, and colourful banners almost covered the red brick walls of the Château Narbonnaise, where Count Raymond and Eleanor lived and held court. Anyone who thought they could make a few sous from the feast-day crowds was there. Jugglers and acrobats performed wherever there was a foot or two of empty space; vendors with trays of food, trinkets and rolls of garish cloth worked the crowd, screaming the benefits of their wares to anyone who would listen; and fortune tellers, beggars and musicians struggled mightily to make themselves heard over the background noise. In one corner, a ragged, mangy bear danced lethargically on the end of a chain while its owner cracked a short whip and small boys darted as close as they dared to taunt it.

Near the centre of the square, three entire pigs—a feast-day gift to the people from Count Raymond—roasted on spits, their fat dripping and sizzling onto the wide bed of deep-red glowing coals beneath. A large, sweating man in a bloodstained leather apron busily carved slices of meat and passed them out to the crowd. A nearby table groaned under the weight of a pile of spiced loaves in a bewildering variety of shapes and colours. John breathed deeply. The delicious smell of roast pig and freshly baked bread filled the air, almost covering the pungent odour of hundreds of sweating, unwashed people.

"Come on," John said, his mouth watering, "let's get something to eat."

Pushing through the seething mass of humanity, John led the way to the roasting pit and accepted a large, greasy slice of meat and a hunk of green parsley loaf. Barely waiting for the meat to cool and oblivious to the fat running down his wrists and dripping into his clothes, John tore off chunks with relish as he headed out to the less busy fringes of the crowd. Working more neatly and slowly, Peter followed him.

John had almost finished his meat and bread, and was looking around for some beer or watered wine to wash them down, when a cheer from the crowd made him turn. The troubadour and his musicians were strolling out onto the wide platform at the top of the steps leading up to the doors of the château. On the flag-draped balcony above the musicians, Count Raymond and Countess Eleanor, dressed in all their finery, stood smiling amid their almost equally colourful courtiers.

William of Arles, a short, skinny, middle-aged man with a mop of straggly light-brown hair, was dressed in a bright, multicoloured tunic that sported wide cuffs and ended below his knees in a ragged fringe. He wore blue boots of soft leather with tiny golden bells sewn around the tops. Other bells, on the edges of his tunic, tinkled lightly as he moved to the centre of the platform. He carried a tambourine.

Four musicians milled around the troubadour, dressed identically in bright green tunics and caps with flaps that hung down over their ears. One played a flute, one the bagpipes, one the tabor drum and the last turned the handle of a hurdy-gurdy.

"Welcome my lord and lady," William said, bowing to the group on the balcony. Raymond acknowledged him with a nod. "And to you, good folk." The troubadour turned to the crowd, who responded with an enthusiastic shout. "I trust that you are in a mood to be entertained." Another shout. "And I hope my songs and stories will be worthy of your time."

The troubadour's voice was high-pitched and carried well over the hubbub of the crowd. "I am William of Arles, here with my companions to transport you on this fine summer's eve with tales of knights and ladies, war and peace, love and death. And"—William leaned forward conspiratorially and jerked his thumb over his shoulder toward Count Raymond on his balcony—"the foibles of the high and mighty." Laughter rolled around the square. "But first," William stood straight and banged the tambourine against his thigh, "I will sing of the troubadours."

The musicians set to work and William began to sing, all the while dancing lightly from foot to foot:

"I sing of the glorious troubadours
And the wonderful styles they espouse.
There's Roger of Bram
A most wonderful man—"

One of the musicians to William's left interrupted with

"Like an oyster dried out in the sun."

As the crowd laughed, William turned theatrically and glared at his companion, who affected to look as innocent as possible.

William continued:

"There's Bernard of Nime
Of most hearty esteem—"

Again the musician interrupted:

"With a voice like a young piglet's squeal."

William glared once more. And so it went on, William introducing every well-known troubadour of the day, only to be interrupted by a rude comment from the musician. The crowd was delighted at the insults and, during one of William's glaring pauses, someone shouted, "What of William of Arles?"

William looked at the crowd. "I see you have impeccable taste," he said, smiling and giving a mock bow.

"This William of Arles.
The master of all—"

He stopped and stared pointedly at the troublesome musician who stayed silent this time and worked extremely hard at looking totally innocent. William continued:

"He plays with such skill,
That the valley and hill,
Both resound with the sound of his music.
His verse is so sharp,
When accompanied by harp,
That his listeners are held in a thrall.
His voice, I've heard tell
Is as clear as a bell—"

The musician jumped forward:

"Like a frog that is trapped in a well."

The crowd roared its approval as William chased the

musician around the courtyard, brandishing his tambourine.

"Look," Peter said, grasping John's arm and interrupting his laughter. "There's Isabella and the others. Let's join them."

John and Peter worked their way through the crowd until they joined their friends on the steps in front of a small church on the opposite side of the square. As the pair approached, Isabella looked up, smiled broadly at John and pushed the boy beside her over to make space. John smiled back, thinking as he did so that someone as beautiful as Isabella should be dressed in finery and sitting beside some great lord in a palace instead of being a handmaid who hung around with the likes of him and his friends.

John stepped aside to let Peter take the seat. He thought he saw a flash of disappointment cross Isabella's features before Adam, on the top step, shouted to him, "John, come and tell us of the debate. Did Foulques make a fool of himself?"

"He did," John said as squeezed in beside the others, "and he had a gang of his Angels with him."

"Those thugs," Adam said. "Raymond should do something about them."

"He should," John agreed, "but for all his corruption, Foulques is a powerful man. He manages to keep in with the Pope. There are many Cathars in Toulouse. Raymond has to be careful."

"I suppose, but we're a long way from Rome. Does the Pope really care what happens here?"

"He sends enough priests and legates to debate with the Cathars," John said.

"But that's just words," Adam said with a frown. "He'd never actually do anything."

"You're probably right," John said. He was tired of talking about debates and Popes. He just wanted to eat, drink and enjoy the evening. He looked down. Isabella, her expression very serious, was talking earnestly to an unhappy Peter. John wondered what was going on.

Across the square, William of Arles and the musicians were launching into a spirited rendition of the epic "Song of Roland and the Battle of Ronceval."

"Charlemagne, our lord and sovereign,
Full seven years hath sojourned in Andalus,
Conquered the land, and won the western main,
Now no fortress against him doth remain,
No city walls are left for him to gain."

John was getting drawn into the troubadour's tale when he felt Adam fidgeting beside him. He turned his head and noticed his friend staring down at Peter. John followed Adam's gaze, half expecting to see Peter and Isabella in the midst of an argument. Instead, he saw Peter twisted round and staring up at them, his mouth open, his face pale and his eyes wide in horror.

"What's the matter?" John asked, suddenly alarmed.

Peter ignored his friend and continued to stare. Slowly he raised his arm and pointed a skinny, shaking finger at a spot above John's head. "Look," he managed to croak out.

John spun round, but there was nothing behind him except the doors of the church and a few people watching the entertainment.

"What is it, Peter?" he asked, turning back.

"Don't you see them?" Peter gasped. "One stands behind each of you."

They all glanced nervously over their shoulders.

"There's no one there," John said, as calmly as he could.

"It is Death that stands behind you all," Peter said. "Each wears a cloak of grave clothes and carries a scythe and an hourglass. Can't you see them?"

John shook his head.

"See! They remove their cowls—skulls, grinning—and they look at me. What does it mean? Am I to die this hour?" Peter shivered violently. "I am so cold."

John leaned forward to comfort his friend, but Peter drew back and turned to Isabella.

"Do *you* see them?" he asked.

Isabella shook her head, as puzzled as the rest.

"What do they mean?" Peter asked again. "If only I can see, it must be that ..." His voice tailed off. His lips were trembling and beads of sweat had broken out on his forehead. For the little group on the stairs, the sound of the crowd's chatter and the troubadour's singing seemed very far away.

Peter continued to stare at Isabella, whose worried frown had turned to a look of fear.

"What is happening, Peter?" she asked. "Why do you stare at me so?"

Peter slowly drew back, his hands clenching and unclenching convulsively.

"Your face ..." he began. "The flesh ..." Peter struggled to find words. "Rotting. The grave opens." His mouth hung open, and drool spilled down his chin.

"Oh, God! Oh, God!" he exclaimed at last, waving his

arms as if trying to push Isabella away. "The worms!"

With a sudden violent lurch, Peter attempted to stand, but his co-ordination was poor. He tumbled down the steps, bumping into the legs of a group of young men standing at the bottom. They all cursed, and one aimed a kick at Peter. The boy ignored them and, struggling to his feet, pushed his way through the crowd, heedless of the curses that accompanied him.

Peter's progress across the square was easy to follow thanks to the disruption it caused. Eventually, even the troubadour and his musicians noticed, but they were professionals and used to disturbances in their audience.

John stood up and glanced at Isabella. Stunned, she stared up at John, her eyes wide and questioning. A desire to go and comfort her swept over John, but he pushed it back. His friend needed him more.

John followed Peter to the far side of the square, where he sat on the bottom step of the Château Narbonnaise, to the right of the musicians, arms wrapped around his knees. He rocked rhythmically back and forth, and low moans accompanied his movements. John sat beside his friend and placed an arm around his shoulder.

For a long time the boys sat in silence, letting the song of Roland's final battle wash over them.

> "Marvellous is the battle in its speed,
> The Franks there strike with vigour and with heat,
> Cutting through wrists and ribs and chines indeed,
> Through garments to the lively flesh beneath;
> On the green grass the clear blood runs in streams."

Eventually, Peter stopped his rocking and calmed down.
"What happened?" John asked.

"I saw Death." Peter lifted his pale face to look at John.
"I am to die. He was a hideous skeleton and stood behind
each of you!"

"That doesn't mean that *you* are to die," John said, trying
to comfort his frightened friend. "It simply means we will
all die eventually."

"Yes," Peter replied. "Death stands behind us all, and
eternal suffering awaits our immortal souls. We play and
frolic without a care, but we are all damned."

John could not have disagreed more with Peter's grim view
of the world, but he kept silent. It was not the time to argue.

"But then I looked on Isabella." A violent shudder
passed through Peter's body. With a great effort, he went
on. "She's so beautiful! I suppose I hoped her beauty would
chase away my visions."

"What did you see?" John encouraged, gently.

"It worked! I looked at her face—her smooth skin, high
forehead, that wonderful half smile she always wears, as if
there is some joke we cannot understand—and I felt calmer.
She is the most beautiful thing I have ever seen, a true
angel. But then it happened."

Peter took a deep breath and continued. "Her face began
to change. The glowing, smooth skin became grey and pocked
with rot, the hair lank and the flesh sagging. Before my eyes,
the beautiful creature of my dreams decayed—the flesh fell
from her, bones thrust through her skin and maggots and
grave worms crawled from her blank eye sockets and lipless
mouth. She faced me—a corpse from the grave—as she

would be on the Day of Judgment."

Peter looked down, and John saw tears on his cheeks. He tightened his grip on his friend's shoulder. He didn't know what to say. He'd heard of hermits and priests having visions, and he knew the stories of St. Anthony's temptations, but he'd never had a vision himself, nor witnessed a person having one. The power of what Peter had seen, or thought he'd seen, was frightening.

Gradually, John became aware of a shadow above him. Half expecting to see the cowled figure of Death, he looked up. William of Arles had moved along the steps until he stood looking down at John and Peter. He was still singing, but the "Song of Roland" was drawing to a close.

"The Count Roland, beneath a pine he sits,
Turning his eyes toward Andalus, he begins
Remembering so many lands where he went conquering.
And Charlemagne, his lord who nourished him.
He cannot help but weep and sigh at this.
He owns his faults, and God's forgiveness bids.
Over his arm his head bows down and slips,
He joins his hands: and so is life finish'd.
Roland is dead; his soul to heav'n God bare."

With a final stare in John's direction, the troubadour danced away.

Peter sniffed loudly and looked up. "I know what I must do," he announced.

"What?"

"I must give myself to God." Peter grabbed John's tunic

and stared into his eyes. His expression was almost pleading. "I see it now. We have a choice: transient earthly pleasure or eternal heavenly bliss. Earthly pleasure is easy and seductive"—for a moment, Peter looked uncertain, then his expression hardened—"but eternal bliss must be our goal. I shall become a monk this very night."

John had often thought that Peter might enter the Church, and the time was certainly coming for all of them to make decisions about how they would find their way in life, but the abruptness of his friend's pronouncement, and the frightening way it had come about, shocked John.

Peter made a move to stand, but John held him down.

"A monk? Now? Is there no middle way? Your vision, or whatever it was, is over! Come back to our friends. They'll support you. The evening's young. We'll play some games and tell jokes. A nice evening of fun and a good night's rest, and these strange occurrences will seem different in the morning."

"No!" Peter tore himself from John's grasp. "You don't understand! Death was telling me there is little time. I must go and pray."

Looking about wildly, Peter rose and stumbled up the steps onto the platform where William was finishing his song. Oblivious to the gestures of the musicians or the shouts of the crowd, Peter crossed the stage and disappeared into the darkness at the edge of the square. John sat and watched him go. He thought of following his friend, but had no idea what he would say.

"Your friend looked distressed." John looked around to see William of Arles beside him. The public performance was over now and the musicians were moving toward the château, where they were to perform later at Count Raymond's dinner.

"He is," John said. "He has had disturbing visions."

"Tell me," the troubadour asked, gathering his multi-coloured tunic and sitting beside John.

"Why should you care?" John asked, slightly annoyed that the man saw fit to barge in on his private worries.

William laughed. "Because I am a troubadour and am interested in the world I wander through. I don't sing only of nonsense about my colleagues and of ancient battles. I pass on news as I travel and tell tales of our world, its troubles and its stupidities. We live in unsettled and dangerous times. Many have visions and, if you are willing to share, I would learn your friend's."

John thought for a while. It was an odd request from someone he didn't know, but John instinctively liked William and his thin open face and easy manner. Besides, maybe if he told someone about Peter's strange behaviour, it might make more sense.

William listened intently and, when John finished, nodded gravely. "I thank you for sharing your friend's distress," he said. "There is much that is strange and worrisome in our land today. God seems to be coming down to interfere in our daily lives more often of late." William stood to leave as he spoke, but John had questions of his own.

"So you will turn Peter's story into a song and sing it on your travels?"

"Perhaps. Or I may incorporate it into a larger tale of visions and troublesome occurrences."

"You're a storyteller as well as a troubadour?"

"They are the same," William said with a smile. "It is simply that some of my stories are put to music."

"You must see some fascinating places on your travels."

William tilted his head and regarded John carefully. "I see many wonders and I see many different places that are all the same. You wish to travel?"

"More than anything."

"It is a hard life. You forsake home and hearth for uncertainty and discomfort, not to mention the dangers of the road. Why would you seek that?"

"I wish to know everything."

William laughed loudly. "Youth has the arrogance of gods!"

John felt his cheeks burn with indignation. "You mock me!"

"No! No." William held up his hands in supplication. "I am sorry. I intend no mockery. Tell me, why do you wish to learn so much?"

"Because I cannot escape the idea that the world is more complicated than the priests would have us believe. I wish to see for myself, to read books, to talk to wise men and women but, mostly, I want to draw."

"To draw? That at least is easy. Simply enter St. Sernin and copy the paintings until you can do them as well as the original artist."

"You don't understand." John shook his head. "I wish to show the world as it is, not as the priests wish it to be. I want to be able to look at a drawing or painting and feel that I could walk into it and live the scene I see."

"That is a tall order, indeed."

"I know. And that is why I must travel, and learn every-thing."

This time, William did not laugh. Instead, he looked thoughtfully at the boy on the steps before him. John was beginning to squirm uncomfortably under the man's gaze when the troubadour finally spoke.

"What of your family? What do they think of your wish to desert them for learning?"

"I have no family. I was taken in at the Priory of St. Anne when I was but an infant. Mother Marie and the nuns are my only family, but I am of an age where I must leave and find my own way in the world."

"Very well," William said, after another pause. "You seem an intelligent boy and you did tell the tale of your friend with some talent and wit.

"My musicians and I leave from the Narbonnaise Gate tomorrow at cock crow. Think on what you wish tonight and, if you are there, you may accompany us and see how you like the itinerant life. It will be hard. I will make you work and, if you are troublesome or do not earn your keep, I will abandon you as easily as I would discard a worn out shoe. You will sleep rough in fields when we can find no benefactor and there will be times when you will wonder at your sanity for undertaking this life, but you will meet a multitude of interesting people, learn the art of storytelling and have ample opportunity in the places we stay to search out wisdom in men's minds or in their books. And perhaps, when you are a famous artist, you will do me the honour of portraying me with such skill that people will wonder at my immortality!"

John stared at William in shock. The troubadour's offer had taken him completely by surprise. Yes, he wanted to travel, but leaving tomorrow? Peter, he might already have lost, but saying such a sudden goodbye to all his friends— to Adam, Isabella and the others, to Mother Marie and the Priory where he grew up? To leave Toulouse, the only place he had ever known, and go off into an uncertain world he knew nothing of? It was frightening.

"It's so sudden," John said.

"It is," William replied, "but sometimes life's opportunities are thrust at us. Some seize them, some do not. Perhaps your friend's visions are his opportunity. In any case, think on what you wish and meet me tomorrow—or not. For now, I must keep Count Raymond waiting no longer than necessary. I bid you good night."

William turned and walked toward the château, leaving John in a turmoil. He felt as if he were at a crossroads: the decision he made tonight would determine the rest of his life. John stood and looked across the square at his friends. They were talking to each other and fooling around. Only Isabella returned his stare, her brown eyes still serious with the memory of Peter's visions. John was about to go over and tell her what had happened when two other boys whirled her up and into a wild dance. John didn't feel at all like dancing, but he hoped the music and the movement would cheer Isabella. With a shrug, he set off in search of Peter. Deep within himself, a tiny kernel of joy was forming. John knew that when the cock crowed tomorrow, he would be at the Narbonnaise Gate.

PART TWO
Gathering Storms

Reunion

St. Gilles

JANUARY 13, 1208

"Peter!" John shouted as he ran down the arched corridor of the cloister, his leather shoes slapping loudly on the stone tiles. It had taken John a minute to recognize his friend dressed in the brown, sleeveless habit of a Cistercian lay brother and with his hair shaved in a tonsure, but there was no mistaking the gangly frame.

John threw his arms around Peter. "What have you been doing? Why are you here?"

Gradually, John became aware that his embrace was not being returned. He looked up. Peter seemed embarrassed. Several other lay brothers and a monk, in his white habit and black apron, stared disapprovingly.

"I'm sorry. It's been two years since I've seen my friend," John explained to the monk, thinking back on that last night in Toulouse. "I didn't mean to create a scene. I was surprised to meet him here, that's all."

"It's all right," Peter said, recovering his composure and smiling. "You took me by surprise, too. What are *you* doing here at St. Gilles?"

"I'm here with Count Raymond's delegation," John said proudly.

"You work for the count?"

"Not really," John admitted. "His nephew, Roger Trence-val, the Viscount of Carcassonne, brought me here as a scribe because I can write and read some Latin."

"The same reason I am here," Peter said.

John glanced at the nearby monk. "You are with the papal legates?"

"I am here to do God's work," said Peter. "As I hope you are? This Cathar heresy that has taken root *must* be eradicated. Count Raymond is much too soft on the heretics. It has angered His Holiness. The legates are here to see that Raymond undertakes his duty as a Christian and excises this evil canker from his lands. There are to be no more half measures."

John frowned. He'd heard that Peter had joined the Church after his disturbing visions in Toulouse, but this person before him sounded unbearably pompous and self-important. And why this extreme, violent hatred of the Cathars? John had never paid them much attention. They'd always been around, a part of Languedoc life as long as anyone could remember. True, they believed differently from most, and the Church disliked them, but there had never been any violence other than the occasional shouting match at a debate.

But perhaps Peter had to say these things when the priest was listening. "We must talk," John said quietly. "There's so much to catch up on! Can we go into the courtyard?"

Peter looked over at the monk and John followed his glance. The man was not attractive. He was short and rat-like with narrow features, a pointed nose and thin lips pulled into a permanent sneer. But what startled John most were the man's eyes. They were wide open and staring, like those of a corpse, John thought with a shudder. As John stared, the eyes blinked, but the action did nothing to change the effect. There was no expression, simply a penetrating glare that both accused and missed nothing. John was transfixed. To his relief, the monk blinked again and nodded almost imperceptibly to Peter.

"Thank you Father Aumery," Peter said as the monk turned and strode off down the corridor with the other lay brothers scuttling after.

"Let's talk. The meeting is not due to begin for some time." Peter led the way through a rounded arch into the small courtyard that lay against one wall of the Abbey Church of St. Gilles. It was square and surrounded by a colonnaded cloister. In the centre was a small fountain, and John and Peter sat on the low wall that surrounded it.

"Did you become a monk because of your vision that night?" John asked as soon as they were settled.

"No. For one thing, I'm not a monk yet, I'm just a lay brother. We do all the mundane work so that the legates can concentrate on prayer and doing God's will—but one day I hope to be fully ordained. And I didn't join the Cistercian brothers because of the visions, they were simply Christ's way of opening my eyes. I joined to glorify God and do His work."

John took a deep breath. He had hoped that Peter would relax once he was away from the monk, but he still seemed serious and distant, almost as if there were a curtain between them. The ease of their old friendship was gone.

"Did you stay in Toulouse?" John asked, resolving to stick with safe topics.

"For a year, yes. I studied at the brothers' house there."

"Did you see Mother Marie at the Priory? How is she?"

"She has gone to Christ," Peter said matter-of-factly. "She passed on about three months after you left."

"I'm sorry to hear that. She was a good woman." John felt a pang of sadness at the news. Mother Marie had been an extraordinarily gentle woman who'd gone out of her way to help John and Peter. They both owed whatever they had and might achieve to her.

"She rests with the Lord, awaiting the Judgment Day," Peter said.

John felt a momentary flash of anger, but he pushed it down. "And Isabella, how was she when last you met?"

Peter looked suddenly uncomfortable. "She is godless," he said.

"Godless?" This time, John could not hold back his feelings. "Is that not harsh? True, I could not see her joining Holy Orders, but godless? Did you talk with her after your visions?"

"I did not."

John frowned. It was odd that Peter, who had been so smitten with Isabella, should not have at least talked to her about the strange visions and his plans. John opened his mouth to question his friend further, but the expression on Peter's face made it clear than any more talk about Isabella would not be welcome.

"How did you get in with the papal legates?" John asked, changing the subject.

Finally, Peter smiled. "I was blessed to be introduced to Father Arnaud Aumery, the abbot of the monastery at

Cîteaux, four months ago, when he stayed at the brother's house in Toulouse. He saw the spark of God in me and offered a chance to accompany him on his travels to convert the heretics."

"He has strange eyes," John commented.

"God has seen fit to give him such, yes," Peter continued, "but Father Aumery is a holy man, as is the senior legate, Pierre of Castelnau. Like yours, my reading and writing has proved of use, and I take notes that the legates use in their reports to Pope Innocent."

"You've done well."

"Yes." Peter's eyes glowed with pride. "And one day I hope to go to Rome itself!"

John smiled at his friend's enthusiasm, but inside he was worried. Peter seemed devoted to Aumery, but John had instinctively distrusted the man.

"But I am being rude," Peter said. "What have you been doing these past two years?"

"Much," John said. "I searched for you that night in Toulouse—at the Priory, in St. Sernin, and through the crowds—but you were nowhere."

"I needed solitude. I left the tumult of the feast and sat by the river, pondering what God wanted of me. I too looked for you after I had been accepted as a lay brother, but you had left by then."

"I left that very morning in company with William of Arles, the troubadour at the feast. You remember him?"

"I do. A godless man, I recall."

John wondered if everyone was godless in his friend's eyes. He ignored the insult and continued. "I travelled with him for more than a year, and learned much. William knows all the history of Languedoc and told it to me, either in songs or in tales around the evening fire. We visited the courts of the lords of Foix—where Adam now works for the count—Comminges and Béarn, and I had chances, never long enough, to study their libraries. I even had time to practice my drawing, copying the pictures in the margins of the books."

"So you still scribble and struggle to find God through earthly pursuits?"

"I still try to perfect my drawing and seek to learn all I can," John said, swallowing his anger once more. "And that is how I ended up here. The library at Carcassonne was particularly interesting and I decided to stay when William moved on. I told myself I could catch up with him later, but my interests came to the notice of Roger Trenceval and he offered me work as a scribe on this venture."

"So you work for a heretic."

"Viscount Roger is not a heretic!" John said. "He is young and clever and trying to do the best for his people. And he attends Mass regularly."

"He supports heretics and allows them to flourish in his cities. In God's eyes that is as bad."

"There are heretics all over!" John was about to defend his employer when he was interrupted.

"Indeed there are," Arnaud Aumery said as he appeared out of the cloister's shadows. His voice was high-pitched with a heavy accent that John recognized as originating across the Pyrenees Mountains in Castille or Aragon. "And that is why we are here at St. Gilles, to stop the spread of this pernicious evil before it corrodes the very heart of Christendom.

"The meeting convenes. Peter, you must take up your quill. And you"—Aumery stared coldly at John—"must run to your master."

Aumery turned and strode out of the courtyard. Without a word or a backward glance, Peter rose and hurried after.

John watched their retreating backs in confusion. He had been so excited when he first caught sight of his old friend in the cloister. As children, they had been so close, sharing everything, including their dreams of the future. John knew that they'd been growing apart even before Peter's visions, but now the gulf between them seemed unbridgeable. Peter was so sure and inflexible! Was that the influence of the strange Arnaud Aumery or did Peter simply need certainty to feel comfortable with the uncertain world in which they were living?

Shaking his head sadly, John walked slowly into the abbey church. Meeting Peter and the legate had turned what John had hoped would be an exciting adventure into something else—something darker. He couldn't help but feel perhaps more than his childhood friendship was at risk.

Threats

St. Gilles

JANUARY 13, 1208

The confrontation between the papal legates and Count Raymond's delegation promised good entertainment value and the abbey church of St. Gilles was busier than it ever was for Mass. The nave and aisles were packed to capacity, and the crowd overflowed out of the three ornately carved doors into the square. The late afternoon sun, appearing fitfully between threatening clouds, sent shafts of light through the rose window above the doors, illuminating the restless crowd and the tables set up on either side of the altar. It would make a wonderful painting, John thought, if only the life and depth of the scene could be captured on a flat surface.

At length, the murmuring of the crowd lessened as the principal actors in the drama entered and took their assigned places. Count Raymond led the way and took his seat at the centre of the long table to the left of the altar. He was a large, bluff man, sumptuously dressed in a deep-purple, fur-lined cloak, and he appeared relaxed, chatting lightly with the young Viscount Roger Trenceval on his left. As befitted his lower station, Trenceval was not as lavishly outfitted as Raymond; still, his youth and open, smiling face made him stand out among the more serious members of the retinue.

On Raymond's right, being pointedly ignored by the count, sat Bishop Foulques of Toulouse, looking just as well fed and self-satisfied as John remembered him. Years of good living had given the bishop several chins, which spilled over the richly embroidered collar of his vestments. His bishop's mitre, sparkling with jewels, balanced precariously on top of his large head.

Foulques was the archetype of the corrupt churchman so hated by the Cathars. He lived a life of unbridled luxury, financed by the tithes charged to the poor. Even worse, he allowed his priests to marry, as well as embezzle money at will and sell indulgences—providing that they paid him his share.

John recalled a popular song that William of Arles had composed about Foulques:

He loves Christ so much
This man of the Church
That he eats and drinks all
'Till his belly shall burst
So there is nothing left
To tempt his poor flock.
He lets his priests marry
So that all girls so fair
May not walk the streets
To seduce the young men.
You see he loves Christ
This pig of Toulouse.

John smiled at the seating arrangements. Foulques was rabidly anti-Cathar, yet because of his position as bishop of Toulouse, he was not sitting to the right of the altar with the papal legates, but next to Count Raymond, who was in trouble for protecting heretics. William would appreciate the irony.

The legates took their places, surrounded by monks and lay brothers. Arnaud Aumery concentrated deeply on some parchments, and Pierre of Castelnau sat by his side, stern and aloof.

John knew a little about Pierre of Castelnau from stories he'd heard on his wanderings with William. For five years, Pierre had been travelling the countryside, sometimes with Aumery and sometimes with the Spanish friar Dominic Guzman, preaching against the Cathar heresy and seeking converts. His failure—John had heard of no more than a dozen illiterate peasants who had renounced the Cathar faith—was due to the man's unyielding stance that allowed for no compromise. He would not deviate from his strict interpretation of the Gospels, an attitude that did not compare well with the much more open discussions the Cathars encouraged.

Pierre's mission was probably not helped by his unpleasant personal appearance. Even if he did convince someone of the rightness of his arguments, John could not see many people wishing to set this legate up as a role model. Pierre was a remarkably ugly man. His skin was pitted with pox marks, and one eyebrow was pulled down by a livid scar that gave him a perpetual disapproving scowl. His nose was large and squashed flat against his face. It sat above a pair of fleshy lips that surrounded a mouthful of rotted, yellow teeth. John had heard tell that Pierre's breath was so foul it could make even the strongest stomach churn. John couldn't help thinking of a vulture, sitting ready to plunge its head into a rotting carcass in search of delicacies. It was probably an image of which Pierre would approve, since he saw himself as plunging into the vile body of heresy to find savable souls.

John and Peter sat at the far ends of their respective tables with quills and ink at the ready. Around them, and to the front of the crowd, local dignitaries and monks from the abbey settled themselves as best they could. The mass of curious onlookers gathered behind, straining for a view.

Finally, Bishop Foulques stood and raised his hand for quiet. Gradually, the crowd fell silent. "We are met," Foulques began in a simpering voice, "to resolve the difficulties between my Lord Raymond, most honourable Count of Toulouse, his nephew Viscount Roger Trenceval of Carcassonne, and the Holy Mother Church of the glorious Pope Innocent III, as represented here by his blessed legates, Pierre of Castelnau and Arnaud Aumery, Abbot of Cîteaux.

"We fervently pray that God will look down favourably upon our conclave here this day and guide our steps as we undertake His divine mission. We call for His blessing upon His Holiness's legates"—Foulques smiled ingratiatingly across at Pierre and Arnaud—"and pray that my Lord Raymond comes to see the error of his ways."

Count Raymond grunted loudly and shifted in his chair, but made no comment. Foulques ignored him and continued. "The problem of heresy in our fair land is a serious one, and our lords have failed over many years to eradicate it from the bosom of the Holy Church."

Raymond sat forward and seemed about to speak, but Pierre's voice rang out first. "Enough of this nonsense," he thundered, standing and thumping the table before him. "His Holiness has given Count Raymond every chance, and the count has sworn, on numerous occasions, to carry out Rome's requests.

"Has he done so? No. The vile canker continues to grow and spread. I read here from a letter written by the blessed Innocent himself: 'Are you not ashamed of breaking the oath by which you swore to eradicate heresy from your dominions? Are you so mad that you think yourself wiser than all the faithful of the universal Church? If we could pierce the wall of your heart, we would enter it and show you terrible abominations you have wrought. What pride has swollen your heart, what madness, wretched man, has seized you, that you ally yourself with the enemies of Catholic truth? You feed on corpses like a crow. Are you not ashamed?'"

A gasp ran through the crowd. John looked up in shock at Pierre's violent outburst. He had expected the discussion to be calm and civilized—like the debates he and Peter used to listen to back in Toulouse. He watched as Foulques sat down abruptly and Raymond struggled to contain his anger.

It was Arnaud Aumery who spoke next, his voice soft and calming. "Perhaps my esteemed brother in Christ goes too far. We all wish only that—"

"Do not presume to tell me how far I may go." Pierre

rounded on his colleague. "I am senior legate here! I am the voice of His Holiness the Pope, and I shall determine how far to go."

John glanced up from his furious writing in time to catch the look of utter hatred that Aumery gave Pierre. Almost immediately, though, the look was replaced by a fawning smile.

"My apologies, brother," Aumery said. "I meant nothing."

Raymond rose then and leaned forward, his fists clenched before him. "How dare you! You come into my lands as a guest, to discuss a problem that plagues us both, and instead of a civilized discourse, I am insulted most foully in my own house! What gives you the right—"

"God Almighty and the Holy Mother Church give me the right," Pierre shouted back. "The time for discussion is long past. We are tired of your dissembling and delays. Burn the evil from the heart of your land at once or suffer the consequences."

For a moment, John feared that Raymond was going to leap across the table and strangle Pierre with his bare hands. Instead, he took a deep breath and spoke in a quieter voice, thick with venom. "You pox-scarred, drooling idiot. You and your carrion brotherhood presume to come into my lands and, in the name of a distant Rome that knows nothing of our situation, order me about. How dare you!"

"In the name of the Pope and the Holy Church," Pierre intoned, "I order you, this instant, to take arms against this Cathar heresy that gives birth continually to a monstrous brood, by means of which its corruption is vigorously renewed, with the offspring passing on to others the canker of its own detestable madness."

Both men were standing and speaking at once. The crowd was straining forward, staring from one to the other in an attempt not to miss a word. John scratched frantically with his quill, trying to get down as much as possible. A brief glance at Peter showed that he was doing the same.

"I came here in good faith," Raymond yelled. "Yet all I have received are orders and insults. What kind of discussion does your master in Rome consider that?"

"For your abject failure to eliminate this harmful filth from your lands, in the name of Pope Innocent III, I pronounce a sentence of excommunication upon you, Raymond of Toulouse."

Pierre's words hit everyone in the church with the power of a mailed fist and shocked even Raymond into silence. Everyone listened in horror as the legate continued in a quieter voice.

"I declare you shunned and deprived of all your lands and properties. No man shall owe you allegiance and all debts outstanding to you are hereby forgiven. Any man who takes arms against you shall do so with the blessings of the Church and, should you die before this sentence is lifted, you may not enjoy the sacraments or last rites. You may not be buried in consecrated ground and your coffin shall lie in the open, a feast for the rats and crows. May God have mercy upon your soul."

The silence in the church was almost a physical thing. Excommunication was a final resort and, if rigorously applied, could destroy the wealth and power of the mightiest lord, not to mention condemn his soul to eternal damnation. This was a much better entertainment than the crowd had hoped for.

"The Lord's work here is done," Pierre said eventually. "We shall leave this night and return and report these proceedings to His Holiness. I shall pray for you, Raymond of Toulouse."

Arnaud Aumery and the lay brothers stood and collected their parchments. Raymond blinked, his face red with fury.

"Do not think you can escape this place with such ease," he said coldly. "I shall watch for your departure whether you go by land or by water, and you shall die before me, Pierre of Castelnau."

With the threat hanging in the air, Raymond turned and strode from the church. A hubbub of conversation erupted behind him.

John looked across at Peter, hoping to catch his eye, but his friend had already gathered his writing equipment and all John saw was a retreating back. John gathered his own quill, ink and parchment and slowly made his way out of the church into the cloister. He was sitting on the wall, trying to gather his thoughts, when Roger Trenceval approached. John jumped to his feet.

"Sit," Roger said with a smile. He was a young man, only a few years older than John, but since the death of his father in 1194, when Roger had been only nine years old, he had controlled large swaths of land and the cities of Carcassonne and Béziers. He ruled easily, without the violence of so many of his kind. As long as the populace kept the peace and paid their taxes he allowed them to go about their business unhindered. As a result, the young viscount was immensely popular with his subjects. His court was famous for its jollity, and the most renowned troubadours in the land came to perform on feast days. John could imagine no one for whom he would rather work. The only difficulty was that Roger's laxity created a haven for heretics, who now preached and worshipped openly in the streets of Béziers and Carcassonne.

"That was quite the entertainment, was it not?"

"Entertainment?" John asked.

"Of course! You do not imagine anyone took it seriously, do you?"

"But the legate excommunicated Count Raymond!"

Roger laughed. "Not for the first time, and probably not for the last. I shall tell you what will happen. That weasel Aumery will write a report to the Pope denouncing Count Raymond and, most probably, me as vile protectors of heretics. Count Raymond will also write, complaining that the legates gave him no fair chance to comply with their demands, swearing that he will do his utmost to eradicate the foul heresy from his lands and bring his people back to Christ. The Pope will lift the excommunication, Raymond will make a few gestures, and things will go on as before. That is how it has always happened in the past and I see no reason for it to be different this time."

"But the legate was so . . ." John searched for the right word.

"Arrogant. Violent. Stupid. Ugly. Take your pick. He is not a pleasant man, either to look at or to listen to. But he is the Pope's creature and will do as he is told. As long as Raymond can keep direct channels open to His Holiness, we need not worry about Pierre of Castelnau or Arnaud

Aumery. But I sought you out for a reason. I believe you know one of the lay brothers?"

"I do. Peter. We grew up together in Toulouse."

"Splendid. The papal party will leave within the hour. I should like you to go with them. Your friendship with Peter will give you the excuse. You can say you are catching up on old times or that you are fed up working for such a friend of heretics as I. I care not. What I wish is that you keep close to the legates, hear what gossip circles them and, if possible, acquire from your scribe friend a copy of the letter Aumery will undoubtedly send to the Pope. Count Raymond and I should much like to see it and, if you think it manageable to wait for the Pope's reply, I should much like to see that as well. Would you be willing to attempt this?"

It was a question, but John knew he had little choice. Roger Trenceval was his lord and he had an obligation to obey any request made, just as Roger had an obligation to reward John once the service was done.

John had the uncomfortable feeling that his life was beginning to spin out of control. Was he now to be a spy? A part of John wished he were still leading the carefree life of a troubadour. But another part of him was excited. He was at the centre of things, associating with the men who had the power in this land. And, maybe, he would be able to rekindle his friendship with Peter.

"I am willing," John said.

"Excellent! Then I suggest you gather a few belongings for the journey. I fear you must walk, as to give you a mount would attract too much attention, but I wish you well." Roger reached into a leather purse that hung from his belt.

"Here are a few coins for your keep on the road. I trust I shall hear from you in due course. Good luck."

Placing the pennies in John's hand, Roger favoured him with one last smile and disappeared into the shadows.

Arguments
Near Arles
JANUARY 14, 1208

John sat on a cold, damp rock, chewing on a hunk of heavy black bread. In front of him the broad, murky waters of the Rhône River swirled past and the boatmen struggled to propel the flat-bottomed ferry toward him. On the far bank lay Arles, William the Troubadour's hometown. It wasn't an imposing place; only three square church towers and the walls of the Roman amphitheatre rose into view above the squat city walls. To the left of the city the weak early morning sun was struggling to rise above the horizon, a pale, colourless circle through the mist and cloud.

In the nearby trees birds called out warnings, and a rabbit screamed as a weasel ended its life. John pulled his leather jerkin tighter around his shoulders. It had been a miserable night. First there had been the abrupt departure from St. Gilles and the dark walk to the river. Then the long, cold wait for dawn and the ferry. It would be here soon now. Perhaps there would be time to stop for some hot soup in Arles, but John doubted it. Neither Pierre of Castelnau nor Arnaud Aumery struck John as men who had much time for luxuries like hot soup. They probably wouldn't even enter the city, choosing instead to skirt the walls and continue north to Avignon.

John stood, stretched his aching limbs and stuffed the remaining piece of bread into the leather pouch that hung from his waist. It would do for lunch on the road. Remembering his purpose—to gather information for Raymond and Roger—he turned to examine his companions. To his right, three Cistercian monks were kneeling at their morning prayers looking, in their white habits with the black aprons hanging behind and in front, like a flock of large, slow-moving magpies. Behind them, a half dozen lay brothers, in their brown sleeveless robes, scurried around, taking down tents, packing bedding and loading mules.

Slightly apart from the activity, the thin-faced Arnaud Aumery also knelt in prayer, hunched forward like a large rodent. His habit was pulled down to his waist and his scrawny hands twisted together in front of his chest. His left hand held a heavy knotted rope and, after each fervent prayer, the hand would break free from its companion and snap up, arcing the rope over the right shoulder and across the skinny back. It must have hurt, yet each time the hard knots dug into the flesh, Aumery jerked his head back and John saw the monk's face twisted not in pain, but in ecstasy. John had heard of monks scourging themselves to rid their lives of sin, but he had never imagined that they enjoyed it.

To John's left, Pierre of Castelnau sat aloof on a black mule, watching Aumery with an expression of distaste. John wondered how the two legates could be so different, and yet so equal in their lack of appeal as advertisements for the Catholic Church. It was easy to see how the Cathars had gained so many converts.

"So, you have come with us!" John turned his head to

see Peter walking toward him. "Are you thinking of entering monastic orders?"

"I would have preferred a monastic cell last night to sitting in the open by the river," he retorted. Despite the differences that had grown between them, John was glad to see his old friend. "Or a place in one of the monk's tents."

"Then become a lay brother. Join us in doing God's work."

John gently shook his head, not wishing to start another argument. "It's not for me. I enjoy the bustle of court life and the songs and stories of the troubadours. And I want to be free to learn everything, to read whatever books I wish and know whatever they might teach me. And do you know the strangest thing? The more I learn, the less clear everything becomes. For every black there is a white and countless shades of grey between. There is so much I need to learn!"

"John, John," Peter said. "You approach the problem the wrong way! Clarity comes not from dwelling eternally on the details. Our purpose here on earth is to adore and glorify God. We worship for His sake, not our own. If you come to know God, you know everything and the details fall into place as a part of His grand scheme. Remember how I used to quote Anselm of Canterbury, 'I believe so that I may understand'?"

"I do," John said with a smile. "And do you remember how I used to counter with Peter Abelard's 'By doubting we come to enquiry, through enquiry to truth'?"

Peter nodded and smiled back. "I remember our debates fondly, even if you were wrong."

John's smile broadened at the gentle dig. "I am glad our paths are crossing again. I have many stories to tell you of my travels." Perhaps they could still recapture the easy friendship of their childhood.

"I am glad, too." Peter said. His smile faded and he looked seriously at John. "You are as close to me as a brother, and I am thankful that God has given me another opportunity to show you the error of your ways."

John frowned. It was as if Peter had relaxed for a moment, but now that old curtain was once again coming down between them. He tried to keep the tone of the conversation light.

"I hope correcting my error doesn't involve whips," John joked, inclining his head toward Aumery.

"That is Father Aumery's way," Peter said seriously. "We must each find our own path to God."

"I agree," John said, worried that his joke had misfired. "It's just that my path is through learning. If God created all that is in the world, He placed truth here too. By searching for that truth, I can come to know God better."

"If!" Peter's voice rose to a near shout. "Do you doubt that God created all?"

"Of course not!" John said hurriedly. "It's just an expression." Clearly his attempts at levity had failed. "I agree with you, Peter, we all need to find our own way, but I doubt if freezing by this river, or hitting yourself with knotted ropes, brings you closer to God. Personally, I would have been much more inclined to dwell on the Lord if I had been warm and well fed last night."

"Father Aumery is a holy man," Peter said indignantly. "He scourges the body to cleanse the soul."

John sighed. He knew he should change the topic to

something less controversial, but Peter was sounding pompous again and it annoyed John. He could avoid a fight with Peter only by slavishly agreeing to his friend's unquestioning certainty. He wasn't prepared to do that.

"Like the Perfects do?" John asked provocatively.

"There's an eternity of difference between the heretics and Father Aumery." Peter spoke angrily. "The Cathars are doomed to the fires of hell, and he will sit with the blessed saints at Christ's feet. You can't possibly believe all this nonsense those Perfects preach!"

"But aren't there a lot of similarities?" John went on. "Both Father Aumery and the Perfects believe that the spiritual realm is the important one and that the physical body is evil, correct?"

"There are *no* similarities." Peter's voice was rising and his cheeks were reddening. "Father Aumery believes, as all true Christians should, that the flesh is weak and that we must be continually on our guard against sinful temptation put in our way by Satan. But the body, like everything around us, was created by God. The heretics believe that the body, and the entire material world, is the creation of Satan and since that is the case, anything you do in this life is all right because the world is by its very nature corrupt. That simply encourages debauchery and sin." Peter made the sign of the cross in the air before him.

John cast a look in Aumery's direction. "I wonder how God looks on the way Father Aumery is treating His creation? It can't be that simple, Peter! A lot of what the Perfects say *is* strange, but it's not all nonsense. And it seems to me that, with their vows of poverty and their itinerant life, they are much closer to the ordinary people than the likes of Bishop Foulques, bedecked in his jewels and finery."

"Do you see Pierre or Arnaud bedecked in jewels?" Peter waved his thin arm toward the two legates.

"No," John allowed. "No one could accuse either of being seduced by the material world, but the church they serve is undeniably rich and some of its members seem to enjoy the wealth too much. Remember the debate in St. Sernin?"

Peter nodded.

"The Perfects won that day because they talked about things that ordinary people could understand—the unfairness and harshness of a world filled with random cruelty. They explained why life is difficult and unfair, why children die, why soldiers suddenly appear and rape the farmers' women, steal their possessions and burn their crops. The world *is* evil, created by Satan. That is how most people see things—a cruel, hard life—followed by death. The Perfects understand that and offer hope: do the best you can in this corrupt world until death comes to release your spirit to an infinitely better place."

John took a deep breath. He knew he should stop, but it was too late. He was angry now and, in any case, a part of him wanted to see how far Peter's new certainty could be pushed.

"On top of that, the people know the Perfects," John continued. "They live among them, simply and without pretension. They live in ordinary houses, not splendid palaces; they conduct services in the common language, not a foreign tongue few understand; and they pray wherever there is need, not in churches that look as though they have been dipped in molten gold. The Perfects live with the people, owning nothing, consoling the sick and answering questions that trouble people frankly and clearly.

"What does the Church offer to counter that? Stories about a far-off day when all the dead will rise out of their graves to be judged on how they have lived their lives. No wonder the Perfects laugh."

"Heretic!" Peter's shout was loud enough for several nearby lay brothers to look up nervously.

"Peter, I'm not a heretic—you know that. I'm simply trying to explain why the legates are failing to win the people. What happened to the days when we could discuss anything and argue for the joy of it?"

"There is no joy in propounding heretical ideas," Peter said loudly and quickly. "Your masters, Count Raymond and Roger Trenceval, tolerate and encourage heretics. These black-clad vermin spread like rats through the streets of our towns, and no one dares stop them. They must be eradicated. You praise the heretics because they own nothing, as if there were virtue in poverty for its own sake. There is not."

"Christ was poor," John replied.

"Christ lived far from here twelve hundred years ago. We have advanced since then, and it is the cardinals, bishops and the Holy Church whom the Perfects mock so much who have led us so far. Without the Church to create order and spread the word of God, you would still be a pagan, living in animal skins and huddling in terror at the unknown noises of the night. Would your Perfects have us return to that?"

"Of course not!" John said, angry at the way Peter was twisting his words. "They argue that, since the world is imperfect, it cannot have been created by a perfect God.

Therefore it must have been made by another—by Satan."

"Dualism!" Peter's voice was almost a scream now. "There is only one God, who created all. All else is Satan whispering in our ears."

"Peter," John said softly, trying to calm his friend. "I do not believe in two gods, but even you must admit that there are things within the Church of Rome that need reform. Why should a privileged few live in luxury and control all knowledge of the Holy Book? Surely Christ himself spoke directly to the masses?"

"Of course he did, and were Christ still walking the earth, I would be the first to say let us go and hear him. But he is not." Peter spoke fast and harshly. "Christ lives in our hearts and, since we are imperfect, we need the Church to ensure that his words remain pure for all and not simply what every individual understands or remembers. The Catholic Church was established by the disciples and therefore its words are the closest one can come to knowing God's wishes."

The pair stood staring at each other. Peter was breathing heavily and his fists were clenched. John could think of nothing to say that would relieve the tension. He lowered his eyes to gaze at the ground between them.

"Beware, John," Peter said. His voice was quieter now, but still filled with anger. "You put your mortal soul in jeopardy."

Peter turned and stalked off before John could think of a reply, leaving him to suddenly wish that he were back at St. Gilles with Roger Trenceval. He raised his eyes and noticed Arnaud Aumery staring at him icily. More immediate than any threat to his mortal soul, John thought, was the need to beware of that man.

Murder

Near Arles,

JANUARY 14, 1208

John's attention was drawn by the shouts of the ferrymen as the boat drew near the shore. The lay brothers had finished packing and the monks were rising from their prayers. As he scanned the riverbank one last time, John noticed that Pierre of Castelnau, still sitting on his mule, was beckoning him. Puzzled and a bit nervous, John walked over to Pierre and stood by the mule's head, stroking its muzzle. They were some way off from the activity by the ferry dock and close to a thick stand of pine trees beside the road. The trees' lower branches were moving in the breeze, but there was something odd about the way they swayed.

As he waited for Pierre to speak, John studied the pines, trying to see into the darkness between the trees, but he could make out nothing other than meaningless, shifting shapes. His attention was drawn back to the legate as Pierre leaned forward and exhaled a disgusting breath in his face. It was all John could do not to pull back, but Pierre's stare held him in place. His eyes were a pale, washed-out grey, and their piercing, unforgiving gaze made John feel guilty, regardless of anything he had actually done. The fact that Pierre might have heard Peter call John a heretic made John's guilt ten times worse.

"You must do penance, boy," Pierre hissed, spraying spittle toward John.

"Penance?" John asked, tightening his grip on the mule's bridle.

"Aye, penance. Your masters are sinful men and will pay the price. If you wish to avoid their sin, you must cleanse yourself. Become a lay brother. Peter tells me you have some reading and some knowledge. That is a good thing—in the service of God. You must leave the path that the arrogant Raymond refused to reject and find the true way."

John listened in shock. Why did *he* have to do penance? Yes, he worked for Roger and Raymond, but that did not mean he shared their sins—did it?

Before he could form a reply, John was distracted by increased movement in the trees. He squinted hard to try to make out the moving shapes.

"Pay attention to me, boy," Pierre ordered.

John ignored him. Suddenly, the moving patterns in the branches made sense.

"There's someone in the trees," he said.

"What are you saying?" Pierre said angrily. "I am talking about your immortal soul and the fires of hell, and all you do is look at trees!"

"But—"

The knight on horseback broke from cover in a burst of noise. He was mounted on a massive charger whose great hooves pounded the ground like distant thunder. The knight was dressed in a long leather coat that was split front and back so he could sit comfortably on his horse. Countless overlapping steel rings were sewn onto the coat to create a protective layer of chain mail. He wore a pointed helmet, designed to deflect sword or axe blows aimed at his head. A nose guard descended from the helmet and was attached to two broad cheek plates, completely obscuring the man's face except for the eyes. He carried a shield on his right arm and a lance tucked beneath his left, but wore no identifying coat of arms either on his shield or on the saddle cloth that hung over his horse's sides. As he spurred his mount forward, the knight aimed his lance at Pierre's back.

To John it seemed as if the world had become a tableau in which only the knight retained the power of movement. For several seconds, everything hung in the balance, until finally, seeing the look of shock on John's face, Pierre began to turn his head. Gripping the mule's bridle, John tried to haul the beast out of the way. He was too late.

The lance entered Pierre of Castelnau's back slightly to the left of his spine. It tore through his heart and shattered his sternum. John watched in horror as the lance point, bloody and evil, ripped out the front of Pierre's chest. The force of the blow hurled the legate out of the saddle and the terrified mule reared, knocking John to the ground. The hooves of the knight's charger thundered past inches from John's face and threw clods of wet earth over him. Rolling aside, John saw the knight retreat at a gallop back up the road toward St. Gilles.

For a moment there was an unearthly silence, then shouts and screams rent the air. John scrambled to his feet, pushed the distraught mule out of the way and knelt over Pierre. The legate lay partly propped up by the lance that still impaled his body, his head oddly twisted to one side. Already his

83

habit was soaked in blood. The dying man's pale gaze met John's as he attempted to speak. He managed one word that sounded like "forgive" before the blood welled over his lips and his eyes glazed.

In shock, his heart pounding and his hands sweating even in the cold air, John stood, unable to think what he should do next.

"Murderer!" Arnaud Aumery's shrill voice came from over John's shoulder. John assumed the legate was shouting at the knight, who had all but disappeared into the morning mist. It took him a moment to realize that Aumery meant him.

"What?" he asked, bewildered.

Aumery pointed a finger at John. His thin face was twisted with hate and his expressionless eyes stared. "You are the worm in the heart of our group! You held the mule steady while Raymond's spawn slaughtered the blessed Pierre, even turning the beast so that the lance would do its foul job more efficiently."

"No!" John shook his head in confusion. "I was trying to pull the mule *away*. I was trying to save him."

"Then why did you pull him to the left? You pulled the mule left and the knight was left-handed. You pulled Pierre onto the lance and made the stroke more certain."

"I didn't have time to think. I just pulled."

"Why were you there at all? Your standing by Pierre was a signal, part of a devilish plot hatched by Raymond in the halls of St. Gilles."

"The legate beckoned me over," John said weakly.

Aumery laughed derisively. "I saw no beckoning," he spat.

John noticed Peter standing behind Aumery. "Peter, tell him I didn't do anything! Tell him I wouldn't kill anyone!"

Peter's glance darted between John and Aumery, but he remained silent.

"It was all planned," Aumery ranted, kneeling by Pierre and cradling his bloody head. "Raymond admitted as much with his threat last evening. His soul is lost. He has sold it to Satan. He never intended to obey His Holiness. He is a heretic and worse, a protector of heretics! And this pup is his servant, sent among us to make the murderer's task easier. I have no doubt that, had the lance missed, this demon in human form would have finished the job himself."

A murmur of agreement swept through the crowd of shocked monks and lay brothers who had gathered round Pierre of Castelnau's corpse.

"No! It's not like that!"

"I even heard"—Aumery drowned out John's protestations—"our own dear brother in God, Peter, call this one a heretic. Is that not so, Peter?"

John looked imploringly at his friend, but Peter simply lowered his eyes. "Yes," he said quietly.

Some of the lay brothers stepped forward toward John.

"Seize him," Aumery ordered. "Fire is the lot of heretics."

A hand grasped at John's sleeve. John swung his fist wildly, felt it connect with flesh and heard a groan of pain. The hand let go of his sleeve. John turned and ran, barging past the lay brothers who were not quick enough to move out of his way.

He had no idea where he was running, he just ran, past the surprised ferrymen and along the river bank—away from the sounds of pursuit, away from the screaming Arnaud Aumery and away from Peter and his past.

John ran unthinkingly, until he could run no more. The muscles in his legs burned and his agonized lungs threatened to explode from his chest. Then he collapsed, face down on a bed of moss between the roots of a broad willow tree.

Gradually, his breathing slowed to normal and the pains in his body eased. The sweat that soaked his clothes cooled and he shivered. Rolling over, he stared up through the bare, black branches of the tree. It was beginning to rain and large, fat drops plunged to the ground around him—as if the tree itself were weeping.

John sat up and looked around. He had no idea how long he had been running, but his surroundings were completely unfamiliar. He was still close to the river, but there was no sign of Arles on the opposite bank. John listened hard, but heard only the rain pattering on the ground around him. He had escaped, but for how long? And what had he escaped from? Certainly Aumery's wild accusations of murder, but he had also abandoned his past. Aumery's abuse John could take, but Peter's silence was harder. His friend hadn't lied—he *had* called John a heretic loud enough for Aumery to overhear—but he hadn't spoken up in his defence. A calm voice of reason might have defused the situation before it got out of hand, but Peter had stayed silent, and John would have trouble forgiving him for that.

What could he do now? The way back was closed. Aumery would undoubtedly take the body of the murdered legate back to St. Gilles. Even if Count Raymond and Roger Trenceval were still there, they could not protect John; they would be having enough troubles of their own. Yesterday Raymond had been excommunicated, and today he would be accused of organizing the murder of a senior papal legate. Whether he was guilty or innocent, Raymond would hardly have the time or the inclination to protect a page who had been in the wrong place at the wrong time. John was on his own.

There was one hope: Béziers, the closest large town where John could lose himself. Arles and Avignon were actually closer, but they were not a part of Raymond's domain and John would be an outsider. Béziers was familiar, and it was on Roger Trenceval's land. Perhaps the young viscount, who had sent him on this mission in the first place, would shelter him. Maybe, by the time he got there, the situation might even have resolved itself. After all, Viscount Roger had said things would go on as normal. But would they? Or had the murder of Pierre of Castelnau changed everything? John suspected it might have, but he had no choice. He stood and walked away from the river.

An Offer
Near Arles
JANUARY 14, 1208

Peter stood in utter shock, staring at Pierre of Castelnau's blood-soaked body. The sudden outburst of violence and Arnaud Aumery's accusations had thoroughly confused him. What *had* happened? The papal legate was certainly dead and his killer had escaped, but what part had John played? Yes, Peter had called him a heretic, but that had been in the heat of an argument. He hadn't meant to suggest, as Aumery had, that John was in some way capable of aiding a murderer.

Aumery knelt over the body, mumbling prayers and making the sign of the cross. A few of the lay brothers had given chase to the fleeing John, but it had been a half-hearted effort and they were now returning to mill about uncertainly. One was leading the dead Pierre's mule.

Peter was glad John had escaped. Still, he doubted they would ever again be friends as they had once been, not after this. Partly it was John's fault—he had developed so many worrying ideas of late—but Peter knew he shared the blame. He regretted the argument they had just had by the river. He had gone over intending to be friendly, but as soon as John had started to disagree with him, he had fallen back on the Church's teachings. He knew he had sounded pompous, but he couldn't help it. He hated being wrong, being made to look foolish, and taking refuge in what the Church told him was true was a comfort when he felt challenged. And it worked with most people, who were too ignorant or scared to disagree with him, but not with John. John kept questioning and pushing and Peter just got more angry.

"You!" Peter was jerked out of his thoughts by the realization that Aumery was pointing a skinny finger at him.

"Yes, Father."

"Come and give me a hand. We must remove the lance from the blessed Pierre's body. Hold him down."

Hesitantly, Peter moved around and crouched by the legate's head. Blood ran from his mouth and nose, and his eyes were wide—very like Aumery's, Peter thought with a shudder. As gently as possible, Peter leaned over and closed the eyes.

"Pierre is already seated with the Lord," Arnaud Aumery said. "Closing the eyes to prevent the escape of the soul is a pagan habit. Are you a pagan?"

"No!" Peter exclaimed in fright. "I am a good Christian."

"Hah! That's what the heretics call themselves. Perhaps you are a heretic like your friend?"

"No! He's not my friend. I mean, I'm not a heretic."

"I don't believe you are. You're just a stupid boy. How are we supposed to combat evil with material such as you? Now, hold the body's shoulders, firmly."

Peter did as he was told, although it was all he could do not to bring up his meagre breakfast. The dead man's clothing was soaked in blood and his fleshy body beneath the fabric already felt cold and limp.

Aumery pulled on the lance, but it remained stuck. He pulled harder. Pierre's body slipped out of Peter's hands.

"Hold him tight," Aumery ordered. "It's wedged in his ribs."

Peter felt his stomach heave, but he clenched his teeth and held on. Bracing himself, Aumery jerked hard. The lance came free, accompanied by a soft sucking sound. Peter turned away and retched.

"Good." Aumery threw the bloody lance aside. "Now load Pierre on his mule. We are returning to St. Gilles."

Peter looked up from wiping his mouth, surprised that they should be returning to the scene of so much argument yesterday. "Will we be welcome there?" he asked.

"I doubt the heretic count will still be there, but it is no matter. We are doing God's work and we have the body of a holy martyr with us—a saint to be, I have no doubt. God will see us trample over our enemies."

Peter wasn't certain. If someone was prepared to kill Pierre, what was to stop them killing the rest of the party? It was a worrying thought, but even more disturbing was the expression of excited triumph on Aumery's face. The man looked almost gleeful as the body was strapped across the mule's back.

The long walk back to St. Gilles was a sombre affair. Peter was mostly occupied with leading the mule, which was upset by the smell of blood from the body on its back, but his task didn't prevent him from reflecting on the morning's events.

He felt sorry for John, and regretted calling him a heretic, but until his old friend discovered God, as Peter had, he would be open to the work of the Devil. As Peter walked, he decided that he would pray for God to send John a revelation as powerful as the one that had changed him in Toulouse. Things would be so much better if John would just accept the truth: all that was good and worthwhile in this world was a gift from God, and it was the Holy Roman Church's duty to uphold that. The Church stemmed from the word of God as given to man in the Old Testament and through the lips of Christ. To deny that, or even to question it, opened the door to chaos at a time when the Church was beset on all sides by unbelievers.

Judgment Day, when the graves would open and the righteous ascend to heaven, could not come until the entire world accepted Christ and his teachings. The crusades to Jerusalem and Al-Andalus were spreading the faith, but to have heresy rearing its head in the very heart of Christendom was the work of the Devil. Surely John would see that! The Church had to be strong and unified if it was to succeed. This was no time for doubts.

Peter could almost hear John's objections in his head. Undeniably, there was rotten fruit within the Church. Bishop Foulques of Toulouse with his sinning priests and vast wealth was one example, but that did not mean that the Church as a whole was corrupt. Pierre of Castelnau— Peter crossed himself at the memory—and Arnaud Aumery were holy men who denied themselves almost all pleasures to be close to God. In time, men like them would root out evil in the Church and restore it to its former glory, and Peter wanted to be a part of that. He dreamed of being ordained and devoting himself to holy work. He would work hard, convert the ignorant masses and save countless souls. That way he would rise, perhaps to become abbott of his own monastery, or even a cardinal in Rome, or even . . .

Peter's musings were interrupted by the mule bucking violently and twisting Pierre's body to one side. Peter calmed the beast and was readjusting the body when Arnaud Aumery approached.

"You have an education, boy?" he asked.

"Yes," Peter replied as he wiped the blood off his hands. "John and I were taught by the nuns of St. Anne in Toulouse."

"John is the heretic who helped the knight murder Pierre?"

"No!" Peter said. He was calmer now and better able to defend his friend. "John wouldn't do that. I am certain he was doing what he said, holding the mule while Pierre talked to him."

"Hmm," said Aumery, nodding thoughtfully, "but he is a heretic?"

Peter hesitated. "No."

"Yet you called him such."

"He's not a heretic, of that I am certain," Peter said, more firmly this time. "I think he simply questions too much."

"And you do not?"

"It is not up to me to question the Church. We must be strong to combat heresy."

"You can read and write well?"

"A little."

"Latin or this corrupt Occitan language that is spoken hereabouts?"

Peter hesitated. The question was strewn with potential pitfalls. It was forbidden to read the Bible in Latin unless you were ordained in the Church. To admit being able to read Latin, unless you were a notary, judge or highborn, was to invite that charge. Yet, to read only Occitan marked you as a Languedoc provincial.

"Mother Marie, who taught John and me to read, was most holy," Peter said hesitantly. "She taught from a copy of St. Augustine's Confessions."

"You are familiar with Augustine! He was a heretic."

"And a pagan," Peter returned. "He also fathered an illegitimate child."

"Not a very good background for a central figure in our Christian thought." Aumery looked slyly at Peter.

"On the contrary," Peter replied, warming to this battle of wits. "It gave him a knowledge of his enemies that better enabled him to defeat them."

"Indeed, and you have a knowledge of this Cathar rabble?"

Peter saw the trap. "Only in so far as it is impossible not to, growing up as I did in the midst of their evil. Could I have chosen the place of my birth, I should have selected Rome."

Aumery laughed. "Birth in Rome is no guarantee of holiness. But what should the Church do when faced with a heresy that it cannot defeat by reasoned argument or example?"

"Listen to St. Augustine: 'Should not the Church use force in compelling her lost sons to return, if the lost sons compelled others to their destruction?'"

Aumery nodded approvingly. "So you *do* know your Augustine. Do you wish to become ordained?"

"More than anything, Father."

"And do you wish to devote your life to the Lord and His work?"

Peter hesitated. The easy answer was yes, but what would he be committing himself to?

"Hesitation is all right. You have not yet been called to service."

"But I have," Peter interrupted.

Aumery looked at his young companion sharply.

"I had a revelation two years ago," Peter went on.

"A revelation," Aumery reflected. "Tell me about it."

Peter told the story of his vision—of how he felt about the beautiful Isabella, of Death pointing at him and of Isabella's decay before his eyes—as Aumery listened intently. After Peter finished, the legate turned his strange eyes on the young lay brother.

"You are lucky," he said, a hint of envy in his voice. "God has blessed you with absolute certainty. For the rest of us, the struggle is harder."

Peter found it hard to imagine Arnaud Aumery struggling with anything less than certainty.

"I too was in love once," Aumery continued.

Peter stumbled and almost fell. The idea of Aumery loving someone, or of being loved in return, was utterly strange.

"You cannot imagine a man who has dedicated his life to God, as I have, being in love?"

Before Peter could think of an answer, Aumery continued. "My father was a prosperous wool merchant in Aragon, and I was to follow in his footsteps. At age twelve, I was betrothed to Dolores, the third daughter of the local count. As was the custom, I had never met her, but I had seen her from a distance and was smitten by her beauty. The future looked bright and I was happy." Aumery turned and favoured Peter with a wintry smile before continuing.

"One day, as my father and mother returned from the local fall fair, they were set upon by bandits and slaughtered. I had pleaded to accompany them, but father had insisted I stay home and study."

Peter thought he detected a catch in Aumery's voice, but the legate coughed and continued. "After I buried my parents, I went, in the company of an aged uncle, to the count to finalize the betrothal arrangements. I met Dolores in the company of one of her ladies in the courtyard. My heart leaped to my throat, and I hurried forward and bowed low.

"'I come to pay my respects to you and your father,' I stammered.

"Dolores laughed, harshly. 'To what end?'

"'So that our betrothal may be finalized.' I looked up, hoping against hope that I had misheard the scorn in her voice, but her beautiful face was twisted in disgust.

"'Do you honestly think that my father would consent to our marriage, or even that I would wish such a marriage, now that you are nothing? Already, your father's business crumbles, and what can you, a child, do about it?'

"'But I love you,' I blurted out desperately. Dolores's hard stare made me feel lower than a worm.

"Do you think I, the count's daughter, could love you, a skinny rat-faced child with the courtly graces of a slug? Go and find a peasant to rut with. That is all you are worth.'

"Blinded by tears of shame, I fled back to my empty parents' house.

"I swore a thousand kinds of revenge on Dolores and her family, but she was right. My father had been deeply in debt to local moneylenders who immediately called in what they were owed. I was soon near penniless."

The legate was a difficult man to feel sorry for, but Peter came close as he listened to his tale of rejection. Even Aumery's grating voice seemed to soften as he spoke of Dolores. A sharp pang of regret stabbed Peter as he remembered his feelings for Isabella.

"In the depths of my despair," Aumery continued, "God sent to me a travelling friar who taught me the ways of the true Church. I threw myself into my learning and devoted my life to finding and eradicating sin from our unclean world."

"What happened to Dolores?" Peter asked.

Aumery shot Peter a sharp glance. "She married an empty-headed young knight. Their house became a noted place of sin and debauchery. At length, their activities came to the notice of the Holy Inquisition, and the woman was investigated. She was found to be in an adulterous carnal relationship with a non-Christian, and both were put to death. Even in her final moments, she was unrepentant and died cursing the Holy Church and me."

"You?"

"Oh, did I not mention?" Aumery turned to Peter, a smile on his face. "I was the inquisitor who brought the charges against the witch."

A chill ran down Peter's spine. Aumery had seemed almost human as he told his story, yet here was evidence that he had harboured a grudge for years and exacted a terrible revenge.

On the other hand, wasn't Aumery's determination to overcome and suppress his natural human instincts admirable? Perhaps, Peter reflected, he too might learn to rid his mind of the painful memories of Isabella that struck when he least expected them.

Aumery's eyes gleamed. His hands clasped and unclasped in prayer as he stared at Peter.

"So God wishes us both to do his work. Are you prepared?"

"I hope so."

"You will need more than hope, but I shall help you. Stay close by me. We have much work ahead, and the Church needs intelligent and dedicated soldiers such as you."

"Stay close?"

"You are much above the stupid peasants who fetch and carry, but you must learn to control this habit of asking questions before you have let your mind work.

"Pierre's death today is a blessing," he continued. "He will become a saint, and Raymond will be damned in all eyes for his role. This tragedy is exactly what is needed. This summer I shall travel north and help preach a great crusade in the name of the martyred Pierre and Pope Innocent. In the following year I shall return at the head of a mighty host and root out this evil from these lands with no mercy. Do you wish to accompany me and do the Lord's work?"

"I do."

"Then learn to hold your peace and stay close."

Aumery strode away, leaving Peter to walk on alone, his head crowded with thoughts. Aumery had obviously been impressed enough by Peter's vision to open up, but why? Peter was certain that the legate did nothing without calculated intent. His intent here must be to mentor Peter and bring him to an important position in the Church. And what was wrong with that? Peter would do as Aumery asked—accompany him to preach the crusade, and be ordained as well. It was a chance to realize his dream, and he would seize it. With friends as powerful as Aumery, Peter saw a life of service in the Church stretch out before him— all the way to Rome.

PART THREE
Crusade

Perfect

Béziers

JULY 22, 1209

John stood on the battlements above Béziers's west gate looking out at the narrow humped bridge over the river Orb. The July sun had already risen with the promise of another hot, dusty day, but the shadow of the massive bulk of St. Nazaire Cathedral behind him protected John from its glare.

After the murder of Pierre of Castelnau, John had travelled a long, roundabout route, over swollen winter rivers and through freezing rain, to the safety of this city. News of the legate's death had preceded him, but Roger Trenceval had welcomed the details of it and sworn to protect John. Opinion was divided over whether Raymond had ordered Pierre's assassination by the mysterious left-handed knight or not, but to Roger, it mattered little.

"If Pope Innocent wishes to use the murder to crush the Cathars," he told John, "he will do so, regardless of whose idea it was."

"Will he call a crusade?" John had asked.

"Quite possibly, but don't be alarmed. Northern knights agree to serve the Pope for forty days in return for remittance of sin and assurances of a place in heaven. Béziers is well supplied, well armed and surrounded by imposing walls. The crusaders will soon strip the surrounding countryside bare of provisions and turn their camp into a foul cesspit. We will sit in comfort and watch them disintegrate into a starving, diseased rabble. The forty days will pass, they will go home, and life will go on."

John hoped Roger was right, especially after the viscount asked him to stay in Béziers and report back to him at his main court in Carcassonne.

As 1208 progressed, word came down that a crusade against the Cathars *was* being preached in the north by Arnaud Aumery. John wondered if Peter was part of it. Most people agreed with Trenceval that the crusade, if it even got as far as their city, would be only a minor disruption of the comfortable life they had led for decades. Besides, Languedoc, even with its population of heretics, was not the heathen east or Al-Andalus. It was a Christian country, and no crusade had ever been called against Christians.

But as the spring of 1209 progressed, news filtered in about an immense host moving in triumphant procession down the Rhône River. Refugees brought tales of local lords, terrified by the size of the army, scurrying to pay tribute and swear allegiance to Aumery and his knights. Béziers' walls would be the invaders' first real test.

John raised his gaze and looked at the crusader army as it awoke. It lay, sprawled along the far bank of the river, like some vast, colourful beast. Bright identifying pennants fluttered from luxurious red, blue and gold pavilions while the blood-red cross of the crusade emblazoned shields and tunics everywhere. Between the pavilions, John could make out servants polishing armour, repairing surcoats and chain mail, sharpening swords and lances and preparing meals. Voices echoed in the morning air, calling on pages to bring food and clothing for the day. Beneath a rising haze of dust the destriers—huge, powerful war horses, specially bred to carry the weight of an armoured knight and his weapons into battle—snorted and stamped as grooms hurried to feed and tend them.

The crusade had arrived at the city gates only yesterday, and it would be several days before they were ready to mount a concerted assault. Siege weapons—trebuchets, catapults, mangonels, towers, battering rams, scaling ladders—had to be constructed, and miners had to try to dig trenches and tunnels up to and beneath the walls before work on breaching the city's defences could begin.

The knights' bright pavilions, interspersed with the plain tents of the monks and lay brothers, sat back from the river on slightly higher ground. On either side of the camp were tethered the thousands of small work horses, mules and oxen that carried those who could afford to ride and pulled the carts laden with everything the army needed, from food and cooking pots to tents, personal weapons and dismantled siege engines. They stretched in a seething, snorting, stinking mass almost as far as the eye could see.

In front of the knights' city and hard up against the bridge lay the much less colourful bulk of the army. Housed in crude lean-tos and rough tents or on the open ground, and already beginning to smell in the warm weather, the infantry managed as best it could. Some belonged to the knights and had come as part of their duty to their lord, but most were mercenary bands—soldiers for hire from all over Europe: brutal, savage and unconcerned by death.

Around and mingled with the infantry lay the host of camp followers. In the morning sun, several thousand pilgrims, freebooters, hangers-on and bored opportunists scratched and began to wonder how they might profit from the day, for profit was the reason they followed this holy army. Some sought spiritual profit from the indulgences the Pope had promised all those who undertook God's blessed work, but most had more material aims. Many, like the tinkers, fortune tellers, jugglers and whores, profited directly from their proximity to the army. Others sought easy plunder as the army devastated the country it passed through or, hopefully, reduced the fortified cities it besieged.

So far there had been precious little plunder for either the mercenaries or the camp followers, but Béziers held promise. The hilltop city was rich, its normal population swollen to well over ten thousand by refugees who had brought with them every valuable they could carry. The problem was getting at the plunder, which was secure behind the impressive collection of ditches and walls that fortified the town.

"The army of the Devil."

John turned to see a female Cathar Perfect standing behind him. The sight itself was not unusual; more than two hundred Perfects, many of them women, lived openly in Béziers. The Perfect leaned on a rough walking staff. Her face was thin from age and from a lifetime of wandering and relying on others' generosity. Her skin, drawn over her narrow features, was weather-worn and wrinkled, yet the effect wasn't hard. A gentle strength seemed to emanate from the slight smile and pale blue eyes. A cascade of snow-white hair lay over the woman's shoulders in dramatic contrast to the black habit she wore. John experienced a sudden urge to draw this woman's interesting face.

John had meant to learn more about these Cathars, who were the source of so much hatred, but he always seemed to be running some errand for Roger or reporting to the court at Carcassonne and had not had much contact with them. He knew little more about the Cathars now than when he'd argued with Peter a year before.

"You think everything is the work of the Devil," John responded.

The Perfect smiled and nodded. "Indeed, and it must be so. Do you think God would create something that will cause as much destruction and misery as this?" She swept her cloaked arm wide to encompass the view of the army.

"They will not destroy Béziers," John countered. "They will sit out there in the sun for a few weeks then lose heart and go home."

"That may be, but in the meantime, there will be much suffering. To feed itself, the army will destroy everything for leagues in all directions, battles will be fought beneath the walls, and disease will sweep through the city as well as the enemy camp. Even after they are gone, there will be no crops for the farmers to return to. It will be a hard winter, whoever wins here."

John watched the Perfect as she talked. Her eyes sparkled and she looked almost delicate, even when talking of death and destruction. She spoke with an intensity that made John uncomfortable, yet the soft cadence of her voice was calming. He had the impression that what she was saying, even though he had heard it many times before, was unutterably wise.

"What's your name?" he blurted out.

"Beatrice," the Perfect said, her smile broadening. "Your next question will be where am I from, and the answer is Albi."

John had never met anyone, especially a woman, so self-assured and confident.

"I am the daughter of James," Beatrice continued, "a lord of Albi and protector of many Good Christians. I grew up with Good Men and Good Women as teachers and took the *consolamentum* many years past."

"The *consolamentum*?" John said.

"It is our dedication to God. Every Good Christian must take it before death if he or she is to enter paradise. But some of us take it early in life and try to live as God would wish. We are the ones you call Perfects.

"But I have told you of me, what of you?"

"My name is John. I was born in Toulouse and I serve as a page for Viscount Roger." John hesitated, wondering whether he should mention being present at the murder of Pierre of Castelnau.

He was saved from making that decision by a commotion in the street below. A rabble of several hundred townsfolk, armed with rusty swords, pitchforks and assorted clubs, was clamouring for the gate to be opened.

"You see," Beatrice said. "Already the common folk, who normally would be living peaceful lives, are lusting after blood. The enemy cannot get in here, so they are prepared to go out there to kill and maim."

With a loud groan, the gate was slowly pulled open and the townsfolk, shouting loudly to keep up their courage, poured out. They ran down the slope and stood, yelling curses at the mercenaries and camp followers at the other end of the bridge. Encouraged by their fellows and confident that they could strike a blow at their enemies before they were organized, other villagers rushed from their houses, waving any crude weapon they could find, and joined the melee.

"What are they doing?" John asked.

"They are proving that they have more of the Devil in them than their enemies," Beatrice answered.

"But it's pointless! They're not going to defeat the crusaders. And it's stupid to leave the protection of the walls."

"Would God create such stupidity?" Beatrice asked.

Across the river, an equally disorganized rabble was gathering and the two groups began yelling insults back and forth. One of the mercenary soldiers—braver, or stupider, than most—ventured onto the bridge. He stood in the middle, waving a sword and hurling curses that John could only imagine through the tumult.

Suddenly, half a dozen townsfolk broke away and sprinted onto the bridge. Taking the mercenary by surprise, they dodged his sword swipes and dragged him to the ground. Others rushed to join in and after a brief flurry of blows, the soldier's bloodied body was raised and flung off the bridge into the racing waters below.

Enraged, the man's companions swarmed across the bridge. A brief scuffle erupted on the Béziers' side before the townsfolk, less inclined to fight with swords than words, began retreating up the hill. As more and more mercenaries crossed the bridge, the retreat became a panicked flight.

John glanced down at the gate where more townsfolk, unaware of the events at the bridge, were still rushing to join their companions. Already people were falling as the two groups milled chaotically and jammed the narrow entrance.

"Close the gate!" someone yelled above the noise.

The soldiers tried, but the confused crush of people stopped them. Already a handful of mercenaries was at the gate and more were swarming up behind them. One man in particular caught John's attention. He was taller than the others and dressed in chain mail, although in his rush to battle, he had neglected to put on a helmet. His tunic was emblazoned not with the crusader's cross but with a blood-red falcon holding a black axe in its talons. The man carried a similar axe in his left hand. John noticed that several others near the big man also wore clothes marked with the falcon crest.

Instead of trying to push through the crowd into the city, the tall man headed for the guards who were still try-ing to close the gate. The first one he reached never knew what hit him. He collapsed in a pool of blood, his chest split open by a single blow.

"To me, Falcons! Kill the guards. Keep the gate open!" The mercenary was screaming at the top of his voice as he hacked about him. Others quickly obeyed and, at their on-slaught, the surviving guards fled into the city.

"They must close the gate," John shouted, moving toward

the steps that would take him down into the street. Only Beatrice's light touch on his shoulder stopped him.

"It is wrong to kill," she said. "Besides, I doubt that you, one unarmed boy, could make a difference."

John hesitated. He looked down at the tall man, who was now fighting through the crowd, swinging his deadly axe indiscriminately. There was something familiar about him, something about his looks, or the way he moved. All at once, John realized what it was: the axe in the man's hand. The mercenary was left-handed! It was the same helmeted knight who had killed Pierre of Castelnau and got John into this mess. John had never seen the man's face before, but he was certain he was the one.

As John stared, the man raised his head and looked straight at him. His face was weather-beaten and cruel, splattered with blood, and featured a long scar running across his right cheek. He smiled broadly, as if he hadn't had so much fun in a long time.

"Come! Now!" Beatrice's voice was urgent as she began moving along the battlements.

As if to underline Beatrice's order, a crossbow bolt slammed into the wall with sufficient force to shower John with rock chips. Without the faintest idea of where he was going, John hurried after the Perfect.

Soldiers were beginning to pass the pair, hurrying from town into the developing battle, but John suspected they would be too late—already the noise of fighting was spreading along the streets. Béziers, the fortress that was supposed to break the hearts of the crusader army against its impregnable walls, was doomed.

Kill Them All!

Béziers

Peter stood to one side of Arnaud Aumery, patiently awaiting the outcome of the debate going on before him. All the
nobility of the crusade were gathered here in this tent at a
council of war. From outside, a group of monks chanting
holy verses provided a background noise:

> *White was His naked breast,*
> *And red with blood His side,*
> *Blood on His tragic face,*
> *His wounds deep and wide.*

> *Stiff with death His arms,*
> *On the cross widespread,*
> *From five gashes in His side*
> *The sacred blood flowed red.*

Few in the tent were listening. These were warriors who
preferred battle and plunder to prayer and forgiveness.
Some would even rather have been fighting each other than
the heretics.

Eudes III, Duke of Burgundy, detested Hervé de Donzy,

Count of Nevers. Both were arrogant and powerful and the disputed borders of their lands had been the scene of open conflict for many years.

"Damn it all," Eudes, a large, bluff, red-faced man, said angrily. He was dressed in his padded under-armour, although he'd covered it with a tunic bearing the Burgundian arms, three alternating diagonal blue and yellow stripes surrounded by a red border. "Order the attack for today! The longer we wait, the better their defences."

"And the better our preparations." Hervé was the opposite of his enemy—thin, precise and fastidious in his dress and manners. He wore a long silk cloak, emblazoned with the Nevers symbol, a yellow lion rampant on a blue background. "We need three days at least for the carpenters to construct the trebuchet and collect rocks large enough to breach the walls. Then we can talk about an attack."

"Three days while you sit simpering in luxury in your tent. And how many more to make the breach? We came here to fight, let's get on with it!"

"Better sitting in a tent than watching our knights be slaughtered on scaling ladders that are still too short to reach the battlements."

"Our knights shall not be slaughtered." A third man stepped forward between the two arguing barons. He was of medium height and build and around middle age, and was dressed for practicality rather than show in a stained and patched leather jerkin, dark blue leggings and scuffed boots. His coat of arms, a white leaf on a red background surmounted by a bleeding dragon, was nowhere to be seen. His greying hair did nothing to soften the hard lines of his face.

"And what makes you so certain of that, Simon de Montfort." Eudes spat the name with obvious disdain. De Montfort ignored the insult and addressed his remarks to Arnaud Aumery.

"It's simple," he said. "We don't send our knights in. Begin the attack with the mercenaries and the camp followers. The former will go for riches and the latter in hopes of salvation. No one cares if they are slaughtered. If they succeed, we will follow. If they fail, we will bury them."

"You cannot listen to him," Hervé sneered. "He's merely a landless fortune hunter. What does he know of honour and knightly battle?"

"I do not know," Aumery replied with a smile, "but I do know he has taken the cross in the Holy Land, where he sent many of God's enemies to hell. That is more than either of you gentlemen can claim. I, for one, would listen to more of his plan."

De Montfort nodded, but before he could speak, a commotion at the tent flap distracted everyone. A priest was struggling to get past the armed guards at the entrance.

"Let him in," Aumery ordered.

The priest rushed forward crossing himself frantically. "God has opened the gate. It's a miracle," he shouted.

"Be calm, my son," Aumery counselled. "What do you mean? What has God done for us?"

The priest fell to his knees in front of the legate, panting excitedly. "The townsfolk came out of the city on a sortie! The mercenaries chased them back, and God held the gates open."

"The gates are open?" de Montfort asked, stepping

forward. "Are any of our men in the city?"

"They stream through the gates now, your Lordship. It is a miracle! God has delivered us the city of the heathen!"

"We must move at once," Eudes shouted. "That rabble will strip the city bare before we can get in."

"I remind you," Aumery said, "that you are here with the blessings of Pope Innocent to do God's work, not to line your pockets."

"But the possessions of the heretics are ours by right."

"Indeed."

"You told us," Hervé said in a sly voice, "that heretics may be distinguished by their reluctance to take any oath or accept the holy sacrament."

"That is true."

"How, though, if the walls are already breached and the rabble running through the streets, are we to distinguish in the space of a sword stroke the Christian from the heretic?"

Aumery stood silent for a long while. The knights fidgeted uneasily, eager to be away to battle. Peter watched Aumery's face. It was hard and uncompromising. Eventually, he spoke.

"Kill them all! God will know his own."

Peter let out an involuntary gasp. Kill them all?

"As you wish," Eudes said with a smile. With Aumery's brutal injunction ringing in their ears, the nobility of France streamed out to prepare themselves to do God's bidding.

Aumery turned to Peter. "You do not approve?"

"It's not for me to question, Father," Peter said. "But there must be many thousands of honest Catholics in the town. Must they, too, die?"

"Yesterday, as you may recall, Bishop Reginald of this very city entered his town, held a Mass in the cathedral and advised the council of citizens to surrender and give up the heretics from within their walls. Do you remember the response he brought back?"

"The bishop brought back a list of the names of known heretics."

"Two hundred names out of ten thousand? Is that the extent of heresy in this land? I think not. Besides, remember the words of the council. They took no more note of Bishop Reginald's advice than of a peeled apple and claimed that rather than submit to our holy demands, they would eat their own children. Well, it has come to that. Let their children suffer!

"Besides," Aumery continued coldly, "I merely follow the scriptures, with which *you* should be more familiar. In Timothy it says, 'The Lord knoweth those that are His.' And in Numbers, 'The Lord will show who are His and who are holy.' We need not trouble ourselves with that aspect of God's work."

"And a goodly pile of corpses will serve our purposes admirably, I think." Peter turned to see that Simon de Montfort had not left the tent with the others.

"That is indeed true, my lord," Aumery said with a smile, "but our young novice may require further explanation."

De Montfort stepped forward and regarded Peter closely. His face didn't have the reptilian coldness of Aumery's, but Peter had no doubt that he was staring at a man who would not hesitate to commit the most horrendous acts if he believed they would further his aims.

"Even with our miracle this morning," de Montfort explained, "Béziers is but the first of many strongly fortified towns and keeps scattered across this godforsaken land. Even the smallest of them can delay us past the forty days our noble knights have signed on for. An example here will ..."—de Montfort hesitated, searching for the right word—"encourage many Languedoc garrisons to see sense and surrender rather than suffer the fate of Béziers."

"But the innocent—" Peter began. De Montfort's laugh cut him off.

"Innocent? Who is innocent in this world? We arrive sinners and die the same way. Only on the Day of Judgment will we be accounted and cleansed.

"But think on this too, young monk. Those who die this day do so that countless others will be spared in years to come." De Montfort, finished with his explanation to Peter, turned his gaze on Aumery.

"We are undoubtedly blessed, Father. If Béziers falls today then all the land round about, and perhaps even Carcassonne itself, will be ours in a matter of weeks. But Toulouse and the mountain fortresses will not fall so easily. To root out the evil of heresy as the Holy Father wishes, this war must be continued over the winter and after the likes of Eudes and Hervé have departed. Someone must stay behind to hold the conquered lands until the next wave of crusader knights arrive next year."

"And you, as a landless baron, would be the one to stay." Aumery finished de Montfort's thought.

"Neither Eudes nor Hervé will allow the other to return and ravage their unprotected homelands."

"Indeed," Aumery agreed. "My thoughts have run along similar lines. But you are not as close to the king as Eudes and Hervé, and the role of protecting our victories must be offered to the highest first."

De Montfort nodded acknowledgement before Aumery continued. "Though, I suspect with much bluster and apology, they will decline the honour. I must then look to a third." Aumery smiled broadly. "But these details must await the fall of Carcassonne. We will talk more."

"We shall, Father." De Montfort bowed to the legate. "But for now I must see to your instructions in Béziers."

Peter watched the knight turn and stride out of the tent. That was how important things were done, he thought. Understandings quietly reached in private with no specific agreements written down, or even expressly stated. Eudes' bluster and Hervé's slyness were in the open and thus easily countered. Aumery and de Montfort held the real power.

Peter had a sense of being privileged to be part of the inner circle of this venture. Gradually, he became aware of Aumery's eyes on him.

"You begin to see how things are done, young Peter?"

"Yes, Father."

"The Lord works in subtle and, sometimes, mysterious ways. All we can do is keep the ultimate goal in sight and work toward it as best we can.

"Now, you need to see more than the workings behind the scenes. You must see the cutting edge of our holy work. I must write tomorrow to His Holiness the Pope, telling him of our great triumph. I wish you to be my eyes and ears on this day. Go with the knights and return to tell me what things happen in the city."

Peter hesitated. He was being asked to enter a holocaust. It was not fear of his personal danger amidst the bloodshed that gave him pause, but he suspected that the sights he must witness would be too strong for his stomach.

"It is God's work," Aumery said. "Would you deny it?"

"No."

"Then go. I will talk with you later. Now I must scourge this loathsome body in thanks for our great miracle."

As Aumery turned away dismissively, Peter exited the tent into the bustle of the knights preparing for battle.

A Hiding Place
Béziers
JULY 22, 1209

John gasped for breath as he followed Beatrice through Béziers' narrow cobbled streets. Despite her age and the walking staff, she set a blistering pace and John had trouble keeping up as they bumped and pushed through the crowds.

Word that the walls were breached had spread like wildfire and panicked people were running in all directions. Some, clutching whatever valuables they could carry, were seeking sanctuary in the nearest church while others simply ran about aimlessly. Still more, trusting that the speed with which the city was falling would protect them from the fury of the crusaders, kept to their houses and peered out into the street with frightened eyes. Here and there, Perfects stood praying and comforting the Credents who knelt around them. All about, almost drowning out the screams of the terrified people, every church bell in Béziers tolled a funeral knell.

Eventually, Beatrice arrived at the square before the great doors of the church of St. Mary Madeleine. John stopped beside her, panting. The square was filled with people, swarming toward the church. Men stumbled along with cloth-wrapped bundles of valuables clutched to their chests. Women, carrying screaming infants, tried to herd their scared older children in the right direction. Everyone glanced fearfully over their shoulder.

"Are we taking sanctuary?" John asked.

"There is no sanctuary for me," Beatrice replied, "or, I fear, for anyone this day."

"Then where are we going?" Although he had only just met her, John didn't question that he should follow Beatrice. She seemed an island of calm in the midst of all the chaos.

"Whatever happens here, there will be no safe place in Béziers for a Good Man or Woman. Many will die, and those who have taken the *consolamentum* are ready. But some of us must escape. There are things to be done. Will you accompany me?"

John hesitated. He had a duty to Roger Trenceval, but dying in Béziers wouldn't help that. If Beatrice could get him out of the city, then at least he would be alive to go to Carcassonne and report.

A sudden commotion at the far side of the square distracted him. People were screaming in terror and struggling away from a narrow alley. As he watched, a group of mercenaries burst into the square, swords swinging in all directions. The group was led by a tall man wielding a bloodstained axe in his left hand.

"I will accompany you," John said hurriedly.

"Then come," Beatrice ordered as she slipped into the alley beside the church and resumed her punishing pace.

They were heading across town, away from the river

and against the flow of people. Everyone seemed to be heading toward the churches, either the cathedral or Madeleine. John supposed they felt safer in familiar surroundings and assumed that their churches would protect them. He wondered if he should be joining them instead of heading off into the unknown with this strange heretic woman. Perhaps he was putting himself in greater danger by following her. After all, unless there had been a particularly long and brutal siege, the rules of war protected women, children and civilian men. Their property could be seized and their valuables taken, but there was no point in killing them. And John had no valuables to lose. For a brief moment, he considered turning back. But then the image of the left-handed knight swinging his bloody axe swept into John's mind. Somehow, he didn't think the normal rules were going to apply today.

Eventually, Beatrice led them to a small gate at the end of a stinking alley. The gate was open, but there was no one in sight.

"Good," Beatrice said. "It looks as if they haven't found this gate yet. It is a blessing that they did not have time to organize a proper siege and block all exits."

"Perhaps God wishes us to escape this way," John suggested.

"Hah!" Beatrice laughed. "We need work to make you a Good Man. The world and all in it are the creation of the Devil. If there is a purpose to this gate being left open, then it is his."

Beatrice smiled at John's worried expression. "But I think there is a more worldly explanation. I had planned to depart this evening, but I see that my co-conspirator has reassessed the situation as well as I have." Putting her fingers to her lips, she whistled three times.

A man, a dozen years older than John, appeared through a doorway to the pair's left. He was filthy, dressed in rags and wore a sullen expression on his broad face.

"'Bout bloody time you was 'ere," he said. "All 'ell's breaking loose back there." The newcomer jerked a thumb up the alley.

"John, meet Adso," Beatrice said serenely. "He has agreed to help us escape."

"Not if you don't get a move on. An' I only agreed to one. Who's this? Another of your ... Good Men?"

Adso managed to make the expression sound obscene, but Beatrice showed no sign of taking offence. "Two travel as easily as one, and you will be paid in Carcassonne," she said. Then, turning to John, "As you see, Adso is not a Good Christian. Sadly, I suspect he is closer to the pagan than anything else."

Adso spat derisively onto the filthy cobbled street. "Well, we can stand 'ere jawing until they come an' skewer us or we can go." Adso spun on his heel and stalked toward the gate. After cautiously peering around it, he disappeared. Beatrice followed quickly and John slipped through after her.

Once outside, John felt a curious sense of relief. Instead of being cooped up between the smoke-stained walls of the city, he was out in the open. A rocky slope, covered in small bushes and cut by irregular gullies, stretched gently down to a wide, flat plain dotted with small villages and patterned into long rectangular fields. About two miles to the east, along a completely straight road, John recognized the large, regular shape of what had once been, eight hundred years before, an extensive Roman villa. The regular lines of an olive orchard spread out behind it.

To John's right, a number of people were frantically scrambling down the slope. Others who had left the city earlier were already spread out over the flat fields. A noise behind John made him turn just in time to avoid being bowled over by a short, dumpy man carrying a sack over his shoulder.

"Close the gate," Adso ordered, harshly.

John obeyed, heaving the heavy object shut on its rusted hinges.

"Fools," Adso said, spitting onto a nearby rock.

"Why?" John couldn't help asking. "Aren't they doing the same as us?"

Adso regarded John as if he had the intelligence of a slug. "Can you outrun a man on 'orseback?"

John shook his head.

"Neither can they." Adso waved an arm at the fleeing people. "Now, shut up an' follow me."

Meekly, John followed Beatrice as Adso led them around the foot of the palace wall until a deep, narrow gully barred their way. The smell of human excrement was so strong it made John feel weak.

Adso stopped and looked at John. "Through that wall," he said, patting the stones beside them, "is where the rich folks live. This 'ere's the wall of the Viscount of Béziers' palace. 'Course, 'e ran away to Carcassonne long ago, but 'is lords and ladies is still there, unless the butchers 'ave broke the door in already."

John wanted to defend Roger Trenceval—to tell this crude Adso that the young viscount hadn't run away—but he kept silent.

"Thing 'bout rich folk is, they smell just as bad as poor folk." Adso pointed to the wall two feet above the head of the gully. A downspout protruded some six inches from the surface, and the wall below it was caked in a disgusting brown mass that spread into the bottom of the gully.

Adso laughed at John's grimace. "That's the thing that separates the rich from the poor—fancy toilets." With another laugh, Adso jumped down into the gully.

"I can't go down there," John said in horror.

"I fear you will have to if you want to live." Beatrice pointed back the way they had come. A group of crusaders was running over the hillside, hacking at the refugees who had fled out the gate.

"All the world is excrement," she said cheerfully and followed Adso down.

John took a last look behind him, where he saw the dumpy man who had almost knocked him over hold his arms up in a futile attempt to halt the sword blow that nearly took his head off. Then, taking a deep breath, he stepped off the edge of the gully.

Holocaust

Béziers

JULY 22, 1209

Peter entered Béziers through the West Gate and, unsure of exactly what Aumery wished him to do, decided to head up toward the cathedral, whose blocky profile dominated the town. He could hear the sounds of fighting in the distance but, with the exception of the occasional knight hurrying to find some plunder, this area of town was deserted—at least by the living. Bodies from the earlier fighting around the gate lay all about in their bloodstained clothing. Most were soldiers and some still clutched weapons in dead hands.

As Peter worked his way uphill, the number of unarmed civilian corpses increased. The majority were men, but many lay on their faces with sword or spear wounds to their backs, as if they had been cut down while fleeing. Here and there a Perfect in a black habit lay surrounded by the bodies of Good Men and Women.

The doors on both sides of the street had been ripped open or shattered by axe blows, and the contents of the dwellings ransacked. A few piles of bloody, dishevelled clothing showed where the occupants had not fled to safety rapidly enough. Several house were on fire, forcing Peter to hurry past on the far side of the street.

As Peter made his way toward the cathedral, the smoke in the air thickened and the number of bodies increased. He began to hear the noises of ransacking and the occasional scream coming from the houses around him. Soldiers staggered past loaded down with sacks of loot. But even with everything he had seen on his journey, Peter's first view of the square in front of the cathedral came as a shock.

The square was large and dominated by the imposing west front of the cathedral, behind whose squat archways and round windows deep red flames were already flickering. It was like a backdrop for a scene from hell.

Amid the swirling smoke, figures ran in every direction. Men, women and children fled aimlessly until caught and cut down by rampaging soldiers. The killing was random and callous. Peter saw two women and a man burst out of the cathedral's main door to escape the flames and be cut down before they had even reached the bottom of the steps. No one was paying attention to any rules of war; the innocent died as easily as the guilty.

The acrid smell of burning wood filled the air and caught at Peter's nostrils, as the clash of weapons and screams of the dying assaulted his ears. Between his feet, a trickle of blood ran down the drainage gutter from the body of a young man not ten feet in front of him. Was this truly God's work?

Peter stood in shock for several minutes before he noticed a group of knights off to his right. One was Simon de Montfort. Peter made his way over, assuming they were discussing how best to stop the massacre and restore order.

"It is a disgrace," de Montfort was saying, "and must not be allowed to continue."

He was talking to a tall man whose tunic was soaked in blood. He carried an axe over his left shoulder. Behind him a rabble of equally bloody killers stood, each wearing a tunic emblazoned with a falcon holding an axe in its talons. Many carried booty in addition to their weapons, several items of which, Peter noticed, had obviously come from churches.

"My Falcons and I broke through the gates," the big man was saying in a heavy, foreign accent. "We took this town for your precious crusade. It is ours by right of conquest and we shall do with it as we wish."

"Yes, you conquered, but in the name of God and only by His grace. The crusade marches and fights under the cross and you will obey the Holy Church."

"Perhaps God will open the gates of Carcassonne, but I think you would do better to trust in my Falcons. They obey me and they fight for what they can get. If they are paid to kill heretics," the man shrugged, "so be it. A sword guts a heretic as swiftly as a Catholic.

"This war will not be over this summer, and someone will have to stay over the winter if this year's work is not to be lost. That someone"—the big man stared hard at de Montfort— "will be well advised to keep some good fighters near him and not be too fussy about how they earn a few extra coins."

Simon de Montfort stood silent for several moments. "Very well. You and your men may keep what you have, but you must, from now on, work with me in preventing any more looting. All valuables must be taken to the camp and their disposal determined by Father Aumery."

"We are at your service," the mercenary said sardonically.

With a shock of disgust, Peter realized that the knights had not been discussing how to stop the killing, but how to share out the spoils. He was about to step forward and say something when a mighty roar drowned out all talk. Peter spun around just in time to see the cathedral roof crashing in on the nave beneath. Violent bursts of flame, sparks and smoke boiled out of doors and windows. Figures, some engulfed by the fire, were thrown into the surrounding streets. For a moment afterwards, apart from the roiling smoke, the scene in the square was a frozen tableau as everyone stood in awe. Then the violence began again.

"So much for their refuge," the big man said with a laugh.

"But there must have been hundreds of innocent people in there," Peter blurted out. Everyone turned to stare at him.

"Who are you?" the big man asked, lifting his axe from his shoulder.

"He is one of Aumery's underlings," de Montfort answered for Peter. "No doubt here to see that everything is done as it should be."

The mercenary smiled, but there was no warmth in it. He pushed his axe forward, poking Peter in the chest.

"Little monk, you go and tell Father Aumery that God saw fit to smite the unbelievers in His cathedral. Tell him also that God's work saved Oddo of Saxony from repeating the work he has already done in the Madeleine."

Peter couldn't move. His eyes were fixed on the blood-stained axe in front of him.

"So," Oddo went on, "you wish to be introduced to my friend, Britta?" The axe pushed harder, forcing Peter back a step. "She has been busy today. I have introduced her to many new friends—some you would call innocent, but Britta doesn't care. Guilty, innocent, it is all the same to Britta. Is that not so, my dear?" The axe forced Peter back another step. The men behind Oddo laughed.

Peter was terrified. Sweat poured off him and the smell of the fresh blood on the axe made him gag.

"But you are not being polite," Oddo said. "You have been introduced to a lady. Should you not kiss her hand?"

Peter stayed silent.

"Answer!"

The sheer violence of Oddo's command forced a response. "Yes."

"That's better. Now kiss Britta." The mercenary turned the axe so the flat of the blade lay inches from Peter's face. The sharp edge tickled his throat. Half-congealed blood was thick on the blade and a tuft of dark brown hair clung to the edge.

"Kiss Britta!" The command was accompanied by a slight twitch of the axe that cut a thin line in Peter's neck. Closing his eyes, he bent his head forward and kissed the cold blade. The blood was sticky on his lips. Stumbling backwards, Peter collapsed to his knees on the cobbles, retching. The sound of laughter from Oddo's men was deafening.

Struggling to his feet and frantically wiping at the blood and vomit on his face, Peter ran from his torturers.

"Oh, leaving so soon, little priest? Britta will miss you."

Peter fled blindly through the chaos and slaughter, tripping over bodies and slipping in pools of blood. Tears burned his eyes as he barged into cursing soldiers and screaming victims.

At length, he found himself in a square in front of another large church. Bodies and discarded treasures lay around, but there was not a living soul in sight. The wide church doors were thrown open, but no one entered or left, and Peter could see no movement in the dark interior. After the noise of battle, the silence was eerie.

Peter moved forward, drawn by the open doors. Perhaps, at last, he had found a refuge. It took a moment for his eyes to adjust from the bright sunlight to the gloom in the church. At first, he could not make out what the shapes covering the floor of the nave were. He stepped forward, and his foot slid out from under him. He would have fallen heavily, except that his landing was broken by a body. In fact, several bodies were piled around the foot of the marble font. Peter pushed himself away and his hand landed in the puddle that had caused him to fall. It was sticky and smelled sweet. Blood.

With rising horror, Peter struggled to his feet and looked about. The church was a charnel house. Hundreds of bodies—men, women and children—lay piled in the aisles, side chapels and round the high altar, where they had huddled in terror. All were covered in blood and many showed the signs of having been hacked at in a frenzy long after death.

Peter was frozen to the spot, breathing heavily. Here and there a voice groaned for help. Suddenly, Peter felt something clutch at his ankle. He stared down to see a bloodied hand reaching out from the pile of corpses beside him.

"No," he screamed, kicking at the hand and fleeing back into the square. Peter ran aimlessly, tears blinding him. The church must be the Madeleine that the foul mercenary had mentioned, but Peter didn't care; he wanted only to escape the cruelty and horror. But he knew there was no escape. He could run forever, but the scenes he had witnessed in the last few hours were burned into his brain.

At last, Peter found himself back at the West Gate. Staggering through, he collapsed, gasping, on the hillside.

"Are not the workings of Divine vengeance wondrous?"

Peter peered up to see Arnaud Aumery standing before him. "They're killing everyone," he choked out. "The dead litter the streets, the cathedral has burned down, the Madeleine is filled with the dead!"

"Is that not appropriate?" Aumery asked. "Today is the feast day of Marie Madeleine and, if you knew your history, you would also realize that the only truly Catholic viscount this citadel of the Devil has ever had was foully murdered by these citizens on this very day, forty-two years ago. Our Lady is taking her retribution through the strong arms of her crusaders."

"But the women and children! No one is being spared."

Aumery sat down beside Peter. "Have you already forgotten what we talked of earlier this day? God offered the citizens of Béziers a chance to deliver up the heretics from their midst. They did not; therefore, they are equally guilty and deserve their fate."

Peter sat glumly gazing at the dirt between his feet, images of death replaying in his mind. Without question, they had the power to shock and horrify him, but it was the embarrassment of his encounter with Oddo that kept bubbling to the surface.

Aumery placed an arm comfortingly across Peter's shoulder. "There is something more on your mind?"

Peter nodded bleakly.

"Then tell me, my son. I have seen much of the world and will understand."

Peter took a deep breath. "I met de Montfort by the cathedral. He was with Oddo of Saxony, one of the mercenary soldiers. I thought at first they were discussing how to stop the killing, but they were merely talking about sharing the loot."

"The spoils of war are sometimes important to motivate the likes of these men to do God's work."

"But Oddo was so powerful!"

"The Lord needs strong arms."

"Not just physically. His will dominated de Montfort, and when I complained, he brushed me aside like a dry leaf in autumn, and his men laughed. He forced me to kiss the bloodied blade of his axe. The man is a brute! He strides through the world as if he owns it, taking what he needs and doing what he wishes. No one can stop him."

"And you envy him."

Peter jerked his head up and looked into Aumery's weirdly staring eyes. He was right; the power that Oddo flaunted so openly was seductive—what *would* it be like to have no restraints, no limits on what you could or could not do? Not to have to work to make people like you, but have them respect you simply for your power?

Peter nodded miserably. "I *do* envy his strength and power. I'm not worthy to become a monk."

"No, you are young and insecure," Aumery said gently. "You do not believe that you are worthy of anyone's respect. So, when you come upon the strong of this earth, you feel weak and uncertain. You lose sight of anything larger than your own worries."

"It's true, Father. If I am honest, the sound of Oddo's men laughing at me caused me more distress today than the horror of the Madeleine. But what can I do? I will never be physically strong. Look!" Peter held out an arm and pulled back his robe. The bones of his wrist and elbow stood out through his pale skin like pebbles under a blanket. "Sticks and string," he said, recalling John's jest about when God had made him. "And as for strength of will, what power can I possibly have to support me?"

"Pierre of Castelnau was one of the most revolting men I have ever met," said Aumery. "Yet he had power, and nobles did his bidding. He is no more and now I have his power."

"You have the power of God."

"And you shall too, once you are ordained. But I have something more immediate. Something that, unfortunately, carries more weight with the likes of de Montfort and that mercenary. I have the authority of the Pope. I can threaten eternal damnation and the fires of hell, and I can call excommunication. Do you know what that means?"

"The excommunicant is cast out from the Church."

"Yes, but all his debtors are released from their debts, his lords are released from their obligations to protect him, and those under him no longer owe him allegiance. At a stroke, I can destroy anyone who challenges the authority of the Holy Mother Church, and that Church is represented through me. That makes even the most troublesome lord sit up and take notice of what I say. They do not have to like me, but they do have to respect my power.

"Your way to power, young Peter, lies through the Church and through me as your mentor. Why do you think I chose you?"

"You chose me?"

"Of course. We are mortal but the Church is eternal. I fear those who say this crusade will last many a year might be correct. Others must follow in my footsteps once I am become dust. I would wish you to be one."

"I would be honoured."

"Do not be honoured too quickly. It will be a hard road and I will not be a gentle taskmaster, but I will teach you the ways of power, how to acquire it and how to wield it. I will teach you how to use the authority of the Church so that the likes of de Montfort and Oddo will do *your* bidding."

Aumery stood and stretched. He looked back at the city on the hill. "I fear the enthusiasm of this morning has gotten even more out of control."

Peter followed Aumery's gaze. Thick columns of dirty smoke were rising from behind Béziers' walls. Large areas of the city were already ablaze and the fires were spreading rapidly through the dry wooden houses. Knights, laden with treasures, were heading back toward the crusader camp.

"It appears God does not wish anything to be left of this abominable city," Aumery said. "I fear not even treasure will survive that holocaust. Still, I do not think there is much treasure in this town."

Peter frowned. There was a vast amount of treasure in Béziers and Aumery knew that. Yes, much would be lost in a fire, but the crusaders would salvage a lot, as well. He was about to ask Aumery to explain when the legate spoke again. "Come, young Peter, let us go and see what de Montfort *has* managed to salvage."

Peter followed the priest across the bridge. Aumery was right: the Church was the answer to Peter's problem. With the power of the papacy behind him, Peter need never feel weak again.

Destinations

Outside Béziers

JULY 22, 1209

"It looks as if there might be a cave behind that bush down there," the first voice said somewhat uncertainly. "We should check it out."

"Might be's not good enough to get me down there," a second voice replied. "I came to this godforsaken city for plunder. I can get covered in excrement anywhere. Let's go find us some heretics to skewer."

John held his breath as he listened to the two men work their way over the stony hillside. His first breath made him gag, but he loved the smell. It had saved his life.

John, Beatrice and Adso sat huddled together beneath an overhang in the stinking gully beneath Béziers' walls. A couple of half-dead bushes pulled over the entrance did little to hide them, but meant that someone would have to come down into the gully to look into the deep shadows and, as they had just seen, few were prepared to do that.

Adso lowered the evil-looking dagger he had been holding in front of him. "I'm almost sorry they didn't come down," he whispered. "Though I doubt you two'd 'ave been much 'elp."

"You know I refuse to take any life," Beatrice said.

"I know, and your friend's got no weapon. Fine pair you are."

"Why do you refuse to take life?" John asked Beatrice. "Those men would have killed us if they could."

"All souls are trapped in their bodies," Beatrice explained. "Death releases them, but to heaven only if the body has undergone baptism by the Holy Spirit in the *consolamentum*. Otherwise, the soul remains trapped on earth in another body, either human or animal."

"Reckon I'd 'ave been doing those two a favour, sending their souls to live in a couple of frogs."

"So you would have sat calmly awaiting death had they discovered us?" John ignored Adso's comment.

"I would," Beatrice replied. "Death is a blessing for those who have taken the *consolamentum*."

"You would not have acted to save either mine or Adso's life, even though our souls are as condemned as the other two?"

John sensed a hesitation. "I would struggle to protect you, but not to the extent of endangering another life."

"Fat lot of good that does," Adso murmured.

"So, if death is such a blessing, why do you flee from Béziers?" John asked.

"Aye," Adso added, "there's plenty back in the city who'd 'appily give you your wish this day."

"I have a task to perform yet.'

"And if you wish to live to perform it, we'd best be silent and rest. It's many 'ours 'til the sun goes down and it'll not be dark long. We need to be far from 'ere afore day breaks tomorrow."

All day the trio huddled uncomfortably in their disgusting refuge. Occasional screams reached them, and twice they held their breaths as footsteps passed nearby, but no one dared brave the filthy gully to search for survivors. As darkness finally fell, they dragged their aching limbs into the open and moved cautiously away from the devastated city. Fortunately, although the night was cloudless, the moon was new and their progress went unobserved.

After several hours of nerve-racking travel, during which John jumped at every sound in the darkness, the three stopped in a small stand of willows by a stream. They washed off as much of the gully's residue as possible then sat on the bank to rest in the warm night.

"How far is it to Carcassonne?" John asked Beatrice.

"I'm not going to Carcassonne," Beatrice answered. "I'm heading to Minerve."

"Minerve!" Adso exclaimed. "No, no. My agreement was to get you out of the city and take you to Carcassonne."

"No," Beatrice said quietly. "The agreement was that you would be paid in Carcassonne. And so you shall be. You need merely go to the Good Christian's house by the main gate and they will pay you what we agreed."

"An' extra for 'im?" Adso jerked his finger at John.

"Of course," Beatrice said. "I am in your debt, Adso."

Adso grunted. "As long as I'm paid."

"One day," Beatrice said, "you will see that money is

but the Devil's tool."

"I daresay." Adso stood and stretched. "Until then, I'll use the Devil's tool to buy an 'ot meal and a soft bed in Carcassonne. You coming with me, lad, or you off to that nest of crazy heretics?"

John hesitated. Was he still bound by his responsibility to Roger Trenceval in Carcassonne? He had agreed to keep Trenceval informed of what happened in Béziers, but Béziers didn't exist any more. The viscount would discover that soon enough without John. And John was frightened. Carcassonne was the next obvious destination for the crusader army and escape might not be so easy a second time.

John also had to admit to a fascination with the calm, gentle Beatrice. She was the first Cathar Perfect he had a chance to really get to know, and the part of his mind that craved knowledge wanted to find out more about her and her strange beliefs. Her mention of a mysterious task also intrigued him.

"I'm going to Minerve," John said.

"You're both crazy. Carcassonne won't fall as easy as Béziers. The foreigners'll work their forty days, take their indulgences and go 'ome. Everything'll be back to normal in a month." Adso shook his head. "But if you insist, 'ead west for a day or two. Keep the black 'ills on your right. When you reach the Cesse River follow it into the 'ills to find Minerve. And stick to the low ground—there'll be crusader foraging parties all over this country soon. I wish you luck."

The leaves rustled as Adso strode away in the darkness. John felt strangely lonely in the silence that followed. Adso may have been crude and abrupt, but he knew what was going on and they owed their escape thus far to him.

"I wish him the best," Beatrice said, rising slowly and with some discomfort, "but we should get moving."

John jumped to his feet and offered his hand. Beatrice took it.

"Thank you. I am not as young as I used to be, and sitting on the damp grass stiffens the muscles. I don't suppose I should be running around burning cities either!"

"Why are we going to Minerve?" John asked as they set off along the bank of the stream.

"Because I have things to do there, and Carcassonne will fall, if not this year, then the next. After that happens the crusaders will move out north and south from the cities. Minerve, Bram, Terme, Laveur and Toulouse will fall eventually."

"Toulouse?"

"Especially Toulouse. Count Raymond may argue with the Church and stall as long as he can, but the crusaders, and that fat slug, Bishop Foulques, will demand Toulouse be cleared of heretics. Either Count Raymond surrenders or he fights. Either way, Toulouse will fall. The Catholics will not give up, even if it takes a hundred years. They hate us passionately."

"But why?"

"Because we exist and thrive in the very heart of Christendom. To them, we are a canker that must be cut out and burned. We threaten them because we follow the old ways. We keep alive the form and intent of the original Christians and of God himself, from a time before the Church was corrupted by Satan. They hate us for that, but deep down, they know we are right and they are wrong. They cannot change—that would mean giving up all their power—so they must destroy us, root and branch. They will not, as Adso and so many others fondly wish, give up and go home. They will stay and more will come until this land is destroyed and the last Good Christian is hurled into the flames of the last bonfire."

John was silent for a long moment, contemplating the bleak picture Beatrice had painted. If she was right, there was nowhere to run. But John didn't need to run. He wasn't a heretic. He wasn't a particularly devout Catholic either, but if he went somewhere, kept a low profile and attended Mass regularly, he would probably be ignored. Perhaps Minerve was as good a place as any.

"What is in Minerve?"

John sensed that Beatrice was weighing her options, deciding on how much to reveal.

"Books," she said eventually.

"But books are material things—the work of the Devil, no?"

"So you've been listening." John could hear the smile in Beatrice's voice. "It's true, all material things *are* the work of Satan and we, as immortal souls trapped in this corrupt world, must reject them. But God's work is spread through the world as well. Wood is material, yet fire, which consumes it, is immaterial and hence pure. Our bodies are evil, yet our souls are trapped within them. Books are corrupt, yet the wisdom within them—wisdom that comes from our souls—can be pure."

"So the books at Minerve contain wisdom?"

"Of course! And Minerve is not the only place with books. But they are all in danger. The Church of Rome excels in the destruction of all knowledge that does not accord with its own ideas. For example, you know of the four Gospels?"

"Of course: Matthew, Mark, Luke and John. Everybody knows them."

"What if I were to tell you that these are not the only, or even the most accurate, gospels? There are others, about eighty in total, written by disciples and by other holy men, that preserve so much more knowledge than is in the Catholic Testament. There are Gospels by St. Thomas, James and Barnabas. There is even one by Judas."

"I have heard of such things, but aren't they forgeries?"

"Some, but not all. Eight hundred years ago, the founders of the Catholic Church sat down and decided which gospels were to be in the Testament. They chose not for authenticity but for congruence with their ideas. The rest they destroyed or suppressed."

"And these are at Minerve?"

"Some, and other things as well. Mankind's soul has been trapped for a very long time, and the wisdom of God has struggled for release in many different ways. Wisdom is not the preserve of a single time or place."

Despite his exhaustion, John felt excitement building at the thought of the library at Minerve. How he would love to read through the knowledge that was collected there.

"So we are going to Minerve to read?" he asked eagerly.

"And other places. There are books in many libraries

scattered over this land, and as many as possible must be saved before the army of Satan finds and destroys them."

"Where will they be taken that will be safe?"

"That's enough questions for now."

"I want to help." John barely had time to think about his words before they were out of his mouth, but he knew his offer was genuine.

"Then you shall. I can use a pair of strong arms and the company will be welcome. In exchange, I shall teach you something of our ways."

"And turn me into a heretic!" John said with a laugh.

"No. Turn you into a Good Christian. But tonight, we will turn into corpses if we do not stop chattering and keep moving."

For the rest of the night, to the regular rhythm of Beatrice's staff hitting the ground with each step, John's mind whirled with the possible wonders he might discover in the lost books. What scholarship and enlightenment did they contain?

Truce

Carcassonne

AUGUST 14, 1209

Peter answered the summons to Arnaud Aumery's tent with some trepidation. In the three weeks since the fall of Béziers, he had been kept busy, but not in the way he had hoped. Despite Aumery's promise to teach Peter the ways of papal diplomacy and prepare him for ordination, the days had been much the same for Peter as for the other lay brothers.

Since the army had left the smoking ruins of Béziers, he had helped pack up Aumery's tent and its contents each morning and reverse the process at the end of the day's march. He had tended the mules and horses, fetched water, helped cook meals, and cleaned and repaired equipment and the large collection of relics and religious artifacts that always accompanied the Holy Crusade. What unpleasant job had Aumery found for Peter to do this time? True, there was less to do now that the army was camped outside the walls of Carcassonne, but many of the tasks, such as cleaning out the mule lines, were even less pleasant.

Oddo had been right: the gates of Carcassonne had not fallen open as miraculously as Béziers, and a prolonged siege had ensued. But, after seventeen days, everyone felt that some kind of resolution was approaching fast. The

147

forty-day term of service for the crusader knights was almost up, and many would soon begin to drift home. On the other side, conditions in the overcrowded city must be dire. It was a question of which side could hold out the longest.

"Ah, Peter, good of you to come."

Peter was taken aback by the cheerful tone of Aumery's greeting. Nevertheless, he pushed into the tent and stood before the legate. As usual, Aumery was flanked by two lay brothers, but Peter was surprised to see de Montfort standing to one side.

"Remove your clothing," Aumery ordered.

"Remove ..."

"You wish to be ordained into holy orders, do you not?"

"Of course, yes!" Peter's heart was suddenly racing. Was this what Aumery had summoned him for? "But I have not studied."

"These are exceptional times, Peter. The Lord will understand our need for haste. Now, remove your lay robe that you may be ordained."

Peter did as he was told, feeling weak and vulnerable as he stood naked before these men.

"Now lie on the ground."

Peter did so.

"Do you repent of all your sins and renounce all your past life?" Aumery intoned.

"I do."

"Do you renounce all sins of the flesh?"

"I do."

"And as you are reborn into the holy order, will you devote what remains of your earthly life to the service of

God and the performance of the seven holy sacraments of Baptism, Confirmation, Eucharist, Penance, Extreme Unction, Ordination and Matrimony?"

"I will."

"Will you abide by the Rule of the Blessed St. Benedict and the laws of the Cistercian Brotherhood?"

"I will."

"Then stand."

Peter stood and Aumery made the sign of the cross on his forehead with holy water from a small vial at his waist. "Now be reborn in Christ and receive the power to offer sacrament in the Church for the living and the dead, in the name of the Father, and of the Son, and of the Holy Ghost."

Aumery, the two lay brothers and Peter said, "Amen."

One of the brothers stepped forward and draped the white habit of the Cistercians over Peter's head.

"Welcome, Brother Peter," Aumery said, embracing him.

As thrilled as he was at the unexpected event, Peter's stomach churned with uncertainty. Normally, ordination was preceded by a long period of training in a monastery, during which one learned the forms and rituals of the priesthood. Peter had been looking forward to this time— to the opportunity to study his calling. He felt unprepared for the work at hand, but as Aumery had said, these were extraordinary times.

"That's just what we need," de Montfort said, stepping forward, "more monks."

"We can never have too many soldiers working in God's army," Aumery replied.

"Well, they're going to have to work in *my* army if this

damnable town doesn't surrender soon."

"It is in hand," Aumery snapped at the knight. "Now, Brother Peter, God has a task for you. We need an emissary to go into the den of Satan and suggest terms for an end to this siege."

So that explained it—Peter's perfunctory ordination. Nothing was ever straightforward with Arnaud Aumery.

"Why me?" Peter asked. "Should this task not be entrusted to someone more important?"

"Do you question that God has chosen you?"

"No, of course not."

"Then be glad you can do his work. Besides, you speak some Latin and this local Occitan language. You will go under a flag of truce and meet with the heretic Roger Trenceval. You will offer him the following terms: if he surrenders immediately and hands over all heretics in the city to justice, then his city and its inhabitants will be spared the horrors of Béziers."

"He will want guarantees," Peter pointed out.

"You will tell him that you are empowered to give him safe conduct and escort him to this tent to discuss the details. Make sure that you offer only safe conduct *to* this place."

"And if he quibbles about the heretics' fate," said de Montfort, stepping forward, "you may say that *all* the inhabitants of the city may walk free as long as they leave everything behind."

"God and the Holy Church cannot agree to that." Aumery turned on the knight. "You had your earthly example of the power of the crusade at Béziers to encourage your men. Now the Church needs a spiritual example. The heretics of Carcassonne must burn."

"Trenceval will not agree to hand over the heretics. Too many high-placed persons in his city are involved, and he is not yet defeated. We have not come close to breaching the main walls, and he has food and water enough. If Carcassonne holds out for another week or two, my knights will begin to go home—then where will your crusade be?

"If the city falls by storm, there will be massacre and looting to make Béziers seem as if it were a child's game," de Montfort continued. "I need an intact city if I am to hold this land for the winter. If I do not get it, then all we have achieved this year is lost and we must begin again next spring. How many of your forty-day knights will flock next year to repeat the work of this? Your precious crusade needs this city un-burned. Carcassonne is worth a few heretic lives. In any case, you will catch them next year or the year after. Do you want to see your treasure go up in smoke?"

The venom in Aumery's stare shocked Peter. How he must hate the idea of letting the heretics go, but de Mont-fort's logic was unassailable. If Carcassonne burned, then this year was a waste and Aumery would have to be the one to tell Pope Innocent that his crusade had failed.

"Very well." Aumery turned to Peter, all traces of the cheery note with which he had welcomed him gone. The voice was cold and hard. "If Trenceval refuses to submit his heretics to the Church's justice, you may offer him what de Montfort wishes. But do not give it easily. You will take these two lay brothers and go now. I want Trenceval here before sunset."

Slightly stunned by the sudden rush of events, Peter left the tent, followed by the two lay brothers. Outside, a squire wearing de Monfort's colours stepped forward and offered him a large white flag on a stout pole. Peter took it and in silence the three marched through the crusader camp toward the walls of Carcassonne. It was only as they entered the city gate that Peter recalled de Montfort's final, intriguing words, "Do you want to see your treasure go up in smoke?"

Peter's walk through Carcassonne was very different from the one through Béziers. The steep, narrow streets, lined with timbered houses that leaned over to almost meet above Peter's head, were crowded, filthy and stinking, but there was life in them. Signs of the siege were everywhere: Skinny mules and dogs wandered about, scavenging what they could from the piles of refuse lying all around. People stared hard at Peter in his fresh habit, their wide eyes betraying strain. But there were no bodies cluttering the streets, and the looks the people gave him were defiant. De Montfort was right, the city was suffering, but it was not collapsing.

The trio was led into the viscount's palace and made to wait in a sumptuous room whose walls were covered with fine, brightly coloured tapestries that showed scenes from the troubadours' songs. Eventually, Viscount Roger Trenceval entered.

Word had obviously reached the viscount of their approach, and he was dressed in a long cloak bearing the

Trenceval arms and bordered in blue and gold. He was followed by an equally well-dressed page and troubadour. Peter was surprised at how young Trenceval was—only a few years older than himself. Despite the man being an enemy, Peter immediate liked his broad, open face, which broke into a smile as he stepped forward to introduce himself.

"Welcome to Carcassonne! I am Viscount Roger Trenceval of Carcassonne and Béziers, and I assume you are envoys of Father Arnaud Aumery?"

"I am sent by him," Peter said as formally as he could manage. "I am Peter and I am authorized to offer . . ."

"Before all that, let me offer you, as guests, some refreshment. Just because we are at war does not mean that we cannot be civilized." Roger Trenceval clapped his hands and a servant bearing a silver tray of wine goblets appeared as if by magic from behind a tapestry.

Peter had the goblet of dark red wine in his hand before he wondered if it was the right thing to do. Did accepting this hospitality somehow undermine his position? Both lay brothers refused.

Roger seemed unconcerned and took a long swallow with obvious relish. "Now, let us hear what you are authorized to offer."

"I am to tell you that you, your people and your city will be spared if you surrender and give up the heretics in your possession."

Peter was startled as the viscount let out such a loud guffaw that he spilled some wine on his cloak. "That is where we were at the beginning of this affair! Let me make you a counter proposal. I will let your crusader army pack up unmolested and return home before disease takes hold in the ranks, starvation follows on from the ravaging of the countryside, and the forty days of service for the papal indulgence are over."

"I cannot accept that."

"Of course not. And I would not expect you to, but you must have come to me with something else. Let us put all our cards on the table."

Peter glanced nervously at the other people in the room. Roger Trenceval smiled and clapped his hands again. His page and troubadour stood. Roger waited expectantly.

"Would you please leave us?" Peter asked the lay brothers with as much authority as he could muster. The brothers looked hesitantly at each other, but eventually stood and followed the page and troubadour out of the room, leaving Peter and Roger alone.

"Now we can speak openly," Roger began.

"If I am to speak openly, then you must too," Peter said. "It is true that the forty days are almost up but, as you can see from your walls, our camp is well situated. We control the entire countryside from Béziers to here. Narbonne and every castle, keep and town hereabouts have sent envoys to pay homage and promise support." Peter was surprised at how easily the words came once he began. "There is no disease and we are well supplied. It is only August; enough knights will stay past the forty days as long as the weather holds and there is hope of plunder. You must still have water and food, else I would not have seen mules and dogs in the streets, but the people have the look of hunger in their eyes. By September, how much water will you have left? How much food? And will Carcassonne look like Béziers when it does fall?"

"I do not worry about your last point," Trenceval said thoughtfully. "Your army wishes Carcassonne preserved as much as I do. However, you are correct in the rest. The desire for plunder is a powerful force and makes dangerous enemies. It will keep enough men here to maintain the siege past the point where I can offer effective resistance. But for all that, I still cannot accept your terms."

"Why not? You keep your lives. All you lose is your treasure, which will be taken eventually in any case, and a few heretics."

"The treasure I do not care for overly, but I am loathe to see the Good Men and Women thrown onto a bonfire."

"Are you a heretic?"

"Sometimes I think we are all heretics, so narrow are the Church's interpretations and restrictions." Roger smiled again. "But no, I go to Mass like every other good Catholic. But it is my job to rule this land, just as it was my father's. It is the Church's job to save souls. I will not go into my sub-jects' houses and tell them what to say in their prayers to the Almighty. If enough of them keep the peace, pay their taxes and answer my call to arms when we are threatened, I am happy and my subjects adjudge me a good and fair ruler. If the old, fat bishop of Toulouse would rather sit in his palace surrounded by his fine possessions and corrupt priests than tend to the souls of his flock, is it a concern of mine?"

"The army camped outside your walls this day and my very presence here would suggest that it is."

"Indeed, but these ones that you call heretics are my people. Many of my liege lords are Good Christians and their wives and daughters are Perfects. Am I to cast them into the flames to save my skin? And were I to do so, would it help me? I have offered to submit, to give up my lands, to pay homage to Rome and do public penance. Arnaud Aumery dismissed me like a peasant. He wishes blood."

"What if there is no blood?"

"No blood! You think this can be resolved without that payment?"

"It might be possible. De Montfort needs your city and he is prepared to allow heretics to live to acquire it." Peter felt strong as he negotiated. Aumery was right, this was real power, not Oddo's blood-stained axe.

"Go on," Trenceval encouraged.

"If you surrender the city and all its contents, your people will be allowed to go wherever they wish."

"Heretics as well?"

"Yes."

"And what is to stop de Montfort's knights rounding up everyone in a black habit after the surrender and slaughtering them?"

"Nothing, if they are wearing black habits."

"The Perfects will never agree to hide in ordinary clothes."

"Yes, but de Montfort wants everything left in the city when the inhabitants leave. If that were to include clothing, the Perfects would not refuse, and who can tell the beliefs of one naked man from another?"

Trenceval smiled. "You are clever for your age." He thought long and hard, his hands clasped before him as if praying.

"And how does Simon de Montfort propose to undertake this surrender?" he asked eventually.

"I do not know, but I am authorized to offer you a safe conduct back to our camp to discuss the details."

Trenceval thought again. At length he said, "Very well. I do not trust your masters, but I trust you. If it will save my people, I shall return with you into the lion's den. But first I must prepare and inform my knights of what is afoot." The viscount rose and left the hall.

The thrill of having succeeded at such an important task, his first, swept through Peter. The only worm of doubt in his mind was that, in suggesting a way for the Perfects to escape, he had overstepped Aumery's instructions. But shouldn't a negotiator have some leeway?

Peter imagined where this might lead. Perhaps he would become the negotiator for the crusade, travelling ahead of the army and persuading impregnable fortresses to bow before the might of God. Think of all the lives he would save—all the lives he had already saved here in Carcassonne, not least of which was Roger Trenceval's! The young viscount reminded him of John; he had the same open mind and broad interest in the world. It may have been misguided, but it was nonetheless attractive. Where was John now? Peter wondered.

"Let us go and see what fate has in store." Roger's return interrupted Peter's reverie. The viscount had changed into a simple suit of brown leather breeches and a deep red tunic that bore his coat of arms on the breast. He was accompanied by the page who had been present earlier and two sullen, yet unarmed, knights.

"You walked here, as befits your station as a monk, but I shall ride, so as not to seem to be surrendering. At times, appearance is more important than reality."

On the way back through the streets of Carcassonne, Roger led with Peter at his stirrup. The page, the knights and the two lay brothers followed behind. The streets were crowded, yet strangely quiet. People stood and watched the small procession pass. It was almost as if everyone were holding their breath, wondering what this new turn of events meant. Peter noticed a number of heretic Perfects amongst the crowd. He felt a momentary qualm. Had he, perhaps, just saved the heretics' lives? And if so, was that a mortal sin?

"So, if I agree to surrender the city and all its contents, everyone will be allowed to leave unharmed?" Roger Trenceval seemed relaxed, even when faced with Arnaud Aumery and the crusader knights. The negotiations for the surrender of Carcassonne had been swift—Simon de Montfort needed an intact city, and Roger Trenceval wanted to save lives. Peter was pleased. He didn't want to see more bloodshed.

"That is the agreement, yes," de Montfort said.

"Everyone?" Trenceval stared directly at Aumery, who glanced over at de Montfort, but nodded. "Yes. Everyone."

"Very well then. I hereby surrender the city of Carcassonne and all its material contents to the army of Arnaud Aumery and Simon de Montfort and I pass my people into the care of his Holiness Pope Innocent III."

"Excellent." Aumery's voice was flat.

Peter stepped forward with the document he had been preparing from his notes. He placed it on the top of the large trunk between the two parties. Aumery, de Montfort and Trenceval crowded round to read it. Peter prayed that he had not made any serious mistakes.

"What's this?" Aumery asked, pointing a skinny finger at a paragraph halfway down the page. "All will leave the city wearing nothing but their sins."

"All possessions are to be left in the city," Trenceval said.

"And without clothing, no one will be able to hide any valuables as they leave," Peter added.

Aumery shot Peter a sharp look, but before he could say anything, de Montfort burst out laughing. "He's a clever one, this little monk of yours. This will save a lot of searching."

De Montfort picked up Peter's quill, dipped it in ink and signed the bottom of the document. Roger Trenceval followed suit. Arnaud Aumery hesitated, but eventually signed. A wax block and lighted candle were brought forward and small pools of red wax dripped onto the parchment. Each of the signatories pressed his ring into the wax to seal the deal.

"Very good," Aumery said, lifting the document and waving it in the air to dry the ink. He turned to Peter. "You offered the viscount safe conduct *to* our camp?"

"I did."

"Good. Seize him!"

Two knights stepped briskly forward and pinned Roger Trenceval's arms to his sides. The young man didn't resist.

His two unarmed knights stepped forward but were met with a wall of drawn swords.

"What are you doing?" Peter asked, shocked.

"Arresting a notorious protector of heretics," Aumery replied.

"But I promised!"

"You promised him safe conduct *to* our camp. He is here now. You did your job well."

"But—"

"Do not argue with me, boy! I will not have this man free as a rallying point while so many heretics still roam openly in this land. Bind him well and guard him until we can place him in one of the city's dungeons."

Crusader knights dragged Roger Trenceval out of the tent while others guarded his escorts. The viscount did not struggle but, as he was being pulled away, he looked straight at Peter and smiled.

Trenceval knew, Peter thought. He knew that in coming here with me, his freedom, and possibly his life, were sacrificed. He was prepared to give that up to save his people. Peter felt stupid that he had not seen Aumery's ploy. His dreams of becoming a famous negotiator vanished.

"Make copies of this," Aumery said to Peter as he handed him the signed document, "and have it nailed to every church door in the city." He turned to de Montfort and the other knights. "Tomorrow at dawn, the population may leave unmolested, taking, as my young friend said so eloquently, only their sins. Your knights will plunder nothing on pain of excommunication. All valuables will be brought here, piled up and guarded. They will pay for the continuing crusade. Escort Trenceval's page and knights back into the city."

The knights filed out, leaving only Aumery, de Montfort, Peter and a few lay brothers.

"So now you have your intact city for the winter and a base for your expeditions next summer." Aumery addressed de Montfort.

"And you have one of the main protectors of heretics in chains," de Montfort responded.

"I do, but I would rather your men were building a bonfire for tomorrow."

"Patience. There will be bonfires a plenty in the summers to come. But what has our young monk here got from the day?"

"Nothing," Peter said bitterly. "I was just a tool."

"But a tool in a righteous cause. And that will take you closer to God. Is that not so, Father Aumery?"

"Indeed, and I believe he has learned yet one more lesson in the art of diplomacy. He has learned much in a short time and will learn more in the coming winter months. He may yet be of service to you in your work here."

"Perhaps. But for now, I must see to our prisoner." De Montfort strode out of the tent.

"And you must to your rest," Aumery said. "Tomorrow you begin to study what you should have learned before your ordination."

Peter nodded and left. Darkness was falling, and the first stars were showing themselves. Word of the end of the siege had passed swiftly through the crusader camp and the sounds of revelry were already beginning.

It had been a strange year, Peter reflected. He could recall every moment of his troubling encounter with Oddo. The image of Oddo's scarred face and Britta's bloody blade still caused shudders of embarrassment, but it also strengthened his resolve to never again be so powerless that a thug like Oddo could humiliate him. Today, he had been a tool in a shameful deed, but his reward, so Aumery and de Montfort seemed to promise, was to be learning over the winter and a place on next year's crusade. As Peter made his way through the dark to his own tent, it seemed a good exchange.

Remembering

Minerve

JULY AND AUGUST 1209

"We shall be safe here. At least for the time being," Beatrice said.

It was a hot late July day and Beatrice and John were sitting on opposite sides of the rough wooden table in the kitchen of the Perfect house in Minerve. The room was rectangular and the table ran almost the length of it. John sat with his back to the huge stone fireplace where pots of all shapes and sizes hung in a hearth large enough for John to stand upright in. The opposite wall was broken by doors leading to pantries, upstairs rooms and a small courtyard. Above John's head, the roof beams were black from the smoke of cooking fires and below his feet, the beaten earth floor was covered in a fresh, thick layer of dry threshed hay mixed with herbs. The smell of wild sage and rosemary filled the air.

The kitchen was also a dining room and meeting place for the twenty Perfects who slept on the floors of the upstairs rooms, but the two new arrivals had it to themselves this afternoon. Beatrice slept upstairs, but John had been given a nook by the fireplace. It was comfortable, but the location meant that he didn't get much sleep—he couldn't retire until the evening service was done, and he had to be up before the morning meal was served, shortly after the sun rose.

After Adso had gone his own way, the five-day journey to Minerve had been tiring but uneventful. The farther they travelled from Béziers, the less chance there was that they might stumble on a crusader patrol foraging for supplies or plunder.

In the days after their arrival, Beatrice had been closeted with the other Perfects, leaving John to wander the steep, narrow cobbled streets of the small town and fend for himself. As soon as it became known that he had escaped from Béziers, John was the centre of attention. For a few days, he couldn't take more than a few steps in any direction without someone approaching him and asking if the stories of the atrocity were true, but things had quietened down now and he'd had a chance to explore.

Minerve was an extraordinary place, surrounded on three sides by deep gorges and joined to the surrounding countryside only by a neck of land some thirty feet wide. The gorges, which held the torrents of the Cesse and Briant rivers in winter, were almost dry in summer. John had even ventured down onto the sandy bed of the Cesse and explored the high, broad caves where it ran underground.

The neck of land at Minerve's north end carried the only road into town and was blocked by the imposing walls and tower of the castle. Walls grew from the top of the gorge and completely surrounded the town. A few determined defenders could hold this town against any army in the world, John hoped.

"Is anywhere safe after what happened at Béziers?" John asked.

"In the long term, no," Beatrice responded, "but Carcassonne should hold them up for a while."

"It might stop them altogether. They might go home."

"I don't think so. The crusaders will try everything to capture Carcassonne as soon as possible so that they will have a winter haven. And, remember, the example of Béziers will encourage surrender sooner rather than later."

"Will they get to Minerve this year?"

"No. Next year, maybe the year after. There are many castles and the crusaders will have to lay siege to each in turn. If the defenders are stout, it will take a long time to subdue this land. But the Church *will* subdue it. The hatred is too great, and the Pope has deep pockets. Good Men and Women will fuel many fires before this is over."

"Why don't the Perfects flee?"

"Where to?" Beatrice shrugged. "We will be hunted to the ends of the earth."

"And you won't resist." John thought back to Adso's comments as they'd hidden outside Béziers.

"No Good Christian will take up arms and fight, but there are many lords who will battle to save what they think is important. And, although I think all their worldly concerns are foolish, I am glad of the time it will give us."

"Time for what?"

Beatrice stared hard at John, who began to feel uncomfortable.

"What books have you read?" Beatrice asked, eventually.

"Only the ones the nuns had in Toulouse. St. Augustine mostly."

"Nonsense," Beatrice said dismissively. "He would have

done better to remain an ignorant pagan than write all that rubbish that the Catholics take so seriously. Anything else?"

"There was one other, in Latin. It was a history by an ancient Roman called Herodotus."

"Do you remember any of it?"

"My favourite bit was the story of Leonidas and the three hundred Spartans. They held a pass against the invading Persians and they all died."

"Yes, but do you remember any of the words?"

John's brow furrowed as he struggled to recall the text. "*So the barbarians under Xerxes began to draw nigh; and the Greeks under Leonidas, as they now went forth determined to die, advanced much further than on previous days, until they reached the more open portion of the pass.*

"There's another bit in here that I can't remember, but then it goes on.

"*Now they joined battle beyond the defile, and carried slaughter among the barbarians, who fell in heaps. Behind them the captains of the squadrons, armed with whips, urged their men forward with continual blows. Many were thrust into the sea, and there perished; a still greater number were trampled to death by their own soldiers; no one heeded the dying. For the Greeks, reckless of their own safety and desperate, since they knew that, as the mountain had been crossed, their destruction was nigh at hand, exerted themselves with the most furious valour against the barbarians.*"

John shrugged. "I remember a few other bits as well."

"You remember the violence and excitement—the bits about the battle," Beatrice said with a smile.

John lowered his eyes in embarrassment. "I suppose

so. It's what interested me."

"That's what we find easiest to remember, what is of interest. But how do you remember?"

John looked up. "I don't know. I just read and reread the interesting bits until I knew them."

"You didn't place them in your mind?"

"I don't understand."

"There is a way to train your mind to remember. It is called the memory cloister. Have you heard of it?"

"No." John could visualize a long, arched cloister, but how that helped your memory was a mystery.

"It takes training, but the idea is to think of your memory as a cloister with alcoves off each side. The alcoves contain what you wish to remember. Thus, if you want to remember the scraps of your Herodotus book, you imagine it placed in, say, alcove number thirty-five on the left. When you wish to retrieve it, you return your mind to alcove thirty-five and imagine pulling the manuscript out and reading it."

"It sounds easy," John said.

"It's not. It requires much concentration, discipline and practice, but the memory cloister can be used to memorize entire books. The possible complexity is endless. Each alcove can become an entrance into a new cloister, which in turn may have other cloisters spreading from it. Even the pillars of the arches can be used to remember specific important facts or lists. I have met adepts who have built cloisters in their minds in the shape of mazes with rooms and branches off almost every archway."

John struggled to visualize what Beatrice was describing.

He understood what she was saying, but couldn't see how it would work. On the other hand, the idea of having all he learned from books organized and easily found excited him.

"Would you like to learn the memory cloister?" Beatrice asked with a smile.

"I think so," John said uncertainly. "It sounds very useful. But why would you teach me? I don't know many books."

"Remember on the road here I told you that we had to preserve books for the wisdom within them?"

John nodded.

"We have collected the physical books, and scrolls of parchment, papyrus and vellum, and placed them in many libraries all over the land—"

"Here at Minerve?" John asked.

"We have only a few here. Most are in high fortresses in the mountains—Quéribus, Peyrepertuse, Montségur—places that are either unassailable or too remote to attract attention. But our libraries will not be ignored forever. The Pope knows of our collections and the crusade is instructed to find and destroy them all."

"Destroy books!" The idea horrified John. He had always regarded books as almost magical things that contained all the knowledge he craved. "Books are precious! I thought the crusaders wanted to burn heretics, not books."

"Books *are* precious," Beatrice agreed, "but the knowledge within them can also be dangerous. The Catholic Church has spent untold energy over the past one thousand years building a single version of the truth. From the vast literature available, they have selected what fits with their story and with it, constructed their religion. They have suppressed the rest, burning the books and the people who have spoken against them. They have listened to Satan whispering in their ears and created a religion that exists in the material world. In the process, they have forgotten the spiritual. But they have been overwhelmingly successful. Satan now sits in Rome and no one notices."

"But the Pope is powerful and the Perfects few."

"That is true, but his power is material and, like all material things, can crumble and fall with remarkable ease. The Perfects *are* few, but our knowledge is vast."

"And, as you said, dangerous."

Beatrice nodded.

"What is this knowledge that the Pope fears?"

Beatrice studied John hard.

"What if Christ were not divine?" she asked, at length.

John's mouth dropped open in shock. This was blasphemy.

"God is perfect, infallible; therefore He cannot create something which is less than perfect," Beatrice explained, slowly. "He created our souls, which *are* perfect, but not our bodies or the material world in which we exist. That is corrupt and fallible and was created by Satan. If Christ was made of flesh and blood, He was corrupt and therefore could not have been of God."

"Perhaps His body was an illusion, so that we poor humans could see Him?" John suggested, struggling to keep up with Beatrice's arguments.

"A clever idea, but if Christ's body was an illusion, that makes a mockery of the Crucifixion and the suffering that the Church makes so much of. And, if God is infallible, how could Christ have failed?"

"Failed?"

"Yes. Even in the Gospels of Matthew, Mark, Luke and John, Christ says that the end of time is coming soon. He says specifically that He is bringing it, and that it will arrive while some of the people who listen to Him preach are still alive. That was more than one thousand years ago."

Beatrice fell silent and watched John. His thoughts were a turmoil. If Christ was not the son of God, where did that leave everything he had ever been taught?

"I don't know what all this means," he said helplessly.

Beatrice smiled. "Of course you don't. If it were that easy to convince people of what I have just told you, then the Church would have crumbled long ago. All I ask is that you open your thoughts. Reread the Gospels with what I have said in mind.

"For now, though, simply assume that what I say is true, or at least that many people fear it might be. Now, imagine a book that told the story of Christ's life as if he were an ordinary man. A man who had an ordinary birth, married, had children of his own, preached and was crucified but survived to realize his ministry was a failure—that all he had taught of the imminent arrival of God on earth was a sham, an illusion placed in his mind by the Devil. What would the Catholic Church think of that book?"

This was almost unimaginable heresy indeed! John knew he should walk away—leave Minerve and Beatrice and find somewhere he could live and not think of all this. Where he could attend Mass with everybody else and live an ordinary life. Where he could forget about the crusade, and the Church, and heretics. But he was fascinated, drawn in by the sheer outrageousness of what Beatrice was suggesting. He had to go on and see where it led.

"The Church would say the book was a forgery," he said.

"And burn it?"

"Certainly." John began to see why burning books might be so important to the crusade.

"And if the book were true?"

"It would destroy the Church."

"Yes. The entire corrupt, material edifice of the Pope's domain would collapse like a castle made of sand when the tide rolls in. Bishop Foulques, Arnaud Aumery and countless others cannot, will not, allow that to happen. If they found such a book, they would destroy it and everyone who had ever heard of it."

What Beatrice said made sense to John, but was she just making a theoretical point?

"Does such a book exist?" John asked, far from certain that he wanted to hear the answer.

Beatrice's shrugged. "I simply give an example of how the knowledge in but a single volume could have the power to destroy the entire Church. And we have hundreds of books in our libraries. If even a quarter of them contain a mere shadow of what I have just told you, then the Pope will never rest until every page is consumed in fire."

"So, that is why you keep your libraries in such inaccessible places. But you said that, sooner or later, every castle and keep will be destroyed by the crusade. Does that not mean that your libraries are doomed?"

"It does, yes. On the road you also asked where we will take the books for them to be safe. I did not answer."

"I remember."

Beatrice tapped her head. "*This* is where we keep the books. That is why we teach the memory cloister."

"To memorize the books!" With a rush of excitement, John realized what he was being offered. The memory cloister was not simply a way to organize what little John knew. It was, when filled with the things Beatrice was talking about, a path to almost untold knowledge.

"Exactly. The physical pages of a book or a scroll are nothing. Parchment and vellum are scarce. It takes a long time for a scribe to copy even a small book. Yet fire can destroy the largest book in minutes. The wisdom that resides in a book is all. A book may be found, read and thrown on a bonfire, but none can know what is in a man's or a woman's mind unless that person chooses to tell."

"So, the Perfects learn the books and preserve the knowledge?"

"That is the way it has been. Some Good Men and Women know the lost knowledge and have kept it safe, but now it is no longer safe in their heads. By the time the next century is passed, if there are any Good Christians left they will be a scattered, hunted remnant. None will be allowed rest until they are dead."

"So who will preserve the books?" It felt to John as if Beatrice's gaze was stabbing right through him.

"You will," she said softly.

John began to protest, but Beatrice raised a hand to stop him.

"Not only you. There will be others, enough so that the knowledge can be passed on and spread throughout the world in the generations after the last Good Christian is ash.

"That is why I offer to teach you the memory cloister. You have a love of learning and, I believe, will make a suitable vessel for our wisdom. If I am wrong, say so now and go upon your way. If I am right, then I will teach you the memory cloister, and you can travel the land placing all manner of wondrous books in your mind."

"I'll do it," John volunteered.

"Do not answer so quickly. Aside from the risks of having such dangerous knowledge, there is a heavier price. To be able to come and go as you please in these troubled times, you must be invisible. That means that all those who accept this role can never receive the comfort of the *consolamentum*. You will not be able to join the Elect and therefore, you will not, unless you are lucky enough to find a member of the Elect on your deathbed, be able to enter paradise. Your soul will be condemned to wander this evil earth until the end times come. It is not a sacrifice to be taken lightly."

John sat in silence, contemplating the offer. The idea of his soul wandering the earth was worrying but, according to the Good Christians, that was what his soul was doing now, and it wasn't so bad. He only had the sketchiest idea of what the Cathars believed, but that was probably why Beatrice had chosen him—unlike the Elect, John had no concept of what he might be losing. And, if he didn't know much about Catharism, the crusaders could hardly call him a heretic. These were frightening times whatever he chose to do, and the idea of developing his memory in the way Beatrice suggested was attractive. On top of that was the access he would get to all kinds of rare and forbidden books.

"I'll do it," John repeated.

"Good." Beatrice's face broke into a gentle smile. "But I must give you one more warning. If you become an adept, there will be consequences. Releasing the memory is like digging for stones in sand. You collect the stones, but you also collect a lot of sand. As you put books in the alcoves, the experiences of everyday life, like the sand, comes too and it sticks to the walls of the cloister. Every carving, window, painting, down to the tiniest mark on the cloister wall, takes on significance. Each triggers a memory from your past life. Eventually, if you become good enough, you can forget nothing."

"That is wonderful," John said, thrilled at the idea of such a powerful memory.

"Perhaps, but it has its cost. There are always things we would prefer to forget, are there not? Memories we would rather lock away or erase than continually be reminded of? You will not have that luxury. If you learn well, you will remember everything you see and do, even that which you would wish not to."

"It doesn't matter," John said, unable to think of anything he wanted to forget.

"Very well then. There is a small collection of books here that we can use for training before you go out to the libraries. We must begin immediately. "

In the two weeks since Beatrice had begun teaching John the memory cloister, he had barely slept. Every waking moment had been spent reading and performing mental exercises to train his memory. John was amazed at the progress he was making. His memory, it turned out, was vastly more powerful than he had imagined. All it had required was the discipline. Now John could read large chunks of text, consciously file them in an appropriate place, and there they were, ready to be recovered in their entirety whenever he wished. At the same time, the Latin he had learned as a child was improving by leaps and bounds and there was little now that he could not read.

Sometimes pieces of text would go missing or John would search a specific alcove and find nothing there, but, like his Latin, his memory had improved immensely—and the things he was learning were amazing. Gospels, some only fragmentary, that he had never heard of; Roman histories and descriptions of all manner of wonders; strange documents from Al-Andalus and the Christian states of Aragon and Castille. It was a whole new world, richer and more complex than any he had ever imagined. John was so excited that he begrudged even the few hours of sleep Beatrice forced him to take. There was so much to learn.

"You are learning faster than I had hoped." Beatrice and John were sitting once more in the kitchen. "You have a natural talent for remembering."

"I love it," John said. "I want to know everything."

"That is good." Beatrice smiled broadly. "But beware two things. Be careful that you do not confuse facts with wisdom. Wisdom comes only through having a place to put the things that you learn. Otherwise, the facts are useless and you fall into the trap of arrogance. That is a sin.

"Also, beware the Devil. He is subtle and knows how to use our weaknesses. Satan is always as clever as the one he is tempting. He places many things in books to mislead us. That is not an argument, as the Catholics think, for destroying books, but it is a reason to gain the wisdom to tell what is false from what is true. And that is a much greater task than mere remembering. For example, the Gospel of Thomas that you read yesterday. It says—"

Beatrice was interrupted by a loud knock on the door to the street. Before she could rise to answer, the door swung in and Adso stepped over the threshold.

"Adso!" John exclaimed, jumping to his feet.

Adso was filthy and looked as though he hadn't eaten or slept properly in days. His cheek bones protruded and his eyes were dark-rimmed and sunken. He was followed by an old man dressed in beggar's rags. The old man was small and hunched over, making him seem no larger than a child, yet his face was deeply lined and his skin as dark as old leather.

John helped Adso to the table while Beatrice assisted the old man and then went to the pantry. She returned with a loaf of bread, a hunk of dry cheese, an orange and two cups of watered wine. She broke the bread in two and gave the cheese to Adso and the orange to the old man.

The old man picked at the bread like a delicate bird, but

Adso demolished everything before him in seconds, drained his wine, wiped his mouth on his sleeve and said, "Weren't nothing that good in Carcassonne, nor on the road 'ere."

"What happened at Carcassonne?" John couldn't contain his questions any longer. "Has there been another massacre?"

"No killing this time, least not other than the knights, whose job it is to kill and die. Town surrendered three days past."

John wanted to know the details of how the battle had gone, but Beatrice spoke first.

"And the Good Men and Women. How did they fare?"

"Well," Adso responded with a smile, "weren't no bonfires."

Beatrice frowned. "Why?"

"Not certain. We was 'olding out well. Still plenty water and we 'adn't sunk to eating the mules and rats yet. De Montfort 'ad attacked several times, but that only left piles o' bodies in the ditches below the walls.

"One day, a damned monk comes into the town, a tall skinny kid, all arms and legs, and talks with Viscount Roger. I expected—"

"What did the monk look like?" John interrupted. The description had made him think of Peter.

"Like I said," Adso replied, puzzled, "tall and skinny."

"Did you hear his name?"

"I didn't learn the name of every monk—no wait, I did 'ear this one's name mentioned. It was one of the apostles, Philip? No, Peter. That was it. Why d'you care?"

"I knew him once," John said. Part of him was glad to

hear news of Peter, but the other was sorry that he seemed to have risen to such an important place in the invading army.

"D'you mind if I go on with my tale, now?" Adso asked. John nodded.

"I expected Trenceval to send this friend of yours packing"—Adso flashed a sharp glance at John—"but, instead, what does 'e do? 'E goes off into the lion's den with 'im. Never comes back. Story is they threw Trenceval in the dungeon—never mind 'im being under a flag of truce."

John gasped at the news. Then a wave of guilt swept over him. He had abandoned his responsibilities to Roger Trenceval to follow Beatrice to Minerve. He had been so wrapped up in his own activities since then that he had barely thought about the young viscount.

"Just as well you didn't go to Caracassonne, lad, else you might be in that dungeon with 'im," Adso said, looking at John.

"But I let him down," John said.

"Don't worry yourself. You made the smart choice. It doesn't pay to put your faith in lords and princes. Trenceval would 'ave made 'is own decisions, whether you was there or not. But what's this Peter to you?"

"I grew up with him in Toulouse," John said. "He had a strange vision one day and went off to become a monk. He was with Aumery at St. Gilles before Castelnau was killed."

"Doesn't surprise me. He must be well in with that devil Aumery to be made a negotiator.

"Anyway," said Adso, turning back to Beatrice, "whatever 'appened at the truce, the next day there's these notices on all the church doors, saying everyone's to leave the city but that they cannot take anything—'carry only your sins' was 'ow it were put. No mention of giving up the Good Folk for burning. I was just appreciating my good luck when this old man comes up and demands that I bring 'im 'ere. Seems I'm making an 'abit of escorting Good Folk round this country. Brought 'im all the way here without a word of thanks—barely a single word of any sort as it 'appens."

"I told him to seek you out should he ever need help." Adso and John stared at Beatrice.

"You told 'im I would 'elp?" Adso asked.

"I knew you would never refuse."

"Huh!" Adso grunted. "What makes 'im so important?"

"He is Umar of Cordova," Beatrice said, as if that explained everything.

"He is a Moor?" John asked.

"And what is wrong, might I ask, with being a Moor?" The old man stared at John, a glint in his eye that belied his age. "The Moors, as you call them, know more of the world than you can imagine. And I"—Umar sat up straighter—"am descended directly from Abd ar-Rahman, greatest of the Umayyad caliphs of Al-Andalus."

John had no idea what the old man meant and was beginning to feel uncomfortable under his penetrating gaze. Fortunately, Beatrice broke the silence.

"A Moor on one side only, and that your mother's, a serving girl four hundred years removed from the great Caliph." Umar shrugged agreement and went back to his orange.

"His father was Gregory of Foix, a Good Christian who led many debates against the evils of the Church."

"This is all very interesting," Adso broke in, "but no one has yet told me what is so important about the old goat and why I should 'ave risked my life to bring 'im 'ere."

The three stared at Umar, who was concentrating on carefully peeling his fruit.

"What?" he asked, as he became aware of the attention.

"Adso wishes to know what is so important about you," Beatrice explained with a smile.

The old man waved his hand dismissively. "There is nothing important about me. I am but an old, cracked vessel that will soon release another soul to a better world."

"We could 'ave released your soul in Carcassonne and saved ourselves this trip," Adso said.

"I dare say," the old man said, "but then I wouldn't have been able to pass on the books, would I?"

"Books?" John asked, looking to see if the old man had carried a satchel in with him. "You don't have any books with you."

Umar cackled roughly. "Can you see the air around you?"

"No," John said.

"Yet you know it is there with every breath you take. Seeing is not all. Beware of trusting only what you see. Your eyes show you material things, and they are the Devil's toys."

"The memory cloister!" John exclaimed with a flash of insight. "You have the books in your head."

Umar nodded and placed a segment of orange in his mouth.

"Books. Books. Books! It's always about books with you people." Adso rose and fetched another piece of cheese and refilled his wine goblet.

"Perhaps you are not as stupid as you look," Umar went on, staring hard at John. "Yes, I have the books in this old head. Are you the one I am to transfer them to?"

"He is," Beatrice said before John could respond. "And you should have been here weeks ago. It was not the plan to have you trapped in Carcassonne."

"These eyes are not what they once were. And there were so many books." Umar spoke to Beatrice, but he never took his eyes off John.

"You were only supposed to get one—*the* book."

John's heart leaped at the emphasis on "the." Could this be the book Beatrice had suggested could bring down the Catholic Church?

"And I have it. And I am here. So all is well. What is your name, boy?"

"I'm John."

"Well, John, we must get to work, if we can get rid of these annoying chatterers." Umar glanced at Adso and Beatrice.

Beatrice nodded approval. "So Adso," she said, standing, "I assume you and Umar are not alone in coming here?"

"Indeed not," Adso agreed. "There's plenty near-naked and 'ungry people streaming up the valley be'ind me. It'll take more than a few 'unks of bread and cheese to see to them."

"Then we must make ready. Adso, if you are sufficiently refreshed, go to the city gates to direct any people who need help to the square outside the church of St. Etienne. I shall go to the houses about town and arrange places to sleep and food to eat."

With that, she was gone. Adso looked at John. "The adventure continues," he said with a sly smile.

"But how will it end?" John asked.

Adso's smile broke into a laugh. "That's the question, and only God—or the Devil—can answer it. I shall leave you with this Good Man."

"Let's get to work," Umar said as Adso left. "Are you adept at the memory cloister?"

"I've only just begun," John explained. "Beatrice has been teaching me and I am learning, but I have some way to go yet, I think."

Umar shook his head and sighed. "It's not like the old days. I remember when people took things seriously. Now it's all rush and bother, and no one takes any notice of what's important. The Devil defeats us by swamping us in trivia so that we lose sight of what's significant. You mark my words: one day no one will care about anything at all. And then where will we be?"

Umar fell silent and stared at John with his watery eyes. John had no idea what he was supposed to say. "I agree," he ventured at last.

"Nonsense!" Umar exclaimed. "This is exactly what I mean! You cannot agree with something if you haven't thought about it. You have a brain with immense God-given power. Use it!" He slapped his hand loudly on the table. John jumped at the noise and Umar grimaced in pain. He massaged his hand.

"Well," he went on eventually. "I suppose we must work with what we have, imperfect though it may be. Sometimes I wish I were back in Cordova. At least there, they appreciate learning."

"You have been to Cordova? Have you seen the

Mezquita? Is it the wonder they say?"

Umar shook his head. "You chatter on like an angry squirrel. How will you have room in your head for the important things if you fill every moment with useless nonsense?"

John dropped his gaze to the tabletop. Already he had disappointed this strange old man.

"But yes," Umar went on, his voice almost wistful. "I have been to the Mezquita and it is even more wonderful than any can say. It is a forest of more than a thousand pillars, of jasper, onyx and marble, many taken from the long-vanished temples of the Romans. When you first cross the orange groves and enter, as your eyes adjust to the dim light, it is as if the pillars go on forever. As if you can walk and walk through this stone forest of trees for the rest of your days and never see two the same."

Umar fell silent for a minute. John was about to ask another question when the old man jerked himself out of his reverie and continued in a much more business-like voice. "But we must continue. There is work to do. Please do not distract me again." Umar closed his eyes and breathed deeply. "*Inasmuch as it pleaseth God the Father, I shall set down my life so that others may learn from it after I am gone to join Him.*

"*In the beginning it was . . .*"

"What is this? What are you saying?" John asked in confusion.

Umar opened his eyes and glared across the table. "You have never done this?"

"What?"

"Transference. Learned a book from the recitation of another?"

"No. I have only learned from reading."

Umar sighed heavily. "Such coarse clay with which to work. Now, listen carefully. The process is the same. Create a space to accept the words, close your eyes and listen hard.

"Inasmuch as it pleaseth God the Father."

"Wait," John said. "What is it I am learning?"

"You truly know nothing," Umar said in amazement. "How long have you been a Good Man?"

"I'm not," John said helplessly. "Beatrice is teaching me the memory cloister *because* I am *not* a Perfect. She says it is safer that way because the crusaders will not stop until all the Good Christians are burned."

The old man gazed thoughtfully at John, drumming his fingers on the table. "So you know nothing of us?"

"I know that you believe that the material world is the realm of Satan, that you don't take oaths, that you believe the Catholic Church is corrupt, that Christ was just a man, that..."

"Enough." Umar stopped John's recitation. "But you don't know of our origins?"

"Not much, no."

Umar rubbed his eyes. "Such strange times," he said more to himself than to John. "I hope Beatrice knows what she is doing." He sighed again. "Very well. I shall tell you something of the burden we Good Christians carry. In doing so, I shall be passing some of that burden on to you. Can you bear it?"

"I can," John said as confidently as he could manage,

although he had not the slightest idea what the burden might be.

"Hmmm..." Umar rubbed his chin. "Our beliefs stretch far back, as far before the Christ as we are after, to ancient Persia and a prophet called Zarathustra. He taught the Five Truths: all are equal; all living things deserve respect; nature is to be celebrated; hard work and charity is the way to heaven; and loyalty is required to all family, friends and clan. He also taught of two gods, Auramazdah, the god of truth, good and creation, and Angra Mainyu, the god of lies, evil and chaos. Humans are the battleground between these gods, our souls and all things spiritual from Auramazdah, our bodies and the material world from Angra Mainyu. Do you follow?"

John nodded, although he was far from certain.

"Good," Umar declared. "Unfortunately, over the centuries, Zarathustra's words were forgotten or changed, and his followers began arguing and fighting amongst themselves. They started to worship other, false gods. The last texts of Zarathustra perished when the armies of Alexander burned the great library at Persepolis, three hundred and thirty years before the Christ.

"A few survivors spread through the world and kept the faith alive as empires rose and fell around them. You know of the Magi?"

"Everyone does. They visited the Christ child at his birth in Bethlehem."

"Nonsense," Umar scoffed. "The Magi *were* wise men from the east, followers of Zarathustra, but they did not come to pay homage at a baby's crib—that is a story for children. They came much later, after Christ had begun preaching and word of his ministry had spread. They came to talk with him as equals to discuss the philosophy of God, but that has been removed from the Gospels you know."

"How do *you* know this?"

"Patience," Umar snapped. "One group of Zarathustra's followers fled to the land of the Bulgars, others, over many hundreds of years, through Greece and Italy to here. They were the first Good Christians.

"Yet others survived in the new world of Islam and moved with the armies around the Mediterranean Sea to Cordova where they lived and studied. I myself studied there with the great scholar Nasir ed-Din, God bless him, in his library at Madinat al-Zahra.

"The material world is evil, but it is also transitory. Manuscripts decay, libraries burn, even carvings on rock flake and disappear with enough time. The only thing that survives intact is the human mind. That is why we memorize everything, why we train adepts in the memory cloister. As long as one remains with the accumulated knowledge of the ages locked in his head, Auramazdah will not pass away."

Umar took a sip of wine and looked at John, who was frowning as he struggled to understand both the history and what was being asked of him.

"So," he began tentatively, "you will transfer the books of Zara..."

"Zarathustra."

"Zarathustra. You will transfer his books to me?"

"Yes. What remains of them, but much more besides.

The battle has been going on for millennia, and countless tyrants and priests have burned all manner of books and scrolls. The task increases with each passing generation and each forbidden book we can rescue from the flames of ignorance and prejudice.

"For example, the book I was beginning to transfer to you is not of Zarathustra. It is much more recent, but in this time and place, it is of immense power and import. To give you but one example: your friend Adso could not understand why Roger Trenceval accompanied the priest you seem to know out of Carcassonne to negotiate with Aumery and the crusaders, even though he knew it meant the surrender of his city and, most likely, his own death. Trenceval went for one reason only—to save my life."

"Your life!"

"Well, not my life, that is of no importance, but what is in my head is. Trenceval knew that the young priest offered the only chance for the Good Christians of Carcassonne to avoid the flames. They would have gone willingly, and I would have too, but what I am about to transfer to you would have been lost, and there are few of us left who know it. Beatrice was right, I should not have stayed so long in the library."

John's mind was whirling with all the news Adso had brought from Carcassonne, the story this old man was telling, and Peter. What was Peter's role in all of this? He forced himself to focus on what Umar had said.

"What is it that is so important?" John asked.

Umar studied John for a long moment. "It is a gospel."

"I have read some lost gospels," John said. "Thomas, the

Apocalypse of Paul, even the one said to be by Judas."

"That is good, but this one is different. This gospel was written by the Christ."

John sat in silence as the meaning of Umar's words sank in. The Gospel of Christ himself! Not just a few stories and parables, but an entire book in the words of the founder of Christianity. Beatrice hadn't made it up! She had been hinting at something real.

"Is it authentic?"

Umar smiled. "That is what everyone asks, at least those whose first reaction is not to cast it or its bearer into the flames! It *is* true, and what is in this book in my head, if it were ever to become known and accepted, has the power to bring down the whole corrupt edifice of the Catholic Church in a single morning.

"You see now why they wish to burn us all, and why Roger Trenceval sacrificed himself?"

"Yes," John gasped, still stunned. A gospel written by Christ. These would be the most powerful words in all of Christendom. He was being offered nothing less than the power to change the world. It was awe-inspiring—and terrifying. If anyone found out that John knew about this, the entire weight of the crusade would fall on him.

"Are you prepared for this?" Umar's voice interrupted John's thoughts.

John took a deep breath. "Yes," he said. How could he not? This was the knowledge, perhaps the ultimate knowledge, that he had sought in all his readings.

"Very well. Now concentrate.

"*Inasmuch as it pleaseth God the Father, I shall set down*

my life so that others may learn from it after I am gone to join Him.

"In the beginning it was ..."

It took John three days to learn the Gospel of Christ. Three days in which he barely slept and simply took in food as fuel to keep himself going. By the time it was done, both he and Umar were exhausted.

"Do you have it all?" Umar asked as the pair sat in the kitchen by candlelight on the third day.

"I think so," John replied. He had just finished running the words through his mind before returning them to alcove thirteen in the cloister. He had concentrated so much on individual words and phrases that the full import of the gospel had passed him by. Now that he was done, the work lay complete in his mind. "Is it true?" he asked once more.

"Yes," Umar confirmed. "The original, long lost now, was written on vellum in Aramaic, the language the Christ spoke. It is older than any of the accepted gospels."

John shook his head in wonder.

"For many years," Umar explained, "it lay in the library of a rich Roman landowner, Marcus Britannicus. He lived not far from here on estates that produced some fine wine that was in high demand in Rome. When the empire collapsed, the library was dispersed and some books, the Gospel of the Christ included, were preserved by a Visigothic lord who wished to emulate the glories of Rome.

His family kept it safe when the darkness of ignorance descended and the land became a battleground between Christian and Moor. Eventually, upon their arrival from the east, some Good Men found the document and began the re-membering. By that time, the manuscript was in sorry shape and, I believe, was finally lost in a fire some three hundred years past.

"But we are not yet done. You now have the most important of the books in my head, but there are many more. Some preserve more of the truth of the early Church and support what you have learned these past days. Others are even older and contain knowledge and wisdom that is lost to our world. You must learn and remember them all. We have a busy winter before us, young John."

"There is so much we do not know!" John felt overwhelmed by the task before him. Only now was he beginning to fully understand what his promise involved: a lifetime of learning. It was exciting, but exhausting.

"Indeed," Umar said sadly. "What we preserve is but a tiny part of all that there was. I once heard of a map, a wondrous representation of the entire world, which showed it to be far vaster than the one we know, with continents, known and unknown, and wonders we can barely imagine scattered across it. I fear it is lost and may never be recovered."

Was this how he would end up, John wondered, an old man with a head full of marvels striving to pass them on to someone else before he died?

"But, Beatrice tells me that you are something of an artist." Umar broke in to John's thoughts.

"I scratch a few drawings in what spare time I have."

"And do you do it well?"

"As well as I can. Drawing has always fascinated me. I used to love the work that illustrated the few books the nuns possessed in Toulouse, even though many of the pictures in the margins were not of religious subjects. Often, they showed ordinary people at work and play—the farmer in his fields, the blacksmith at his forge or the miller at his wheel. Sometimes mythical animals, fire-breathing, winged dragons for example, writhed around the text."

Umar nodded encouragement.

"I used to sneak away from my duties or studies whenever possible and visit the great churches of Toulouse. I adored the brightly painted murals of saints and scenes from the Bible, the play of light on the blues and reds and the luxurious shine of the gold that made the holy men's haloes."

"Rubbish," Umar scoffed.

"The content may have been," John said, "but the form had a beauty that I admired. The problem I had was not with what the pictures represented, but with the way they did it. Despite the detail and the accuracy of many of the scenes, there was something about them that was dissatisfying."

"What was it?"

"I don't know." John struggled to explain. "They seemed flat and lifeless. In some ways, I was more drawn to the painted statues of the saints and holy men that adorned the doorways. The figures were long and serious—less accurate in many cases than the paintings—but their carved reality gave them a depth that was missing from the murals."

John shrugged helplessly.

"Once, many years past," Umar said, "I saw a book in Cordova that you would find of interest. It talked of different ways of painting and of representing our world, and it contained some strange drawings. I do not agree with this interest of yours, but I do understand some of what you say. Some drawings in the book were of such exquisite beauty that they made men breathless."

"Did you learn this book?" John asked with rising interest.

"Some, but it was not easy. Words are easy, drawing not so. How do I tell a drawing? I cannot."

"Where is the book now?"

"I do not know. Perhaps it is lost. The Moors do not treasure the representation of life. For them it is a sin that offends God. They prefer designs, so they would not care for such a book. If it still exists, it would be at Madinat al-Zahra in Nasir's library."

"Nasir is still alive?" John had assumed that Umar's teacher was long dead.

Umar shrugged. "It is possible; he was not all that much older than I. In any case, his library would still be there. Shabaka would know."

"Shabaka?"

"A Nubian, with skin so black it glows. A most interesting person. He is devoted to Nasir. When I was last in Cordova, it was Shabaka who took supplies to Nasir in his library at Madinat.

"But I ramble on. It is a sign of age and exhaustion. I

must to bed if we are to work more tomorrow."

Umar stood and stretched stiffly. "And you should sleep as well."

"I will," John said, "but I must calm my mind first."

"Very well. I bid you good night."

Umar picked up one of the candles and shuffled out of the room. John remained seated in the flickering light, staring into the darkness. His body ached with tiredness, but his mind would not let him rest. The things he had learned, and their possible consequences, whirled around his head.

He had just managed to convince himself that, despite his racing thoughts, he should lie down and try to sleep, when the door to the street opened and Adso entered. John only just managed to protect the flickering candle flame from the draft.

"Well, well," Adso said cheerfully as he went to the pantry and grabbed a piece of bread. "Finished work for the day?"

"Yes," John replied, glad to see his happy-go-lucky friend after the intensity of his time with Umar. "I've learned some incredible things."

"No doubt," Adso said. He sat at the table and broke off a piece of bread. "That old Umar 'as been around in a lot of places for a lot of years. 'E must 'ave picked up all manner of things. What is it you 'ave been so wrapped up in these past days?"

John hesitated. Should he tell Adso? Was the book he had learned a secret from everyone, or just those who did not support the Cathar cause?

"Was it that Gospel of the Christ?" Adso asked through a mouthful of bread.

"You know about that?'

Adso shrugged. "I keep my ears open. A lot of folk certainly seem to put a lot of store in it."

"It could change the world."

"The world'll change for sure, with or without your memory books."

"But this book is in Christ's own words," John explained eagerly. "It turns what the Gospels say upside down."

"Much turns the Gospels upside down. Nothing new in that. I doubt the cardinals in Rome'll pay it any mind."

"They'll have to," John said. "This book proves that Christ did not die on the cross, that he was taken down alive and nursed back to health by Mary Magdelene. He did not want to live on in this world and felt that his time here had been a failure. The End of Days had not arrived with him, and people were going about their business wrapped up in their petty cares, just as they had before he preached and was crucified."

John felt the words rushing out of him. It was a relief to tell someone about the burden he had been given.

"Mary and Jesus travelled and learned. They read and talked with holy men of all faiths, trying to understand. Jesus pondered much on what he had discussed with the wise men from the east. He came to appreciate the ancient wisdom they had talked about. He collected books and with Mary came here to Languedoc to study and think. At the end of his long life, his ideas were very close to those of the Cathar Perfects."

"Good story," Adso said.

"Good story! Is that all you can say? This book under-

194

mines the entire Christian faith. Christ was a Cathar—the first heretic. If it gets out, the Catholic Church will collapse. This is the most important book in the world!"

"Per'aps. Per'aps not. For a start, 'ow do you prove that it's true and not just some tale made up to cause trouble? And even if you can do that—" Adso held up his hand to prevent John's interruption—"even if you can prove it to be true, do you think the likes of Arnaud Aumery will ever allow it to become known? He, and plenty others like 'im 'll move 'eaven and earth to destroy that knowledge. The bonfires of books and men and women will make this crusade seem like a picnic.

"And, even supposing that you are right and the Gospel is true and believed and not wiped out by the Inquisition, and the edifice of the Church comes crashing down around all our ears, the world'll go on."

"How can you say that?" John asked indignantly. "Without the Church in some form, where would we be?"

"Somewhere. Look, John, you think too narrow. I 'ave heard tell of a god, far to the east, who 'as six arms and in each of them he carries a weapon that can destroy the world. I doubt *that* god'll worry too much about your Gospel.

"I even met a man once," Adso continued, "'airy he was and from the north where it's dark for 'alf the year and the snow lies to the rooftops. 'E believed in an ancient god what carried a war hammer and an 'eaven where warriors went to wench, drink and fight after they died. That's a god I could believe in.

"Point is, there's a lot of gods out there in this world. If one falls, even if it's yours, the others'll go on doing what

195

they've always done and so will the people who believe in them."

"You don't believe in God?" John asked, horrified.

"I wouldn't say that. I'm just a simple man who 'as precious little time for anybody's god or devil. If all the brilliant men and women in the world cannot decide what God's like, what chance do I 'ave? Best to just get on with life. There's enough 'appening every day to keep us busy without looking for trouble, and there's enough trouble in the world without killing those what thinks different."

Adso stopped speaking and broke into laughter—so hard that he collapsed in a fit of coughing and choking. John jumped up and poured him a goblet of wine. Adso took a long draft and calmed down.

"You looked so comical," he said eventually, "better than a travelling jester! But don't be so shocked, I'm not about to try and convert you to my 'eathen beliefs, and I won't be here long enough to give Beatrice a chance to convert me. My strength's almost back. A few more days and I'm off."

"Where to?" John felt a pang of regret that his friend was leaving so soon.

"Bram, Cabaret, down that way. There's plenty of bands roaming the country, just waiting for a few of these northern jackals to stray too far from their castle walls. Should be some good plunder." Adso winked broadly at John.

"You'll become a robber."

"In a manner of speaking. Tho' I don't see it as robbing. These crusaders came down 'ere uninvited. They wish to burn our towns and slaughter innocent people. They deserve whatever they get, I say. Better to do something and 'ave fun doing it than sit around worrying if God'll approve.

"But I think I've upset you enough for one night! I'm off for some sleep. The shed out back's not the most comfortable, but at least I don't 'ave to get up at the crack of dawn to pray. I bid you good night."

Adso took a candle off the mantle, lit it from the one on the table, and retreated through the house. Again John was left with his thoughts.

Adso's view of the world was the opposite of Beatrice and Umar's, but there was an attraction to what he planned to do. Adso would be free, roaming wherever he wished— and he'd be doing something active to fight the invaders. John was certain that preserving the ancient writing was important and he was looking forward to the other books Umar could give him, but what if Adso was right? What if it all made no difference in the grand scheme of things? One part of John craved the clash of swords and the life of adventure. Another wanted to head straight down to Cordova and try to find the drawing book of which Umar had spoken. But John had made a promise to Beatrice and Umar. He would have to follow that through.

Yawning hugely, John stumbled over to his alcove and fell into his bedding. A good night's sleep was what he needed.

PART FOUR
War

Angels

Toulouse

MARCH 1210

Despite the familiarity of the surroundings as he walked through the narrow streets of St. Cyprien at Arnaud Aumery's side, Peter didn't feel as if he were coming home. It was the place he had grown up, and he had many happy memories but, as Aumery had pointed out, the Holy Mother Church was now his only home. Peter wasn't here to relive old times; he was here simply to pressure Count Raymond to weed out the heretics in his city.

No one had found any evidence to link Count Raymond to the murder of Pierre of Castelnau and, since he had recanted the angry statements he'd made at St. Gilles and done penance, his excommunication had been lifted. The count had promised to support the crusade and drive all heretics out of his lands, but so far he had done nothing. While the crusaders had been dying under the walls of Carcassonne, Raymond, as reported in numerous harsh letters from Bishop Foulques, had allowed Cathars to meet and worship openly in Toulouse. Over the winter, he had stalled and delayed on his promise to send knights to help Simon de Montfort subdue the land around Carcassonne and now, as Foulques reported, things had degenerated to the point where there was almost open civil war in the streets between Raymond's followers and Foulque's own Angels.

As he looked around, Peter could see few signs of war. St. Cyprien looked much as he remembered it: not wealthy, but not dirt poor either. The houses were well maintained, the streets relatively clean, and the smells of humans and animals no worse than in any crowded city. The people were nicely enough dressed and they watched the small party of monks and lay brothers pass through their neighbourhood with only mild interest.

Peter knew that pride was one of the seven deadly sins, but he couldn't help holding his head high and hoping that someone in the watching crowd recognized the poor orphan boy returning as a full Cistercian monk. Peter had studied hard over the winter and now felt able to perform some of his duties—hear confession, perform baptism, administer last rites. He was still a long way from leading a full Mass but that was not a major part of his duties. Mostly, all that was required was a quick blessing of the knights as they prepared for battle.

In any case, the most important learning Peter had done recently had nothing to do with blessing knights or comforting the dying. It had come during the long, cold evenings when Peter and Aumery had sat in the legate's tent and spoken about wielding power. Aumery had done most of the talking, telling Peter long stories of his work as Abbot of Cîteaux and his visits to Rome. Peter's lessons were continuing now as the pair wended their way through the narrow streets.

"If there is one thing you need to remember at all

times," Aumery said, repeating the winter's main message, "it is that, no matter how powerful a lord may seem, every man has a weakness. Find that weakness and, when the time is right, exploit it. And be ruthless. Be like a terrier who, once it gets hold of a rat, may be beaten senseless before it lets go. If you are right, and if God is with you, you will triumph."

"And yet," Peter responded, "the negotiations at Carcassonne allowed the heretics to escape. Had de Montfort been more of a terrier, would we have won both an intact city and the heretics?"

"Possibly, Peter," Aumery said thoughtfully. "Maybe I miscalculated there. I thought that sending you in to the city would do no harm. I did not expect Trenceval to submit so easily. Why do you think he did?"

"To save his subjects the slaughter of Béziers?"

"In part, but he could have done that by giving up a few score heretics to the fire at the beginning of the siege."

"Then it was the heretics that were important to him?"

"That is what I have come to believe. Have you heard of the Cathar Treasure?"

"I have heard some wild tales," Peter said, hauling old bits of gossip into his mind. "Some said it was riches beyond our wildest imaginings. Others that it was the Ark of the Covenant itself. Some said that the heretics brought the treasure with them from the east or from the Holy Land."

"And what did you think of these tales?"

"That they were just imaginings. The heretics never struck me as ones who would hoard treasure."

"My thoughts exactly," Aumery said. "The heretics set

little store by material possessions. They have no chests of gold or precious stones, but what if they have a small treasure of immense power?"

"Like what?"

"What is the holiest object in Christendom?"

Peter searched his memory. There were countless relics of saints that were associated with miracles—he'd even heard that a church in Rome possessed the preserved head of John the Baptist—but the holiest object would have to be something from Christ himself. It couldn't be his body as he ascended to heaven, and the cross on which he had suffered, or a large piece of it, was said to lead the crusaders into battle in the Holy Land, so it couldn't be that. There was only one other alternative.

"You mean the Grail?" Peter asked.

"I mean nothing else," Aumery said, smiling broadly. "The holy cup from which Christ drank at the Last Supper."

"And you really believe the Cathars possess this?"

"It must be. It is the only thing small enough to be easily hidden and transported."

Peter was thrilled at the idea that the Grail might exist, and even be close by, but there was a problem. "Why would the heretics preserve the Grail? They do not recognize the divinity of Christ."

Aumery stopped walking and stared at Peter with his strange eyes. "They do not preserve the Grail because *they* worship it. They preserve it because *we* worship it. Think of the Grail's power! What could we not do if the Pope possessed the Grail? It would revitalize the church and sweep the corruption of those like Foulques away. With the Grail at their head, the armies of Christ would sweep triumphant across the world! Heathens would bow down and Christ would reign in glory! It would herald the Judgment Day. The tombs would open and the dead rise to stand naked with their sins before Christ."

Aumery's voice rose and his eyes gleamed with fervour. Passersby were stopping to pay attention.

Peter was caught up in the odd monk's enthusiasm. "Could it be true?"

"It is! It is the only answer. I have read the holy books in Rome and talked with the greatest minds in Christendom. I am in no doubt. The Cathars possess the Holy Grail. And *that* is the real purpose of this crusade, to regain the power of the Grail for the Holy Mother Church."

A horrible thought struck Peter. "Could the heretics not simply destroy it?"

"They would not dare!" Aumery exclaimed. "The Grail has power. It has touched the lips of Christ Himself. The heretic rabble fear what we, the true Church, could accomplish with it. They will do their utmost to hide it from us, but they will not destroy it. And one day, in one of their pitiful castles, I shall find it and announce the coming of the End Days, just as is foretold in the Revelations of St. John."

Aumery strode along the street and Peter had to hurry to keep up. He felt an extraordinary thrill. This was better than his wildest dreams! He was at the forefront of the battle against evil, and he was going to win. When Aumery found the Grail, together they would use it to remake the world.

Aumery slowed and his breathing eased. He began talking again, almost as if to himself. "Clues that I had collected over the years led me to believe that the Grail was in Carcassonne, but it was not. As you arranged, the heretics left with nothing but their sins, and a thorough search of the city has turned up nothing."

"Then the clues you followed were wrong?"

"Perhaps. Or there is another explanation. The clues could refer to the key to finding the Grail rather than the holy object itself."

"But the key could be anything, a book, a map, a scrap of paper."

"Yes, and perhaps those exist, somewhere," Aumery reasoned. "But we know the Cathars left the city naked. Therefore, they hid the key, destroyed it, or else they did take it out and we never saw it."

"How?"

Aumery tapped his forehead.

"Of course," Peter said in sudden realization. "One of them knew the location."

"That is what I suspect," Aumery mused. "Probably an old, respected Perfect. I regret not being able to apply some persuasion to the heretics in order to flush this Perfect out—if indeed there is only one—but we will find him or her again.

"In any case, the Grail must be at one of the heretics's remoter strongholds, perhaps Minerve, Peyrepertuse or Montségur. In the long term it is of little consequence. We have time and, eventually, every Cathar will burn and the Holy Church will recover its most treasured relic."

"But," Peter said, "the Cathars are fanatical. They may be willing to die without revealing the location of the Grail."

"That is true. In which case, it is God's wish that we do not find the Grail yet. Perhaps the Church is not ready. All we can do is try, and in the process, cleanse Christendom of this rabble."

Peter was silent as the implications of Aumery's speech sank in. To discover the Cathar Treasure, Aumery, with the blessings of the Pope, was prepared to conduct a war that might last decades and kill everyone tainted with heresy. Even if the Grail was not found, the land would be cleansed of anyone who might know something dangerous to the Church. It was a huge task, but a noble one. "It will take years," Peter said.

"Indeed. It will not be easy, and it may not be completed in our lifetimes, but the Church deals with eternity. And if only a few dedicated souls, such as you and I, devote our lives to the task, it will be completed and a day will dawn when not a single heretic will wake to see the sun."

Peter thought about what Aumery had said. The idea of finding the Holy Grail excited him, the thought of spending his life chasing down every last ragged heretic in this remote corner of the world less so. That hardly seemed the best way to achieve power within the Church. Peter had looked forward to triumphing rapidly. Even without the Grail, a few speedy victories at Aumery's side might result in a more important position, as an abbot of a small monastery, for example. That would be the first step on a ladder that, with luck, could lead anywhere. Peter would have to be careful not to become wrapped up in the ever more difficult hunt for an ever smaller but increasingly elusive number of enemies.

But that was not the only thing on his mind. He was quickly learning that nothing came without a cost. The ways of wielding power were not always as clean as one would wish. The betrayal of Roger Trenceval, even if the man had been complicit in the process, had been one such example. Peter had been sorry when news of the young viscount's death in the dank dungeons of Carcassonne last November had reached him. There had been talk of murder, but it was much more likely that the man had succumbed to bad food, cold and filth.

"You must harden your heart to do God's work," Aumery had said at the time. "The Devil often wears a smile. You liked Trenceval, that is understandable, but behind that smile was a demon doing Satan's work. Had he undertaken his Christian duties and rooted out the vile heretics from his domains, he would be alive, sitting today in Carcassonne, basking in the blessings of His Holiness."

Peter understood that, but it was hard. He had liked Trenceval, yet the man had been doing the Devil's work. He hated and feared the cruel Oddo, yet he was on the side of righteousness. What if it was a friend who was corrupt and doing the Devil's work—say John, or Isabella?

Peter pushed these unpleasant thoughts out of his mind as the party crossed the bridge over the Garonne River and approached the gates of Toulouse. The walls above were hung with brightly coloured banners bearing the coats of arms of the city's important families. Flags and pennants snapped in the wind from the battlements of the towers on either side of the gate.

"Bishop Foulques' Angels are waiting to welcome us,"

Aumery said, waving his arm to indicate a group of men standing on either side of the gate. They were dressed in white with a black-outlined cross on the chest. "Foulques calls them his White Brotherhood, but the common people call them his Angels."

Peter shuddered. He had known the Angels as a boy and they had scared him then. On one occasion, three Angels had attacked him and John as they had walked home at night. Peter had been terrified into immobility, but John had taken on the largest attacker and knocked him to the ground. The three had fled, and the boys had been spared a beating. Afterwards, Peter had felt ashamed and inadequate and had fought with John over something insignificant. The memory made him very uncomfortable.

Peter took a deep breath. Why was he so bothered by an old memory? He wasn't a scared boy any more. He was a servant of Rome with the power of the Catholic Church behind him. He need never fear the ignorant rabble again.

He took a good look at the Angels. Most were pox-marked and many exhibited the white lines of old battle scars. Each man carried a club, several of which had nails or other irregular pieces of iron hammered into their surfaces. These Angels looked more like the scum of the worst taverns as they gazed sullenly at the approaching monks.

As Peter watched, a side gate opened and Bishop Foulques stepped through. He was dressed in sumptuous robes embroidered with silk threads and precious stones that glittered in the March sunlight. As he threw his arms wide in a theatrical welcome, Peter was distracted by a commotion on the walls above. A group of figures, young boys, as far as he could see, were struggling to manhandle three large pots onto the battlements.

"Toulouse! Toulouse!" the boys cried as they tipped the pots. "To hell with the Bishop's Angels."

Foulques skipped back under the gate's archway in time, but his men were caught by the full force of the pots' contents. A yellow waterfall of urine, mixed with excrement and rotting animal intestines, cascaded down on the Angels, soaking hair and staining robes. Pulling Peter's arm, Aumery moved to one side of the road.

The boys on the battlements were laughing uproariously and flinging insults down. The Angels were swearing and hurling curses back as they struggled to organize themselves. Several were on the ground, having slipped on the piles of glistening entrails.

Eventually, the Angels managed to get to the gate and, waving their spiked clubs, poured through in an attempt to catch the boys, who vanished along the top of the wall.

From his safe position on the side of the road, Peter struggled to sort out his feelings. A part of him was shocked at the disrespect shown to the bishop's men, but he also felt a thrill that they had been humiliated so easily. On top of it all was relief that they were gone.

"My apologies, my apologies!" Bishop Foulques remained under the arch. "You see what we must endure from the Cathar rabble that Count Raymond refuses to eradicate from the bosom of the Holy Church. But rest assured that my White Brotherhood will find and suitably punish the perpetrators of this outrage."

Aumery, Peter and the others carefully picked their way

through the disgusting debris, lifting the hems of their habits to avoid the worst of the mess. Once through the gate, everyone relaxed.

"Again, my apologies," Foulques said. "Come to the Château Narbonnais. I have had a lunch prepared that I think you will find to your liking."

"We did not come for lunch, your Grace," Aumery said. "We wish to meet with Count Raymond as soon as is convenient."

"Of course, of course. I shall see to it." Foulques turned to a short priest who was hovering at his side. "Please take my compliments to Count Raymond, and ask if he would be so good as to attend the meeting at the Château two hours earlier than we had previously discussed."

"*Tell* him!" Aumery ordered.

The priest looked confused.

"We carry the authority of His Holiness Pope Innocent III," Aumery went on. "We require the count's attendance at *our* pleasure, not his."

The priest still hesitated until a nod from Foulques sent him on his way.

As the group walked to the Château Narbonnais, Peter realized that his mentor had just taught him another valuable lesson. Aumery had told him that the best way to handle Bishop Foulques was through flattery, but the incident at the gate had exposed one of the bishop's weaknesses. Foulques had chosen to meet the delegation at the gates rather than wait in the Château because he wanted to show off his White Brotherhood and their power. It had backfired horribly. The boys' attack had shown, in the most dramatic way, that Foulques did not control the streets of Toulouse and it had left the bishop deeply embarrassed. Aumery had taken full advantage of that, dropping the idea of flattery in favour of flaunting his own power and ordering the bishop to change his plans. At least for this visit, Aumery had the upper hand.

Peter felt a pang of nostalgia as he turned the corner into the square in front of the Château Narbonnais. Here was where he had seen his vision, where he had turned away from Isabella and John, and where his life had changed forever. Only three years had passed since that night, yet he was returning at the side of a papal legate working to recover the most holy relic in the Church. Peter strode confidently across the square at Aumery's side.

The Château Narbonnaise was more a fortress than a palace. It was constructed of red bricks and built into an angle of the city walls. Round towers, dotted with threatening arrow slits, rose above the squat walls. Only the entrance made any allowances for decoration, the round arch being surrounded by carvings of shields and armour. Above the arch the largest shield bore the cross of the counts of Toulouse. It was a strange design, a complex cross with arms of equal length. Each arm ended in three points and all twelve points ended in a nob of stone.

"It is said," Aumery commented, seeing Peter's gaze focused on the cross, "that the present count's ancestor, who went on the First Holy Crusade to recapture Jerusalem from the heathen, brought the design of the Toulouse cross back with him for his family's coat of arms."

"But if Raymond is a heretic, he would not allow a cross on his coat of arms," Peter said. "The heretics hate the cross in any form. They say it is merely an instrument of torture and that our Lord Christ did not die upon it." Peter crossed himself as he mentioned this heresy.

"Indeed, but remember, Count Raymond says he is not a heretic, and that may be true. He may simply allow them to preach their evil sermons. But also consider this. Some say that this is not a true cross. They say it has a pagan origin from long before the suffering of our Lord. See, it is not a solid carving, but merely a carved outline—a hollow cross—and the twelve points on the arms represent the signs of the pagan zodiac."

"So, it may be a heretic symbol after all?"

"It may. Do not be too ready to take things at face value, young Peter. The Devil continually conspires to trick us in new ways."

The party climbed the steps and entered the courtyard of the château. It was small and dark, surrounded as it was by the high brick walls.

"The count gave me the château last year," Foulques said, waving his arm to encompass the buildings around.

"A bribe?" Aumery asked, acidly.

"No, no." Foulques went on with no sign that he had taken offence. "Merely as a convenient place from which to undertake the Lord's work."

As they stood, a group of musicians entered the yard

from a doorway opposite. Peter was surprised to see William of Arles, the same troubadour he had seen on the night of his vision and with whom John had gone travelling. As the musicians began, William banged his tambourine and began singing in his high-pitched voice. The language was Occitan.

> *"I go to her with joy*
> *Through wind and snow and sleet.*
> *The She-Wolf says I am hers*
> *And, by God, she's right:*
> *I belong to her*
> *More than to any other, even to myself."*

Bishop Foulques smiled at his arranged welcome, and despite there being nothing religious about the song of longing and lost love, Peter found his foot tapping to the tune. Aumery stepped forward, however, and Peter stopped his tapping, expecting a violent diatribe. Instead, to everyone's complete astonishment, Aumery began to sing in Latin. His voice was surprisingly deep and quickly drowned out William, who fell silent. To the musician's tune, Aumery sang:

> *"It's hard to bear it*
> *When I hear such false belief*
> *spoken and spread around.*
> *May God hear my plea;*
> *Let those, young and old,*
> *Who cackle viciously*

*Against the law of Rome
Fall from its scales."*

As Aumery finished, William stepped forward and acknowledged the legate's performance with a nod of his head and a sweep of his arm. "I am William of Arles and I bow before such a voice. Should you ever leave the Church, you could make a fine living as a troubadour."

"I am Arnaud Aumery, Abbot of Cîteaux and legate to Pope Innocent III, and I use the gifts that God gave me to do His work and praise His name. You would do well to consider a similar path rather than wasting your life on frivolous nonsense that encourages debauchery and sin."

Aumery pushed past the troubadour and scattered the musicians as he strode up the steps into the hall. For a moment, Peter found himself standing before William. The troubadour stared at Peter for a moment, then nodded in recognition. "Your visions gave you a hard taskmaster," he said with a smile.

"God is my master," Peter replied, striding after Aumery.

Peter's stomach grumbled noisily when he saw the sumptuous meal laid out on the long oak table in the château's main hall. The centrepiece was an entire roast boar, and it was surrounded by an assortment of pies, plates of quail, eggs of all sizes, and breads. Servants stood respectfully to one side, holding decanters of wine, and the rich smell of roasting meat wafted through from the archway that obviously led to the kitchens.

Aumery approached the servants. "Clear this away. Leave only the bread and wine," he instructed.

The servants hesitated, but at a nod from Bishop Foulques, they sprang into action. In no time, the table was clear except for loaves of bread, decanters of wine and goblets. Aumery sat and bowed his head in prayer to bless the food. The others joined him.

"You live well, Bishop," Aumery commented as he broke off a piece of bread.

"I find," the bishop replied between swigs of wine, "that living at a certain standard engenders respect among the upper classes. And, without them, we cannot hope to combat this pernicious heresy."

"I think you will find that God's help is of more use in our struggle than a few minor lords whose wives are, probably, closet Perfects."

"Of course, of course. But I think you misjudge them."

"And how many heretics have they, or you, converted of late?" Aumery asked.

"Such things are hard to judge," Foulques said. "The Perfects, it is true, will never change their corrupt ways. However, there are many plain folk who were sympathetic to the heretics and now greatly favour us."

"Those would be the boys who emptied the contents of chamber pots on the heads of your Angels?" Aumery asked sarcastically. "Perhaps, as we speak, those very Angels are now subtly converting them to the true faith with the clubs they carry?"

"Come, come," Foulques blustered. "The situation is not as simple as—"

The bishop was cut off by a commotion at the door. Peter turned to see Count Raymond enter the hall. As host in his own territory, he was more sumptuously dressed than he had been at St. Gilles. Raymond was a tall man, and his presence was accentuated by his clothes. He wore an ankle-length tunic of startling blue, decorated with a diamond pattern picked out in gold thread. In the centre of each diamond, a golden Toulouse cross glinted. The tunic was bound at the waist with a heavy chain of gold, and from a lighter chain around Raymond's neck hung a large medallion with the Toulouse coat of arms in cloisonné. The clutch of retainers who followed the count were almost equally well dressed and a small whippet, wearing a collar of red velvet, frolicked at their feet. The count had obviously designed his entrance to say: "Here is a lord the equal of the King of France."

"My dear Aumery," Raymond said as he reached the table and held out his hand to the priest, "I see you declined Bishop Foulques' generous repast. Probably wise. I always find that the mind works more clearly on an empty stomach."

Out of the corner of his eye, Peter saw Foulques grimace at the implied insult, but his attention was held by Raymond. The count was unrecognizable from the blustering, threatening man he had seen two years before. Obviously, he could play games as well as Aumery.

"Count Raymond." Aumery stood and clasped the count's hand in both of his. "So glad you could accommodate our schedule. We have little time. The battle against the Devil is ceaseless."

"I am certain it is," Raymond replied. "And I can think of no one who is better fitted to lead that struggle than you."

The insincere pleasantries over, the two men sat at opposite sides of the table. A page poured Raymond a goblet of wine, which the count sipped appreciatively.

"In deference to the pressures of the continuing struggle against evil," Raymond said, wiping his mouth with his tunic sleeve, "we should get down to business. To what do I owe the pleasure of this visit?"

"Since your pledge to support the Holy Crusade and root out the vile Cathar heresy from your lands, His Holiness has written to me on a number of occasions, requesting details of the actions taken. Unfortunately, I have been unable to provide him with any."

"His Holiness must understand," Raymond said, smoothly, "that the situation here is not simple. I have had only a few months to address this complex situation, and my power over the city itself is not absolute. I have made the city fathers aware of your request to give up the heretics within our walls for interrogation, and they have complied." A page placed a document in Raymond's outstretched hand. "I have here a list of the known heretics in Toulouse." He slid the document across the table.

Aumery scanned it. "I thank you, but this is not satisfactory. There are a mere score of names here. Do the city fathers expect His Holiness to believe that that is all there is in this hotbed of heresy?"

Raymond shrugged. "I can speak for neither the expectations of the city fathers nor the beliefs of His Holiness."

Peter watched, fascinated, as the two men sparred. He knew that they detested one another. Yet they hid behind politeness and the wishes of the Pope and the city fathers.

"What is de Montfort's position?" Raymond asked.

"He is sworn to carry out His Holiness's orders. To that end, a mighty army from the north is assembling."

"And to what use will this army be put?"

"It will be a righteous sword that will sweep through the nests of heretics, *wherever* they may be found."

If Raymond heard the veiled threat to Toulouse in Aumery's statement, he gave no sign. "And I shall aid this noble cause to the fullest of my capabilities. Perhaps Bishop Foulques might offer the services of his White Brotherhood to the crusade?"

Foulques looked startled, but recovered quickly. "Of course, of course. They should be honoured. But they already fight in the cause, battling the heretics at their heart, in the streets of this very city."

Aumery smiled. "Very generous of you, but I am certain the Brotherhood are performing God's work admirably here in Toulouse.

"But, as to the matter of handing over the heretics: His Holiness has instructed me that you have six weeks in which to submit them—their bodies, not simply their names on a piece of parchment—for interrogation and punishment."

"And if this should prove impossible?"

"Then Toulouse and all its inhabitants shall be placed

under an interdict. All places of worship shall be closed, Mass will not be said and no sacraments—Baptism, Marriage, Confession or Last Rites—given."

Peter stifled a gasp. Aumery was threatening the excommunication of an entire city. Raymond showed no reaction, merely gazed thoughtfully at Aumery.

"I believe that to be harsh," he said eventually, "and I shall petition His Holiness directly on the matter. However, I shall attempt to carry out his instructions. I thank you for informing me of them.

"Now, if there is nothing else," said Raymond, standing, "I shall attend to my business. You are welcome to stay as long as you wish. Perhaps you would consent to say a Mass in the Cathedral of St. Sernin this afternoon? I am certain Bishop Foulques would be happy to arrange it."

"Thank you for your hospitality," Aumery said as he also stood. "It has been a most instructive meeting."

Aumery kept his smile in place as Raymond and his entourage left the hall.

"I would be honoured to arrange a Mass," Bishop Foulques said.

Aumery's smile vanished as he turned to face the bishop. "I do not wish to perform a Mass in a half-empty church while heretics mock us in the streets," he said angrily. "You would do better to persuade the city fathers to give up the heretics. When the interdict takes effect, you will be a bishop with no power and no flock.

"Now, I wish to cleanse myself and pray. Please show me to a cell. Peter, fetch my scourge and attend me."

Peter followed Aumery and a servant to a tiny bare

room with only a single narrow slit high in the wall to allow light. Aumery knelt and prayed briefly. Then he loosened his habit. Peter shuddered at the intricate pattern of knotted white scars that covered his back.

"My scourge," Aumery said, holding out his hand. Peter passed him the knotted rope he had collected from one of the lay brothers.

"There is so much evil in the world," Aumery said sadly as he swung the rope hard over his shoulder. Tiny flecks of blood showed on his pale skin where the coarse rope hit. "Peter, why did we come here today?"

Peter was momentarily confused by the question. "To force Count Raymond's hand?" he guessed.

"Only partly." The rope swung in another arc. "Our main purpose was to humiliate Bishop Foulques."

"But he is a bishop of the Church," Peter said.

"A corrupt and weak one." The rope arced and the spots of blood on Aumery's back grew. "Raymond will pretend to do something while doing nothing. He will appeal to His Holiness and attempt to delay the crusade with words. As long as he does so, de Montfort, even when he is strong enough, will have no excuse to attack Toulouse. However, should Toulouse fall into chaos, both de Montfort and Pope Innocent will be forced to act.

"If Foulques feels threatened, as surely he is by the possibility of an interdict, then he will fight for the only thing he cares about—his own power. He will use his Angels to spread fear through the streets. The heretics—not the Perfects but the common herd— will respond, as you saw this morning they already do. There will be bloodshed and violence. With luck, Raymond will be unable to control it and we shall be forced to step in. De Montfort will mount a siege with His Holiness's blessing and the heretics will burn on the banks of the Garronne River."

Aumery's plan was becoming clear, and once again, Peter found himself amazed at Aumery's resolve. He was fomenting uncontrollable violence to get his way. "But at St. Gilles, when Pierre of Castelnau met with—"

"Do not mention that man's name in my presence." The rope swung in a wide arc. "He was weak. Were he still alive, there would be no crusade, and I would not lead it."

"But he is a holy martyr."

"He was a fool." The rope slashed into Aumery's back with particular force. Drops of blood sprayed onto the floor. "He deserved to die."

"Deserved?"

"You have not yet learned to think things through, Peter. Do you imagine it mere chance that the murderer knew exactly where we would be camped?"

Peter was too stunned to reply. Had Aumery told the knight or Count Raymond where Pierre could be found so that he could be murdered? Certainly, Aumery had benefited by the deed. He had used it to raise the crusade he now led. In two years he had risen from a junior papal legate to one of the most powerful men in Christendom. Arnaud Aumery was devious, yes, but would he stoop to murder?

"What do you mean?" Peter stammered.

"I mean just what I say," Aumery said dismissively. "Now leave me. I would pray."

As Peter closed the cell door, the last sounds he heard

were the soft thud of the rope digging into Aumery's flesh and the sigh of satisfaction that escaped his thin lips.

Peter walked back through the narrow stone corridors, his mind crowded with thoughts of the day's events. There were times—many, lately—when he felt that he understood Aumery, his ways and his goals. At other times, though, like today, he wasn't so sure. If Aumery had truly arranged for the murder of Pierre of Castelnau, how was that God's work? He knew that Aumery worked toward God's goals, but murder as a way to get there? Peter was startled from his thoughts by a figure stepping out in front of him. It took him a moment to recognize who it was.

"Isabella," he said, taking a step back.

"Hello, Peter. I saw you at that strange monk's side. You've done well since last we met."

Peter's mind was a chaos of conflicting emotions. For three years, the only contact he had had with the world from before his visions had been his fraught meeting with John. He had deliberately pushed down all memories of the games, jokes and songs of his friends, and all thoughts of Isabella. Now, with no chance to prepare himself, here she was, standing an arm's reach in front of him, as darkly beautiful as ever and with that mysterious half smile playing around her mouth and eyes that used to make his knees go weak.

"I do God's work now for Father Aumery and his

blessed Holiness, Pope Innocent." Peter silently cursed himself. Once again he was falling back on the self-important phrases that had so annoyed John.

Isabella's smile broadened. "Are you happy in this work?"

Peter hesitated. He'd never asked himself that question. Doing God's work was a reward in itself; happiness had nothing to do with it. "The work of rooting out this foul heresy in the heart of Christendom must be done if we are to prepare for Christ's coming."

Isabella nodded, but her smile faded. "Have you had more visions since that night in the square?"

"God has not seen fit to favour me with more."

"As I recall, it did not seem much like a favour at the time, but"—Isabella hurried on to prevent Peter's interruption—"I have wondered many times since then if the visions were my fault."

"Your fault?"

"If you recall, our conversation on the steps that night was not to your liking. You declared your love for me and, I believe, were about to ask that we become betrothed."

Peter didn't say anything, but it was true. That night—troubled by the debate and his discussion with John, excited at the festive atmosphere in the square and undecided as to his future—Peter, when faced with Isabella's beauty, had babbled on inanely about love. And, yes, had Isabella not interrupted him, he would have asked for her hand.

"I said that I was not ready for such a declaration of love," Isabella went on. "I was young and had led a sheltered life. I wanted to see more of the world. I wanted desperately not to hurt you and was about to suggest that we remain friends and see what the future would bring, but you were not listening. Your visions of death held you in thrall by then.

"What I have often wondered is whether you saw my response as rejection and if this, in some way I do not understand, caused thoughts of death to overcome your mind and allow Satan in to corrupt your sight."

"Satan!" Peter was taken aback. "It was *God* who sent me those visions. They caused me to become a priest and fight the Holy Crusade against heresy. Is that what Satan would have wanted?"

"Only if the crusade is wrong."

Anger flooded through Peter. "The crusade *cannot* be wrong! It is Christ's work, blessed by His Holiness himself. This vile canker in the heart of Christ's earthly kingdom *must* be burned out, else how can we defeat the heathen overseas? You put your soul in mortal jeopardy by even thinking such thoughts."

All traces of Isabella's smile were gone now, replaced by a sadness Peter could not recall ever seeing on her features before. "I am sorry," she said. "I was wrong to doubt your visions. I do not wish us to part with bad words between us."

Peter breathed slowly and tried to calm himself. He didn't want bad words between them either. He wanted to sit down as they had years before and just talk, but he couldn't. Talking brought out ideas, and ideas could be dangerous. That was John's problem—he put no limits on what he thought, simply allowing any and all ideas to surface and giving them equal weight. It was much easier, and safer, to be certain, to build a shield of the correct doctrine to protect yourself from hurt and embarrassment. But some people didn't seem to understand that.

"I am truly glad that you are doing well on the path you have chosen." Isabella's smile had returned to her lips, but it didn't reach her eyes. "Have you seen John since that night?"

"Our paths have crossed."

"He is well?"

"It was some time ago, but his body was well enough." Peter's mind went back to the last he had seen of John, fleeing for his life down the riverbank after the murder of Pierre of Castelnau. How did *that* fit with what Aumery had told him a short while ago? "I fear for his soul, though. He worked for the heretic Roger Trenceval and consorted with all manner of Cathar filth."

"Do you know where he is now?"

"I don't, but why should you care?"

The sad expression flitted across Isabella's face again.

"If you see him," Isabella said, "greet him for me."

"I doubt I'll see a heretic like him."

"You never know," Isabella said, her mysterious smile back. "You met me. But I must be off. Go well, Peter."

Before Peter could ask what she meant, Isabella was gone.

Leaving

Bram and Cabaret

MARCH 1210

John tramped along the dead straight road to Bram, his shoes slapping on the wet stone cobbles laid by Roman legionnaires more than a thousand years before. It was only March and the bitter winds from the mountains still blew strongly. At least the last rain squall had stopped before it wet John's tunic and trousers, but his dark-red woollen cloak was saturated and heavy. To its weight was added a large satchel, hanging from his shoulder and balancing on his left hip. In his right hand, John carried a long, knotted walking stick with which he marked his strides. He shivered as another icy gust chilled him. Although he knew they would be sparse, John looked forward to the companionable comforts of the Cathar house at his destination.

To dull the discomfort of his present state, John thought back over the events of the previous winter. It had been a busy time learning from Umar. The old man was a hard taskmaster; nevertheless, the winter had been one of the most peaceful in John's life. Minerve had been quiet and its inhabitants protected from the violence sweeping the surrounding countryside. For more than half a year, John had been comfortable: not living in luxury, but safe and fed adequately, and all he had to do in return was learn. It was a good life, but a tiny worm of discontent wriggled in the back of John's mind.

What was Adso doing? As he had promised, he had left Minerve a few days after he and John had last spoken, heading south to find a band of robbers to join so he could seek plunder and harass the invaders. He had gone cheerfully and John had envied him a little. What an adventure it would be, living rough with a close band of companions, attacking the crusaders when there was an advantage and disappearing into the forests to rest and await another chance. Beatrice and Umar were wonderful and very wise, and John loved the life they had given him. Still—

There had been fighting all around Carcassonne most of the winter. Simon de Montfort, and those crusaders who had stayed with him, had made sure that anywhere within easy marching distance of Carcassonne was subject to raids. De Montfort had surprised everyone, not least Beatrice, by continuing his campaign into the previous autumn. He never had enough men to mount a serious siege of a major castle or town, but the few knights who had remained, led by Oddo and his Falcons, had rapidly gained a reputation for ferocity. Through a combination of rapid movement, brutality and the memory of Béziers, they had forced the surrender of Fanjeux and Montréal. Even Toulouse and Albi had paid at least token homage. On the other hand, with not enough men to garrison his new conquests, de Montfort had had to rely on the promises of local lords, and many had reverted to their old ways and allegiances as soon as the crusader knights rode over the nearest hill. Had Adso been involved in all that?

"De Montfort will have to reconquer all the small fortresses again come the spring," Beatrice had prophesied only a few days ago, "but this time he will have a new army from the north and he will wish to teach his faint-hearted vassals a lesson."

"Will he come to Minerve this year?" John had asked.

"He will first subdue the land around Carcassonne," Beatrice explained. "He will probably begin by making examples of a couple of minor castles, but, to be secure next winter, he will have to reduce a major fortress and that means Minerve. We are probably safe until late summer, but by then, water will be a problem for a besieged town swollen with refugees, and de Montfort's task will be easier. You must go before then."

"Where?" John had asked.

"De Montfort cannot attack every stronghold. He will concentrate on the ones that are big enough to hold sufficient knights to mount raids when he is occupied elsewhere. Small castles like Montségur or Quéribus are virtually impregnable, but they cannot support a large garrison and are too remote to threaten him directly. Many of the smaller fortresses have books that must be rescued."

"And memorized."

"Indeed." Beatrice smiled at her pupil. "You have done better than I could have hoped this winter. You have learned all of Umar's books?"

"All the ones in languages I can understand," John said proudly. "But there is one he has told of but does not have— a book on drawing."

"I have heard of it."

"Do you know where it is?"

"If it is anywhere, it is in Al-Andalus."

"Umar says he has seen the drawings in it and would copy some down for me, but he delays. He says there are more important books, and copying drawings is harder than reciting words."

"And in that he is correct, but there is another reason. Umar is very proud. It is not a good characteristic for a holy man, but he comes from a proud people. In any case, his hands pain him greatly. You have seen how they are twisted and how he rubs them constantly?"

"I have."

"He fears that he has not the skill left to copy the drawings from his mind and he does not wish to seem weak before you, so he hesitates. He will do it eventually."

John hoped so. The religious books were wonderful and undeniably important, but he craved what the drawing book might teach him. He still practised whenever he could, attempting to draw the streets and buildings of Minerve, but learning books took all his energy and it was hard to find the time or the materials. It was exasperating and John looked forward to the day he would have time to sit down and practise. Maybe one day he would even go to Al-Andalus himself and search for the mysterious drawing book.

Despite the rain, the cold, his sore feet and his frustrations at not having enough time to draw, John was happy. The memory cloister sat in his mind, loaded with wonders and ready to receive more. He thought over all that Umar had taught him. The Gospel of the Christ had been the most important and the most shocking. Despite Adso's disparaging comments, John still believed in the power of the work. Not only did it undermine the whole Catholic faith, but the issues that Christ wrote about as an old man in Languedoc greatly supported the idea that the Cathars were the ones who preserved the true Christianity. John believed that the Gospel was true, but he struggled with how it would be possible to convince enough others of its authenticity. Although it didn't really matter if it were true. True or false, Adso had been correct in saying that the Church would stop at nothing to suppress the Gospel's contents.

John looked up and caught a glimpse of the walls of Bram on the horizon. It was a small, not particularly well-fortified town, one that Beatrice thought de Montfort would pick off easily before he tackled the harder nut of Minerve. That was why John was on his way. There were two books in Bram that needed rescuing.

One had been written by a man called Origen, a mystic who had lived some two hundred and fifty years after Christ. Using texts that were old even in his day, Origen had written that the early Christians believed that every soul came from God, and that through reincarnation, each soul came closer to returning to God. Origen's writings had been popular once, but the Emperor Justinian had been convinced by the Church cardinals that they were heresy. They said that every soul could not be direct from God, because that made them equal to Christ and, if reincarnation was the way to become closer to God, what was the point of Mass and going to church? Many of Origen's most controversial writings had been burned, but a copy of one was preserved in Bram.

The other book was not religious. It was a copy in Latin of a Greek book on mathematics by Aristarchos of Samos, who had lived some three hundred years before Christ. It was said to prove that the earth was a sphere and that it travelled around the sun rather than vice versa. Understandably, the Church, which believed in the idea that the earth was a mirror of heaven, a flat land with Jerusalem at its centre, would not take kindly to it.

John would reach Bram that evening and begin reading immediately. To keep his mind active, he went to the memory cloister. John closed his eyes as he walked and looked inward. He saw a heavy oak door that swung open easily at his touch, revealing a long corridor of stone. Arches led off on either side. John walked a short way along the corridor and stopped beside the thirteenth archway on the left. Within it was a shelf and on the shelf lay a book. John lifted the book and looked at the title: The Gospel of the Christ. He opened the book at random and began reading:

Chapter 8: 1. Had I not been so near to death, I would not have permitted it. In the hours on the cross, my doubt had blossomed.

2. At first I attributed it to the works of Satan, but as time passed and my Father remained hidden, I began to believe that I had misled myself, that I was forsaken. I looked down upon the people coming and going below me, soldiers, peddlers, the curious. To them, as they went about their mundane and worldly pursuits, I was simply one prophet among many—and a failed one at that.

3. I had preached as I believed was my duty. I had

done all that my visions in the desert had required of me. I had healed the sick, preached to the multitude and offered myself as the door through which heaven would prosper on earth. And yet the End of Days was not here. The earth had not opened and released the dead, the sun had not been extinguished, Satan had not been defeated in the final battle, the world with all its petty cares went on.

4. Perhaps the holy men from the east, with their ancient beliefs in an eternal struggle between Good and Evil, had been right and I misled. I hung my head and awaited death. But I was not even to be allowed that luxury.

5. At the coming of dark, Mary and the women came and took me down from the cross. I knew nothing of it, otherwise I should have made them leave me to my solitary, defeated fate. But they wrapped me in cloth and took me to the house of a friend where they tended me back to health.

6. They put around the tale that I had been buried in the stone tomb that had been prepared, and attempted to keep my continued presence in the city a secret. It was not possible. The curious went to the tomb and found it empty. Thomas, the doubter, stumbled upon me. He tried to persuade me to continue preaching, but I was too sick in body and mind.

7. As I lay on my cot and as Mary mopped my brow, I decided that I had to leave Jerusalem as soon I was strong enough. I would preach no more, but instead I would travel and learn. The world was much larger and more complex than I had believed living in this small

corner. Somehow, I had misunderstood the message God had sent me in the desert.

8. Perhaps my labour upon this earth was to learn all things. Perhaps only through discovering my own inner peace and what those from the east call Enlightenment, could I understand what was required of me by God.

9. And so I began my travels. I first went east to—

"Hey! Watch where you're going."

The book slammed shut and flew out of John's hands, back into the alcove. He opened his eyes to see a band of soldiers standing in the road before him. They were dressed in a motley assortment of armour, chain mail and helmets and carried a selection of long pikes, axes and the occasional sword. John's first fearful reaction was that he had been captured by a crusader party, but none wore the red cross on their tunics. They were more likely either soldiers from Bram or common robbers.

"Where are you heading?" The leader was a short, stockily built man. His face was round and his features bulbous and pox-scarred except for his chin, which was cleft and jutted forward aggressively.

"Bram," John replied.

"You must know the way well to be able to walk there with your eyes closed." The men behind the leader laughed.

"I was thinking," John said defensively.

"Ah, a thinker. Well, I think too. Do you want to know what I think?"

John stayed silent, but the man went on anyway. "I

think you might have something worth stealing in that bag of yours."

"I don't." Instinctively, John raised his staff.

"So you want to fight for the bag," the robber said, smiling and hefting his axe. "*Must* be something valuable in it." He stepped forward.

"Bertrand. I know 'im."

John peered past Bertrand to see who had spoken. One of the soldiers stepped forward.

"Adso!" John exclaimed, delighted to see his friend.

"Still doing Beatrice and that old Moor's bidding?" Adso's smile undermined any insult there might have been in the question.

"They have taught me much," John said.

"I have no doubt. Beatrice is a very clever woman and old Umar's head contains more knowledge than the library in Rome.

"'E escaped with me from Béziers last year and 'e works for the Good Christians," Adso said, turning to Bertrand. "'E's no crusader and he won't have anything worth stealing."

Bertrand looked disappointed and spat pointedly in the dirt. Then his face broke into a smile and he made a mock bow to John. "Then let us escort you to Bram," he said.

As they walked, Adso and John talked.

"The autumn was 'ard," Adso said after John had told him about the winter in Minerve. "De Montfort 'ad knights everywhere. They call themselves Falcons and are led by this brute of a man called Oddo."

"He's left-handed and his men wear the crest of a falcon clutching an axe."

"'Ow did you know that?" Adso asked. "Not in one of your books."

"I saw him at Béziers. He led the charge through the gates. I didn't know his name was Oddo, but the falcon's his symbol. I think he may also be the knight who killed Pierre of Castelnau and started all this."

"Then 'e 'as a lot of blood on 'is hands," Adso said thoughtfully. "'E'll be a hard man to stop and no mistake. 'E even led an attack on Cabaret for de Montfort, but 'e weren't strong enough for that one. 'Ad to go 'ome with 'is tail 'tween 'is legs.

"After that it got better for us—good pickings. We ambushed a party of knights back before Christmas. Turns out the leader was Bouchard de Marly, one of de Montfort's most trusted lieutenants."

"Did you kill him?"

"Naw, 'e's sitting rotting in a Cabaret dungeon. Thought at first we could swap 'im for Trenceval, but we was too late."

"Roger Trenceval is dead?"

"November last's what I heard."

"How did he die?" John was saddened by the news that his protector in Carcassonne was dead. He also felt a returning pang of guilt at the way he'd abandoned Trenceval after Béziers, although he couldn't see how anything *he* could have done would have made any difference.

"Murdered, most like. De Montfort and Aumery wouldn't want 'im lingering on as a symbol for the rest of us."

"That's terrible."

Adso laughed out loud. "Terrible, is it? You've a lot to

learn, lad. War's a brutal business and this one's worse 'n most. We 'ad two men captured this February past."

"What happened to them?" John asked.

"Tortured," Adso said bitterly. "These damned priests said they was 'eretics and cut up their faces something dreadful. Then they burned them. Seems if you think someone's bound for an eternity in 'ell, what you do to their bodies in this world don't matter. Mind, we sent a few of them to their 'ell in exchange."

"Beatrice says a new army from the north will gather this summer."

"Sooner than she can imagine. De Montfort 'as met it near Béziers. Word is, they're already on the way back to Carcassonne. After that, who can say? De Montfort'll want a quick victory to begin 'is year, and Aumery'll be craving some Cathar flesh to roast. They won't be ready to take on Minerve yet, but they could take any one of a dozen smaller castles."

"Bram?"

"Could be, if 'e comes west, Cabaret if he goes north, or Aguilar if 'e decides south. Only time'll tell. My guess is 'e'll go in all different directions, try to clear around Carcassonne. The towns in most danger'll be the ones closest in, Alairac for example, but where 'e goes first only 'e knows."

"How long can Bram hold out?" John asked, worried at how little time he might have.

Adso shrugged. "For a time. But a lot of folk want to surrender. They think de Montfort'll spare them if they do. And they might be right, 'least the regular folk, but anyone who doesn't swear allegiance to the Pope's doomed."

"And you? What will you do?"

Adso looked at John. His smile was firmly in place and his eyes sparkled. "You know me, I'm not one for regular Mass, but I'll bend a knee to the Pope if it'll save my skin.

"Look, you thinkers worry too much. Did Christ say this? Does God wish us to do that? Whatever God wants from us, 'E's doing a good job of keeping it a secret from regular folk, and I don't know that the rich bishops in all their finery or the 'oly Perfects are any closer to knowing the truth than I am. Oh, I'd rather sup with Beatrice than Bishop Foulques, although I dare say I'd be better fed by the bishop, but I'm not about to throw myself on either an' say, 'Oh yes, you're right. Tell me what to do.' All a man *can* do is look after 'imself and those 'e cares about the best 'e can, and hope that that's enough for whatever God 'e chooses."

The pair lapsed into silence as they trudged toward the walls of Bram. Adso was right, John thought, most people *didn't* care about the things Aumery or Peter argued for, or what Beatrice had told him over the winter. The day-to-day struggle for existence took up all their energy. Still, in the face of the brutal crusaders, preserving the knowledge in the old books was something worthwhile, wasn't it?

"You might not 'ave time," Adso said as he and John walked the odd, circular streets of Bram. Built on a low hill, the town featured streets that ran in ever increasing circles around the central church, like ripples on a pond.

"It will take three or four days to memorize the books. Surely we have that long." John had found Origen's book and the other one exactly where Beatrice had said they would be, in the cellar of the Cathar house near the centre of town. The Aristarchos book was small, no larger than a slim prayer book, but it was full of symbols and complexities that would take time to learn. Origen's work was simpler, but it was a massive tome. Its memorizing, even with all the practice John had, would be a larger, and he feared, duller, task than he had expected.

"The refugees are saying that de Montfort's only a day or two away and 'e's certainly coming 'ere first rather than Cabaret or Alairac. Bram's not the strongest fortress, but it might be able to hold for a week or two. Bertrand's got more'n a hundred knights 'ere. Problem is, if de Montfort arrives tomorrow, you'll be trapped, and then what use'll all that learning in your 'ead be?"

Adso made a good point. If John took the books to Cabaret, fifteen miles to the northeast, he would have time to read and learn them in safety, however long Bram resisted. He would also be almost halfway back to Minerve.

"I'll leave tomorrow morning."

"Good idea. Leave the fighting to soldiers." Adso smiled, displaying his broken teeth.

A thought struck John. "If Bram's not very strong, why is Bertrand committing his knights to defending it? Wouldn't he be better to take to the woods and harass the crusaders from there, as you did last winter?"

"Maybe we'll make a soldier of you yet. That's exactly what I argued for. But Bertrand'd 'ave none of it. Seems 'e 'as sworn some sort of oath to Raymond of Toulouse and at least 'alf 'is knights are Raymond's men. Don't 'old with oaths myself, but what can you do?"

"But that means you'll be trapped when Bram falls."

Adso laughed. "Don't worry 'bout me. Remember Béziers? I'm not one to get trapped anywhere. You 'ead off to Cabaret and learn Beatrice's books. You've got a strong 'ead, so you're a scholar. I've got a strong arm, so I'm a soldier. Our paths'll cross again. Now go and read."

John watched Adso head down to the town walls. He knew what he had to do, but he still felt that he was deserting his friend. He hoped Adso was right, and that they would indeed meet again.

Cabaret was the most northerly of three small keeps spread along a rocky ridge. They looked impressive and each was an independent fortress, but the lower slopes of the ridge were cluttered with the houses and workshops of a small village. Cabaret had been an important place for centuries, and an ancient, Roman path ran along the opposite valley side, linking several small iron mines. Agricultural terraces were scattered across the surrounding hills and there was a continual bustle of people tending to them or fetching water from the streams in the valley bottom. John could see why de Montfort had failed to subdue the place the previous year. It would take a huge army to seal off all approaches to the community and there was precious little flat ground where siege engines could be located.

After the long walk from Bram with his bag of books, John had found a warm welcome in a Cathar house beneath the walls of the keep. The mention of Beatrice's name ensured that he was given a quiet corner in which to work and was allowed to join the Perfects at their vegetarian meals. He began reading immediately and, after three days, finished Origen's book. Despite its imposing size, it had proved unremarkable and had contained little John had not read elsewhere.

On the afternoon of his fourth day at Cabaret, John was struggling with Aristarchos's book when he was disturbed by a commotion at the door.

"I'm told that young John of Toulouse is within," a familiar voice said. "Tell him that the greatest troubadour in all of Languedoc is here to see him."

"William!" John exclaimed, jumping to his feet and running to the door. The pair embraced. "But you are alone," John said, a trace of a smile turning up the corners of his mouth.

"I am. I could not feed my musicians in these troubled times. What of it?"

"Where is the great troubadour of whom you spoke?"

William burst into gales of laughter and playfully punched John on the arm. "I see you have not learned manners in your months away from me," he said when he had calmed down.

"And you have not learned modesty," John replied. "But sit, have some bread and wine."

The pair seated themselves at the table and William poured them both a goblet of wine while John broke off a couple of pieces of bread.

"What brings you here?" John asked when they were settled.

William's face became serious. "Hard times. I was on the road from Toulouse, where Count Raymond and that fat slug Foulques paid me too little for too much work. I was headed for Pamiers and Foix, where they say men are not yet killing each other and still appreciate good songs. But I ran into some crusaders north of Bram and was forced to spend a night singing Catholic dirges in Latin for the legate Aumery."

"Aumery is at Bram?"

"Aumery, de Montfort and an entire army are at Bram. There was also a young priest friend of yours I seem to keep bumping into."

"Peter!"

"Indeed. A humourless lad, I thought, but in a weak moment he did ask me to pass on his greetings should I run into you on my travels."

"Peter is well?" John asked.

"As well as anyone can be who is forced to spend their days with Aumery. The man has a beautiful voice, but he has the face of a surprised ferret and the soul of a rabid fanatic." William paused and shook his head. "But I also have a message from a much more pleasant friend."

"Who?"

"She approached me in Toulouse and asked how you were and if I knew of your whereabouts. It seems she was there the night we first met."

"Isabella?"

"The very same, and with looks that could turn the head of even that rat-faced Aumery."

"How is she?"

"She is well, and showed uncommon concern for your well-being. Personally, I do not think you worth the effort, but she seemed determined to make me tell what I knew of your story since last you two met, and I have never been one to resist such beguiling eyes."

"Tell me how she is," John ordered. He found himself strangely eager to hear news of Isabella. He had thought about her a lot on his travels; if he were honest, she probably crossed his mind more than Peter, but he had assumed their paths would never again intersect.

"She is well," William repeated with a sly smile. "I told her of our adventures that first year, but despite my witty relating, your recent doings appeared of greater interest. I did not know you were here, but I had heard on my wanderings that you had escaped the unpleasantness at Béziers with Beatrice and that she had established herself in Minerve, so—"

"You told Isabella that I was in Minerve?" John felt a thrill pass through him.

"You didn't want me to?" William asked innocently.

"Of course I do, I did! I don't know! Why should she care?" John babbled in confusion.

"For a smart boy who is learning so much, you sound perilously close to a village idiot. Even I, a mere scribbler of musical entertainments, would guess that she cares for you."

"But she cares for Peter."

"Your stick friend? If she did, I doubt she does now. The young lady did not strike me as one who is attracted to visions of death and religious certainty. In fact, when I saw her, she was living in a Cathar house."

"She is a Perfect?"

"No, but I think she might be called a Good Christian."

John felt strange. Did Isabella care for him? Did he care for her? He had never asked himself either question. Isabella had been one of the group of friends and Peter had been utterly smitten by her. John would be happy to see any of his old group of friends, but this happy? John felt like hugging William for bringing him this news.

"You came all the way here to tell me this?" he asked with a silly grin on his face.

"Don't flatter yourself," William said. "The affairs of a couple of puppies who barely know their own minds are no concern of mine. I came here because Bram will fall soon. The attacks on the walls are brutal and ceaseless. The ditches are filling with blood faster than water in a storm. Word is that after Bram, they will head for Alairac and then, maybe, south to Aguilar. It seemed to me that the north would be a safer place for one of my talents to seek a living. I shall head to Minerve, where I can at least have a sensible conversation with Beatrice, and then, who knows. Too far north and they don't appreciate a troubadour's talents. Perhaps I shall go to Aragon—I hear both Good Christians and good singers are still welcome there."

"Then you had better become a Good Christian," John said playfully. Then, more seriously, "So, de Montfort is not coming to Cabaret?"

"Not this year, it seems. I suspect his failure last winter rankles, but he cannot afford too many such." William paused and his eyes narrowed in worry. "But Aumery did say a strange thing."

"What?"

"He said that there would be a gift for Cabaret when Bram fell."

"What did he mean?"

"I cannot imagine."

"Your presence is gift enough," John said. "Will you stay and entertain us for a few days?"

William drained the last of his wine and stood up. "I am honoured by your flattery, even though I suspect you are more pleased with my news than my presence, but I must move on. I had not intended to stop here at all, but I fell into conversation with a Good Man and from his description of the ugly boy who had suddenly appeared to scrounge a bed and meals, I assumed it must be you."

"I see I did not learn flattery from you!" John rose to stand beside his friend.

William bowed in mock gratitude. "But tell me, do you still draw? You have not forgotten your promise to immortalize me?"

"I have not forgotten my promise, although I fear it will take more than mere human skill to create a work that will match your opinion of yourself. I practice when I can, but those times are rare these days. I fear my skill is not improving much."

"Maybe you need a worthy subject. Someone of Isabella's beauty, perhaps," William said slyly.

"That would certainly be a more pleasing task than attempting to capture your sorry face on a wall, but what I need is a book. I hear there is one in Al-Andalus that contains wondrous pictures."

"There are many wondrous things down that way."

"You've been there?"

"I have. There are few places I have not been in search of stories and songs. If things get much worse here, perhaps it will not be long until I am seeking refuge down there again. At least the Moors appreciate talent, but for now I must be on my way." William moved toward the door.

"I am glad you dropped by," John said. "Say hello to Beatrice when you are in Minerve and tell her I am near done and shall return in a few days."

"I shall do so," William said as the pair walked outside. "Do not read too much. It strains the eyes and the brain. And do not spend your hours dreaming of that girl in Toulouse. I do not doubt you will meet again and, perhaps, by then you will have learned to draw well enough to do her beauty justice."

"I shall try. Travel well, William. I hope we shall meet again in happier times."

"As do I, young John. And when we do meet again, you must tell me of the mysterious gift from Bram. Perhaps it will be worthy of a song."

The pair embraced once more and John watched the troubadour head down the rough path across the hills to Minerve. It had been good to meet his friend again and, although the news from Bram was disturbing, John was happy as he returned to the table. Both Peter and Adso were at Bram, but the first was safe enough beside Aumery, and the other's skills and cunning would serve him well in a crisis. Isabella was in Toulouse and was asking for him—that was the thought that spun happily around John's brain. He sighed contentedly and returned to his book.

The candle flame spluttered out in the final pool of melted wax. It was still dark outside, but the sounds of birdsong announced that dawn was near. Soon the Perfects would rise to begin their devotions and eat their meagre breakfast. John sat in the darkness, his mind a turmoil. He had finished Aristarchos's book more than an hour before and he was tired, but his brain would not allow sleep. New ideas—literally new ways of looking at the world—were swirling around his head.

Aristarchos's mathematics had been beyond him, but the ideas behind it were earth-shaking. As Beatrice had suggested, the book held that, instead of the sun travelling around the earth, which was what everyone knew to be true by simply looking in the sky, the opposite was the case. The earth was not the centre of God's universe, the sun was, and the earth and the other planets were merely objects spinning around it. What's more, the moon was simply a lesser object spinning around the earth. And the stars were not set in a crystal sphere above the earth at all, but were points of light almost immeasurable distances away.

The Church would scream heresy, but what if it were true? Would that not be as shocking in its own way as the Gospel of the Christ?

John looked down at the book in his hands. He could see it now without the candle flame; the pale light of pre-dawn was filtering in through the window. Above him, he could hear the sounds of the Perfects beginning their day. Soon they would be down to set the fire. John didn't want to be caught up in that. He needed time to think— and to draw. Strangely, the urge to draw had been growing since William's news, two days before, that Isabella was asking after him. He wanted to draw the world around him, yes, but mostly he wanted to draw Isabella. Her face hovered in his mind as clearly as if he had seen it yesterday and he wanted to get it down on parchment. But the Perfects of Cabaret had no parchment, or even ink or quills.

John turned the mathematics book over in his hands. The back cover was fine leather and blank. He went to the hearth and the black remains of yesterday's fire. He selected a suitable piece of burned wood and made a few experimental lines on the cover. They took. Stuffing the small book into the pouch at his waist, John collected several more pieces of charcoal, wrapped himself in his fur-edged cloak and let himself out into the morning.

John walked along the ridge and then down the path that followed the narrow valley in the direction of Bram. The sky was clear and it was the first day in weeks that the rain had stopped, but the wind coming off the hills was knife-edged and the ground beneath his feet muddy. John pulled his cloak tight around him, but he still shivered whenever he stopped walking. His feet and legs were soaked and filthy almost to his knees, and he was beginning to lose the feeling in his toes, but it was good to be outside.

John followed the path for nearly a mile, until the valley widened out before him. The weak sun bathed the landscape and mist rose in thick swirls from the wet ground. John stopped at a rock half as tall as he was. Long before, it had tumbled down from the surrounding hills and come to rest by the path, providing a spot sheltered from the wind. John sat and gazed toward Bram. The view was empty as far as he could see, except for some distant travellers winding up the valley toward him.

John looked up at the sun and tried to envisage the solid earth beneath him moving around it. It certainly seemed as if the opposite was happening. The sun was moving through the heavens but, if the earth were turning, John supposed the effect might be the same. He took out the mathematics book and began making tentative marks on the cover. As the sun rose, he sketched the shape of Isabella's face with her dark hair cascading down on either side. He drew in her high forehead, narrow nose, eyes and mouth. He got the proportions right, but it looked nothing like the image in his mind. The eyes were lifeless and his attempt at giving Isabella her mysterious smile simply made it look as if she had eaten something distasteful. The face was the same as all the mosaics and paintings in the churches, magnificent if you painted it in bright colours and surrounded it with gold, but nothing like a real person.

In frustration, John smeared out the charcoal lines and stuffed the book back in his pouch. He wished once more that he had the drawing book Umar and Beatrice had mentioned. Maybe it would teach him how to draw what he saw the way he saw it.

He would also have to study the mathematics book more. He knew its conclusions, but not how Aristarchos had come to them. Maybe John could find a mathematician who could explain some of it, but who? Peter had always understood figures and numbers, but he would probably just say the book was heresy and burn it.

John frowned. Would Beatrice and Umar be any happier with his questions? They obviously thought the mathematics and drawing books were much less important than the gospels they had given him to learn. Would they approve of him spending his time trying to understand Aristarchos's ideas, not to mention drawing? Probably not. The earth and the sun were material things and thus the Devil's work, and certainly Umar would regard further study as an unnecessary distraction from John's main purpose, which was to fill the memory cloister.

But was that what John really wished to devote his entire life to? To fill the pot of his memory with ancient books? It was without question a noble thing to do, and John was completely in favour of preserving books that people wanted to burn, but there were so many other things! John still wanted to see the world, he wanted to master drawing, if he ever found the book, and he wanted to understand the world and the sun and all that the strange book in his pouch seemed to promise. And there was more. John wanted the free life Adso led and he wanted to do his part against the crusaders who were ravishing his land. Yet, it was impossible to do all those things and still be what Beatrice and Umar wanted him to be.

The thought of Adso made John wonder how his friend was doing and what was going on at Bram. He desperately wanted to know, to get up and walk down the valley, past the winding procession that was much closer now, all the way to Bram. There he would find Adso and Bertrand, learn what was going on, and fight beside his friend to rid the land of its invaders.

John leaned his head back against the rock and felt the warmth of the rising spring sun on his face. It was an impossible dream. John knew he had to go back to Beatrice in Minerve. But once he was back, would he ever escape? Beatrice's soft voice and calm logic would convince him that his idea of joining Adso was nonsense. She would say that fighting was never the answer and simply played into the Devil's hands. The only way to truly fight the crusaders was the path she had pointed him on—collecting, learning knowledge and wisdom so that, whatever happened here, future generations would have the chance to see the truth and learn from the mistakes being made now.

John sighed and lowered his head. A song thrush, lured into the open by the sunny weather, sat on a nearby branch. "What should I do?" John asked the bird. The thrush tilted its head and stared at him curiously. "You're right not to answer," John went on. "It's my decision and, in any case, I *know* what I should do. I should get up from this rock, have some breakfast at Cabaret and set off for Minerve.

"But I *want* to go to Bram." John's raised voice startled

the thrush and it hopped up to a higher branch. John's gaze wandered to the road. The travellers were closer now. It seemed to be some sort of procession, but exactly what sort, John couldn't make out as the walkers appeared and disappeared around corners.

"Bram is where the action is. Maybe Beatrice is mistaken. Maybe the crusaders can be beaten and driven home. I should go and do my bit to make that happen.

"I wish I could fly like you. Then I could just fly to Bram and see what is happening to Adso and Peter."

John lapsed into silence, vaguely embarrassed that he had been talking to a bird. He watched the procession wend closer. There was something odd about it. A line of figures in single file, so close to each other as to be almost indistinguishable, and all with their heads down. Perhaps they were religious penitents; there were lots of people with strange ideas around at the moment.

The procession entered a stand of stunted pines and disappeared from view. John gazed at the puffy white clouds scudding across his view and let his thoughts wander. Lucky people were those who were certain about things. Beatrice and Aumery were lucky—both were certain. About different things, but that didn't seem to matter. Now even Peter seemed to be acquiring certainty. Was John destined to live his life questioning? But how did one know what to be certain about? Maybe God would appear to him one day in a blinding flash of light and tell him.

John shivered and stood. It was time to get back; some hot wine by the fire sounded good.

The figures were emerging from the trees. As John took a

final look at them, the leader stumbled and fell. A low moan rose from the group and reached John on the wind. The rest stopped and began turning their heads as if looking around. But they weren't looking at anything. And there was something wrong with their faces. Curious, John began walking down the track toward them. The thrush took off in a flutter of wings.

The leader of the procession was back on his feet and had resumed his stumbling progress. There were dozens of people in the line. Each had a hand reaching out onto the shoulder of the one in front. John broke into a run. Realization of what was coming dawned slowly, but he forced it back. It couldn't be. It was too awful.

Eventually John reached the shuffling men and stopped in horror. At the sound of his skidding feet, the leader raised his head. It was all John could do not to collapse on the path. The man's bare feet were caked in mud and blood, and the skin, where it showed, was white with the cold. He was dressed in a padded, bloody tunic that John recognized as the sort knights wore beneath their chain mail. But it was what was left of his face that made John's stomach churn. Someone had deliberately mutilated this man almost beyond recognition. His ears and nose had been sliced off. His lips too were gone, leaving a bloody hole that exposed his teeth. One eye socket was just a black, blood-filled hole. From the other, a bloodshot eyeball stared at John.

John glanced at the man behind the leader. He was the same. No, he was worse, both eyes had been removed. The rest in the line that stretched back into the trees were the same, blind and hideously mutilated.

John looked back at the leader. Despite the man's mutilations, he recognized him. The cleft, jutting chin was distinctive.

"Bertrand?" John asked.

The man inclined his head painfully. These were the knights of Bram. A gift from the crusaders—a hundred mutilated and blind, led by a one-eyed man. A warning: if you resist, this will happen to you.

"Adso?" John asked with a sick feeling in his stomach.

Bertrand shrugged. The effort almost caused him to fall over.

John stepped forward and placed Bertrand's arm over his shoulder.

"Come on," he shouted to the rest of the line. "You're almost at Cabaret. People will help you there."

A low groan rose behind him as the procession started moving again. A host of emotions swarmed through John as he took Bertrand's weight and staggered forward. Rage that human beings could perpetrate such an atrocity on others. Anger that Peter might have been a part of it. Worry that Adso could be one of the helpless wrecks behind him. But there was, finally, certainty too. Beatrice could take the way of peace, but he could not. He could no longer hide in books. He had to fight, to resist the monsters that could perform such a horror. He would go back to Minerve, he owed Beatrice that, but then he would find a knight who would teach him the arts of war.

A Mission

Alairac

MAY 1210

Peter stared at the pile of half-naked bodies in the field below the walls of Alairac. There were about a dozen of them, stripped of their chain mail and weapons and piled unceremoniously in a heap that could be seen from the muddy road leading north. It was early May, but it felt more like January. The fifteen-day siege had been in the teeth of a raw, howling gale, but the castle had fallen the night before. Realizing they were doomed, the defenders had tried to sneak away under cover of darkness. Oddo's Falcons had had a fine hunt in the darkness and the results formed the pile that Peter now contemplated.

The gale had finally died down, but freezing rain was blowing in from the west in bitter sheets and Peter felt unutterably miserable. Apart from the trip with Arnaud Aumery to Toulouse, accompanying Simon de Montfort on the spring campaign against the heretics had been brutally hard work. Perhaps one day Peter would rise to a position of great power and sit in a comfortable abbey, but for now he was a lowly monk, given a host of grinding tasks. Aumery's distrust of luxury in any form meant that the monks had to work hard and devote their spare time to prayer and contemplation.

Not that Peter objected to the prayer; it was, after all, what monks did and was a vital conduit to God. Peter also found it strangely relaxing. Even in the black pre-dawn, kneeling on the frozen ground and shivering in the wind, the monotonous repetition of the memorized words took Peter out of himself. Aumery said that, during prayer, a monk's mind should focus on a love of God and the sacrifice and suffering of His only son on the cross, but Peter found that by concentrating his mind on the words of the prayer, everything else left his head. Eventually he found that he could, for brief moments at least, experience an extraordinary sense of peace and well-being. The sense of loneliness he also felt was a bit frightening, but the peace convinced him that the place he went during prayer must be somewhere closer to God than the brutal world in which he spent his days. Peter wondered if Aumery's scourging his back with the knotted rope was the priest's way of searching for that same place.

"That's one more castle we won't have to worry about." Peter turned to see Simon de Montfort standing beside him looking at the bodies. He was wearing a red cloak against the weather and held the reins of a large horse. A heavy cart, loaded with timbers for a siege engine, lumbered past, splashing mud over Peter and de Montfort's legs. The crusader's horse stamped in annoyance, but the man ignored it.

"There are too many damned castles on hills in this country."

"And too many heretics," Peter ventured.

"And not enough bonfires, according to Aumery." De Montfort looked up at the leaden sky. "Even God would have His work cut out getting a heretic to burn in weather like this. This is truly a godforsaken country. At least in the Holy Land we were always warm."

"That must have been wonderful, to go on a crusade against the infidels."

"Wonderful? I don't know if that is the correct word. Bloody, exciting, frustrating, holy—it was all those things and more—and those infidels are damned fine warriors. We could never get them to stay in one place long enough to fight a proper battle—always raiding our knights, killing one or two and then disappearing over the next hill. We were fine as long as we sat in our castles or ventured forth in strength, but too small a party was inviting disaster. At least the Moors of Al-Andalus fight our kind of war." De Montfort wiped the rivulets of rain off his forehead. "Still, God knows best, so we must move on."

"Where to now?" Peter asked.

De Montfort regarded Peter with his cold eyes. "I am tired of these minor outposts and spending our time burning wet villages. More knights from the north join us every day. We will spend another month clearing the country around Carcassonne and then we will be strong enough to attack a major fortress."

"Which one?" Peter asked eagerly.

"Minerve," de Montfort replied. "Aumery will have his bonfire."

The pair stood in silence before the bodies for a moment. "Have you always wished to be a monk?" de Montfort asked at last. "Did you have a message from God instructing you to lead this life?"

257

Peter was startled by the abrupt change in topic. "All who do the Lord's work are called by Him in one way or another."

De Montfort laughed. "You are young, but already you have learned the art of playing with words. I am not seeking to trick you, I simply wish to know what draws you to Aumery. He cannot be an easy man with whom to work."

"Father Aumery is very holy."

"I do not dispute that. I have seen how his back bleeds for the love of Christ. I merely observe that you do not appear to be one who is drawn to such mortification of the flesh."

Peter thought for a long moment. De Montfort was right; he had no desire to beat himself into ecstasy as Aumery did, but how much was it safe to tell this man? "I believe there are other ways to get close to God."

"And if those ways should advance you in this world, so much the better?"

Peter stared at his feet.

De Montfort laughed. "Don't worry, young monk. All of us advance ourselves as best we can. Oddo does it through sheer, naked power. Aumery uses the mysticism of God. Both, I believe, have the same end in view, personal advancement, although I suspect Oddo will settle for what advancement is possible on this earth, while Aumery has his eyes set more on the next.

"You have done well for one so young. That was a heavy load Aumery placed on your shoulders at Carcassonne and you carried it. You are intelligent and you learn quickly. I may have need of you in the future. Would you be prepared to serve if I called?"

"If the duties did not conflict with my calling to God."
Peter answered carefully, but inside he was excited. De
Montfort was powerful and being close to him might ad-
vance Peter's ambitions.

"You are a difficult man to tie down!" de Montfort said
with a nod. "That is a good characteristic. It means you can
keep secrets, and that means that people will tell you
things—valuable things. Knowledge is power, never forget
that. But you have not asked how I strive to advance my
own cause."

"It is not my business."

"Of course not, but you will listen if I tell you. I do not
seek naked power such as Oddo craves. He enjoys watching
others cower before him, and that is a transient pleasure at
best. Nor do I seek the uncertain comfort of a position in
the next world.

"Oh, do not look so surprised. I am convinced there *is*
a next world, it is simply that there are many competing
paths toward achieving a position in it and I am not sure
which is the most certain.

"My hopes for immortality lie with my son, Simon. I
have been deprived of my lands in England by the king, so
I must rebuild. That is why I chose to remain here and lead
this venture last winter when no one else wished to do so.
It has been a hard season and there will be others, but now
the knights flooding south for their forty-day indulgences
must bow a knee to me. It will take many years, but if I can
secure this land, I will have something worthwhile to pass
on to my offspring—a power base from which he can build
without the struggle I have been subject to."

De Montfort fell silent and gazed again at the pile of bodies. "That is how we are all destined to finish," he said eventually. "Does your God make the prospect easier? Certainly, the heretics seem happy enough to embrace their end. I will go naked to the tomb if I have something to pass on to my son.

"But"—de Montfort roused himself from his reverie— "for now we must be on our way. Power must be exercised, else it becomes rusty and of no use. And I would ask a favour of you."

"If it is within my power," Peter replied.

"It is not a large thing, and it might greatly ease our work later. However, it will entail removing your monk's habit for a short time."

Peter remained silent.

"What I need," de Montfort said, staring hard at Peter, "is a spy. As I said, when summer eventually arrives, we shall attack Minerve. I know something of its situation and it is formidable, at least on the outside. What I need to know is if there is a softness at the centre. Is there disaffection with the lord, are the granaries full or empty, where does the town's water come from? Those are things I need to know if I am to capture the town without destroying my army on the ramparts. Will you help?"

Peter pondered what he was being asked. It would certainly be more exciting than the long trudge north with the army, and it didn't sound too difficult. There were refugees all over the land this year. If he shaved his head to remove his distinctive monk's tonsure, it would be easy to pass himself off as one more displaced person. In addition, doing a favour for de Montfort would place the knight in Peter's debt, and there was no telling how useful that might be in the future. The only difficulty was Aumery.

"I will need to talk with Father Aumery," Peter said.

"Of course," de Montfort replied with a smile. "I foresee no difficulty. Speak with Aumery and then return to talk with me. I would wish you to leave soon."

The crusader hauled himself into his warhorse's saddle. "You will go far." De Montfort turned his horse's head and moved away up the track.

Peter watched the retreating back and recalled de Montfort's words: knowledge is power. Aumery had often told him the same thing. The trick, he assumed, was to acquire the right knowledge. Perhaps this task for de Montfort might be one way to do just that.

Return

Minerve

MAY 1210

The clang of metal on metal rang through the warm, late-May air and echoed across the gorge below Minerve's castle walls. Sweat poured off John's forehead and stung his eyes; dark patches stained the back and underarms of the padded jerkin he wore for protection. It was becoming increasingly difficult to wield the heavy sword, yet his opponent showed no signs of tiring.

John swung his sword low across his body and parried a blow that would have taken his left leg off below the knee. Remembering his training, he twisted his sword up and over, trying to force the other man's weapon out of his grip, but his adversary was clever. Almost faster than John could see, he transferred his sword to his left hand, pushed John's sword wide and away and moved in close. John could feel the man's breath on his face—it smelled strongly of wild garlic—and see the glint in his eye. He was about to push him away when he felt a prick on his neck. The man smiled. "You're dead," he said.

John looked down to see a narrow, evil-looking dagger in Adso's right hand. He sighed, dropped his sword and sat down heavily on the dusty ground. "Damn," he said. "You always have another trick!"

Adso joined John on the ground, replaced the dagger in the sheath by his waist and took a long draft from the wineskin beside him. "If you're not big or strong enough to overpower your enemy, tricks is what'll keep you alive," he said, offering John the skin. "Remember, in the 'eat of battle, most soldiers just rush forward and 'ack about madly. It might be frightening, but there's no skill to it. You can always out-think a man like that."

The pair sat on the low hill at the opposite end of the narrow neck of land from Minerve's castle and caught their breath. Below them was a hive of activity. A small group of soldiers was practising with crossbows, while others sweated to deepen the ditches beneath the castle walls. A continuous stream of carts, loaded with sacks of grain, barrels of olives and squealing pigs, rumbled up to the gates and were admitted.

John had arrived back in Minerve from Cabaret two weeks before. To his delight and relief, Adso had beaten him by a full day, having snuck away from Bram the night before it fell.

"It was obvious what was going to 'appen," Adso had said after John told him of meeting Bertrand and the others. "The defences of Bram never 'ad a chance of standing up to the siege engines de Montfort 'ad with 'im. Massive they were. I told Bertrand that our only chance was to try and fight our way out, but 'e says no. Said 'e would rely on the rules of chivalry and throw 'imself on de Montfort's mercy after they surrendered." Adso laughed bitterly. "For a rogue, old Bertrand is stubborn in his belief in honour and rules.

I suppose 'e 'as paid more'n enough for 'is mistakes. Seems there's no rules in this war."

John had persuaded Adso to teach him all he knew about fighting, and they had been outside the city walls every day since. Those two weeks had been a chaos of fevered preparation for the town. No one doubted that de Montfort and his crusader army would soon arrive, which left two choices: either flee or prepare to fight. Most chose the latter and set to with a determination firm in the belief that Minerve was one of the strongest fortresses north of the Pyrénées. Rooftop cisterns were filled with water, and food was stored everywhere. The earthy smell of the farm-yard hung over the town as farmers brought their animals in from the surrounding countryside. It was becoming increasingly difficult to walk the steep, narrow streets without having to kick pigs, goats and chickens out of the way. Refugees from outlying villages camped in every spare room and open space, and more knights, many escapees from Carcassonne, trickled in each day to offer their services.

"How long until they arrive?" John asked, eventually.

"Week or two at most," Adso replied. "Word is they're moving north from Alairac, but slow. De Montfort's in no 'urry. The longer he takes to get 'ere, the bigger his army gets, the more subdued the countryside be'ind him is, and the more strain there'll be on us with all these extra mouths to feed. But that also gives us more time to prepare a welcome that'll break the crusader army once and for all."

"That's what you said about Carcassonne."

"And I should 'ave been right. If Trenceval 'adn't given

up the city for that old man and his books, we'd still be there. Minerve'll be different. Even after Béziers, people didn't take the crusade seriously. Everyone thought they'd get tired and go 'ome 'fore they got to 'is village. Last winter and Bram changed all that. Now everybody knows they're 'ere until we beat them and force them to go 'ome. Minerve's where we'll do that."

John wished he could be as optimistic as his friend, but the tales told by refugees from other towns made it hard. "What about the siege engines?" he asked. "Bram's walls only held out for three days against them."

"They'll make life unpleasant, no doubt about that, but Minerve's much better situated than Bram. Siege engines or not, de Montfort will have to assault us eventually, and the only way in is along this causeway. As long as there's twenty men with crossbows left alive, that'll be suicide. We'll break the crusader army's spirit right 'ere. One serious defeat and that army'll melt away and the Pope'll make peace."

John fervently hoped Adso was right. A part of John's mind was thrilled to be learning to fight, and he was proud of how good he was getting, despite the fact that every time he mastered something, Adso had a new trick to get around it. But the rest of John's mind wouldn't let go of the strange books he had read and the knowledge they seemed to promise.

Despite Beatrice's injunction to leave the books behind once he had memorized them, John had brought the mathematics book with him to Minerve. He had all the words in the memory cloister, but there were many numbers he didn't understand. The book was important, John realized, and he wanted to master all of its secrets.

"Well, come on then," Adso said, getting to his feet. "There's still time left today to learn that trick with the dagger."

John jumped up. That was something else that had changed. Two weeks ago, after a hard day's training with Adso, John's muscles would have ached horribly. Now they simply responded as he required. His body had hardened with the work.

"Right," Adso said. "Left 'anded swordsmen always 'ave an advantage 'cause they come at you different than you expect. Why do the stairs of a keep always spiral to the right?"

"So a defending swordsman has the space to swing against an enemy coming up."

"Exactly, if the swordsman is right-'anded."

John thought for a minute. It was true, keeps were built to be defended and the advantage always lay with a right-handed man if he were uppermost on a right-handed spiral stair. A right-handed man fighting his way up the stairs, or a left-handed man defending, would be at disadvantage. His sword arm would be crammed up against the pillar at the centre of the staircase, and he would be continually bumping his arm against the wall.

"I 'ave 'eard tell," Adso went on, "that there's a family up north where the lords are always left 'anded. They had a keep built with the stairs going the opposite way. They say the keep's never been taken.

"Now, I'm not left-'anded, and I'll never be good enough on that side with a sword to take a natural left man, but I've practised and I can perform passably well. Certainly well enough to confuse my opponent when 'e's tired and not thinking too good. Just 'cause God gave you a good right 'and, don't mean your left's useless."

Without warning, Adso swept up his sword in his left hand and attacked John. John managed to parry the blow only because he had been expecting something like this. The first lessons he had learned were to never let your guard down with Adso and to always expect the unexpected.

The swords clashed loudly as John tried desperately to parry Adso's swings with his left hand. It was hard work and Adso often got past John's defences. The swords were round tipped and blunt, but a blow in the heat of combat still hurt, even through the padded jerkin. Adso's lessons were written in the patchwork of bruises, in various states of healing, on John's arms, legs and sides.

"So you're a soldier now." Both John and Adso stopped and turned to see Beatrice standing beside the road.

"I'm trying to be," John said sheepishly.

To John's surprise, Beatrice had barely attempted to persuade him not to learn to fight. In a sense, that had been worse than if she had shouted at him and called him stupid. Then he could have gotten angry and stormed off to do what he wanted, but it was impossible to get angry at Beatrice. She never gave cause. Still, John had guiltily avoided her as much as possible since his return from Cabaret.

"Well," Beatrice said with a smile, "if you learn the art of soldiering as well as you learned the memory cloister, I'm sure the crusaders will be in trouble."

John felt himself blush at the compliment. "I'm sorry," he mumbled, dropping his gaze.

"Never be sorry," Beatrice said. "I offered you a path through this life. You chose another, but paths sometimes wind in ways we cannot anticipate. Perhaps one day your two paths will meet."

"Enough talk of paths," Adso said. "My path now is to a cool spot and some of this food that we seem to 'ave so much of."

Adso picked up his wineskin, sheathed his sword and strode toward the town. John hesitated. He felt he needed to explain what he was doing to Beatrice.

"I *do* appreciate all you have taught me," he said, eyes fixed on the ground, "and I shall remember all I have learned. I can be a soldier *and* work with the memory cloister."

"It is hard to serve two masters," Beatrice said softly. "You have a good mind, John, and now it contains things of value. I understand why you need to fight by Adso's side, but be careful. Try to stay alive. I have a sense that your mind may yet do some good in this world, and it would be a pity to lose it to some mercenary's crossbow bolt or sword."

"I will try." John raised his head and looked at Beatrice. "Do you know which of all the wonders you and Umar have told me of is the one I crave most?"

"The book on drawing?"

"Yes! I know you think the material world is evil and that we should not be seduced by it, but if the Devil created the entire world about us, why did he make some of it so beautiful?"

Beatrice remained silent.

"A sunset over the mountains that turns the sky to fire can uplift the spirit to wondrous heights," John continued. "The ruins of the ancient Roman temples and villas, grown about with vines and scented with wild herbs, capture a lost past so strongly that it brings a lump to my throat. The stained glass windows in the cathedral of Toulouse were made by the Catholics you so despise, yet they are a wonder to behold even to the pagan eye. Would the Devil put these things in the world when they would give us poor mortals such comfort?"

"The Devil seduces in many ways."

"Perhaps. Or perhaps God slips a little beauty into the Devil's creations to give those who can see it some comfort as they struggle through their lives. If that is the case, then the ability to recreate that beauty in art on a wall or a page would be a great gift. It would spread the beauty before the eyes of many and increase the good in the world. I think, if the book Umar talks of can teach me to draw, then, through that, I might bring some hope into the world.

"Oh, I will remember the mystical texts of Zarathustra and the Gospel of the Christ and the others, and wherever I see an opportunity, I shall pass on that knowledge and try to use it to confound the plans of these crusaders and their minions. But I want to understand the world and to draw it."

John fell silent in embarrassment after his outburst. He had never really thought all this through before, it had just come to him as he spoke. Even though he had begun by trying to explain how he felt so that Beatrice wouldn't be angry with him, he was afraid that he might have horribly offended her. But Beatrice was still smiling.

"You have a fine mind, and that is something that comes from God. I think you are mistaken, but I do not regret teaching you. Perhaps you have been given the tools to come to the right conclusions on your own." The smile faded. "I am sorry I shall not be here to see that happen."

"You are leaving?"

"I have things to do."

"Are you afraid that we will lose here?"

"I cannot say, I do not have a military mind. Perhaps Adso is correct and you will win. What I do know is that winning or losing here is of no importance. In any case, I wish you luck and hope that our paths cross in the future."

"I do too."

With a final smile, Beatrice tapped her staff on the ground, stepped onto the road and set off against the flow of traffic.

John watched her back until it was lost in the dust. He was so intent on watching Beatrice that he didn't notice the ragged refugee with the shaved head who hesitated and stared at him for a long moment before continuing on into Minerve.

The Spy

Minerve

JUNE 1210

Peter trudged up the narrow cobbled streets of Minerve. On either side of him, the rough limestone walls of the houses reared like castle battlements, broken only by small, deeply set windows. People going in both directions jostled past him and skinny goats bumped his legs. The town was crowded, but so far Peter had discovered nothing that would give his masters any comfort. There was plenty of food, the cisterns were all full of water, despite there being no evidence of communal bucket wells or pumps in the streets, and the inhabitants seemed determined. The Perfects he frequently saw walking the streets were comfortably accepted by the populace, and the services they held in their houses were well attended.

Peter had been in Minerve almost a week and May had turned to June, but so far no one had questioned him. He was dressed in rags and sheltered behind a story about being a refugee from Carcassonne who had been wandering and begging around the countryside all winter. His only worry was that he would bump into John. Seeing him as he had arrived at the city gates had been a shock, but so far there had been no further sign of his old friend.

Peter would have to leave soon, whether he had any information or not. Simon de Montfort's army had to be close by now and the last thing Peter wanted was to be trapped in the besieged town. Unfortunately, Peter had fulfilled neither of his tasks. After his conversation with de Montfort outside Alairac, Aumery had agreed to the spying idea. He agreed so readily, in fact, that Peter suspected that the two men had been discussing it before he was even approached. Aumery blessed Peter's task, making only one condition to releasing him temporarily from the priesthood. While in Minerve, Peter had to try to find out all he could about the Perfects within its walls. How many there were, how popular they were with the townsfolk and whether there were any who had arrived recently and were held in special regard by the others. "Look for a Perfect, probably aged, who travels from town to town," Aumery had advised. "That may be the one who knows the location of the treasure."

Peter was slightly concerned that he was spying for two masters, but resolved his worry by reasoning that they were all on God's side. He was also thrilled that the Grail might be in Minerve, even though Aumery didn't think so. How wonderful it would be to find it, or at least be the one who discovered where it was!

But Peter had found no weakness in Minerve's defences nor any clue as to the location of the Cathar Treasure. He wondered how he would explain his failure to Aumery and de Montfort. He desperately hoped he could find something out; to return with nothing wouldn't help him curry favour with either.

Peter turned a corner and froze. John was heading toward

him down the hilly street. He was carrying a yoke over his shoulders, from which swung two large, empty buckets, and he was having trouble negotiating the crowded thoroughfare with his unwieldy burden. He was also deep in conversation with an old Perfect who scurried along by his side, tapping a gnarled staff on the cobbles.

Peter hunched over and moved to the edge of the street, where several beggars were loitering, half-heartedly holding out their hands for alms. Out of the corner of his eye, he watched John approach. It felt odd to see him again after so much had happened. Peter almost wished he could step forward and swap stories with his childhood friend,

John and the old Perfect passed without even glancing at those around them, and Peter fell into step behind them. He followed in part because he was curious about his friend, but also because John appeared to be on his way to collect water. The source of the town's seemingly endless water supply would no doubt interest de Montfort.

Following John and his companion was easy in the crowded streets and the pair soon arrived at an old metal gate in the town walls, near the southeast corner. The gate was open onto a set of steep stairs that descended into a dark tunnel. John spoke a few words to the Perfect and disappeared down the steps.

Peter waited a few moments and then approached the old man, who had settled himself against the wall to one side of the gate.

"Hello, Father," Peter said respectfully.

The Perfect looked up, squinting against the bright sunlight. "Good day. Are you here for water from the well?"

"No," Peter said, crouching beside the man and doing his best to hide his excitement. A well! "I am just taking the air."

"As am I. I find being cooped up indoors causes the mind to become dusty. Fresh air blows away the cobwebs. Are you from here?"

"No. I am from Carcassonne. I left when it fell last year and I have been wandering ever since. My name is Peter." Peter had told the story so often that it came easily.

"I am Umar. Are you a Good Christian?"

Peter hesitated for a moment. "Yes," he said. It was all right to lie if you were doing God's work.

Umar nodded thoughtfully. "And have you sworn the oath to defend Minerve and her inhabitants with your life?"

"I have," Peter said, although he had not heard of such an oath. It seemed a harmless enough lie.

"Excellent," Umar said. "We need all the fighters there are to combat the evil that comes to attack us. You have my blessing."

"Thank you," Peter said, uncertain whether he should bow. He knew better than to cross himself—heretics never did that—but he didn't know what they did. "Are you from this town?" he asked.

"I am not," Umar said. "Like you, I am a recent arrival."

"Where are you from?"

"I am from everywhere," Umar replied with a smile. "I travel much from town to town."

Peter's heart leaped. First the well and now this—an old Perfect who travelled a lot. Did he hold the location of the Cathar Treasure in his head? "You must learn many things on your travels."

"Indeed. I see much of the Devil's work as I venture through this corrupt world, as you must have over this past winter."

"Yes, of course, but you must also see wonders."

"Ah, yes, but worldly wonders are nothing—books are my great joy. I have been blessed with frequent opportunities to read many books and I have learned wondrous things." Umar tilted his head and looked slyly at Peter. "It is gratifying to have one so young take such an interest in an old man."

Peter's pulse raced. Had he made a mistake? Was the old man suspicious? But Umar went on calmly. "Do you read?"

"A little," Peter replied.

"That is good. There are some books at the Good Christian house by the town gate. Perhaps, if the forces of Satan give us enough time, you might like to visit and I would gladly show them to you."

"I should like that," Peter said. He was nervous. He was certain that he had found a Perfect who knew at least a part of the secret of the Cathar Treasure, but he knew that if he talked much more, sooner or later he would make a mistake. Also, he needed to check out the water supply.

Peter nodded toward the gate. "I think I shall visit the well. A cool drink would be good."

"Indeed. Go in safety. Perhaps we shall meet again."

"Perhaps."

Peter headed toward the gate, pleased with himself. At last he might have something to tell de Montfort and Aumery.

The steps—worn and slippery with spilled water—led

down a short tunnel and then levelled out to a covered path along the base of the town wall before descending steeply once more. Peter moved cautiously, sticking close to one side where he could touch the cold stone of the wall and keep out of the way of anyone going up. The steps were mostly carved out of the rock of the gorge wall, but in some places they had been built up or repaired. The walls and roof of the tunnel were man-made from large blocks of local stone, and light was let in through occasional narrow windows cut in the walls. The effect was of going from bright light by the windows to almost complete darkness between them, and Peter's eyes were continually adjusting. This was good as it meant that, should he run into John coming back up, it would be unlikely that he would be recognized.

Peter assumed that he was climbing down to the river bed and that the tunnel was to hide and protect the route from observers and enemies across the gorge. This explained the lack of wells in town and might prove to be a weakness.

The stairway took several sharp turns as it descended, but eventually, Peter arrived at the bottom. The tunnel opened into a low, dark room with a stone floor. The gloom was normally broken only by the light from four narrow windows, but a heavy door in the far wall was open and a broad shaft of light illuminated Minerve's water source. The air was cold and damp, and the walls and floor were covered in slippery moss. Peter stood by the wall at the base of the stairs and took in the scene before him.

On the rock wall to Peter's left, some three feet above the ground, a spring of clear water bubbled out of a fissure in the limestone. The water ran down into an artificial pond from which John and a couple of others were filling buckets.

So this was the town's water supply. If it was the only source—and Peter had certainly seen no other—it might be possible to capture or destroy it. At this time of year the river was almost dry. If some men could force their way in and hold the area for long enough, they might be able to somehow contaminate the well or pull down the walls around it. Without water in the dry summer, Minerve would not be able to hold out long.

Peter turned to ascend the stairs before John was finished at the well. Instead, he found himself face to face with the old Perfect, leaning on his staff and watching him curiously.

"Are you not going to have a drink then?" Umar asked. "The water is fresh and cold."

"I ... I'm not thirsty any more," Peter stammered.

"I think that's only one thing you are not. No Good Christian would ever take an oath, even a fictional one to defend Minerve, and calling me Father proves that you are a Catholic. Do you come here to spy on us?"

"No! I mean, I am a Catholic. I was scared." Peter floundered, trying to think of a convincing story.

"Well," Umar interrupted him, "perhaps on your travels over the winter, you have seen something of the crusader army and might be willing to tell us of it. John," Umar raised his voice to call to his companion and stepped toward the pond.

Peter panicked. John knew he worked for Aumery. He didn't think that anyone in Minerve would hurt him—least of all John—but they certainly wouldn't let him leave. If he was going to escape, he had to escape now.

Peter's choices were limited. He could run back up the stairs, but that would just take him back into the heart of the town and there was only one way out. John would follow and raise the alarm. A couple of guards on the gate and Peter would be trapped.

His other choice was to get out the door onto the river bed. He knew that one branch of the river ran underground nearby. There must be at least a few places where he could climb the gorge walls. His choice was made.

Umar was waving at John, who had put down his buckets and stepped toward the old man. Others were watching curiously.

"I think I have found a spy," Umar was saying. "He is too young for me. Do you think you could apprehend him?"

It was now or never. Peter lunged toward the door. He took one step and his foot landed on a patch of slimy moss. His leg shot out from under him and Peter fell painfully to the rock floor. His sliding foot caught the old man in the middle of his shin and catapulted him over. Umar spun around and fell heavily, his head hitting the rim of the pond with a sickening thud that echoed in the confined space.

For an instant, silence descended. Umar's limp body rolled to a stop and Peter scrambled to his feet. Pushing people out of the way, he made for the door. John grabbed at him, but recognition dawned on his face, and he hesitated just long enough for Peter to shove him aside and leap through the door.

The bright sunlight hurt his eyes after the gloom of the

tunnel, but Peter didn't stop. Glimpsing water to his left, he turned right and ran. His feet sank into wet sand, but he kept going. No one seemed to be following.

Eventually the walls of the gorge met above his head and Peter found himself in a broad tunnel. This one had been carved ages before by the river and was much larger and brighter than the stairs. Peter stopped to catch his breath.

His course was obvious: follow the dry river bed until he could find a way out and then make his way south until he met the army. Peter was elated, partly because of the adrenaline in his body after the excitement of his escape and partly because he had succeeded in his mission. Even so, he was upset about the old man. He hadn't meant to hurt him and he hoped he wasn't dead. Aumery would certainly be interested in the secrets Umar carried in his head.

Taking a deep breath to calm himself, Peter set off over the sand. There was no sound of pursuit. If he kept a steady pace, he would be back with de Montfort and Aumery in a couple of days.

The First Casualty

Minerve

JUNE 1210

John stood stunned, staring at the bright doorway, the empty water buckets rolling at his feet. The figure who had pushed past him had been Peter, he was certain, but what was he doing here? Why had he run? Was he the spy Umar had called to him about?

Umar! John turned to see the old man's body, small and fragile, crumpled beside the pond. One arm was raised and rested against the wall, the hand groping feebly for purchase, as if trying to haul the body upright.

John knelt and cradled Umar's head. Blood seeped from a deep wound in his temple where his skull had cracked against the wall. Umar's eyes were open, but his gaze was unfocused. The other people at the well crowded around John.

"Move back!" John shouted. Umar seemed to hear John's voice and struggled to fix his gaze on him. His lips moved and John leaned forward, trying to catch what Umar was saying. It took a moment, but eventually John understood: the old man was repeating a single word over and over, almost as if it were a chant: "Remember."

When John drew back, Umar's eyes were closed. His

lips had stopped moving, but his chest rose and fell shallowly and the blood continued to flow. John stared at the blood, transfixed. The old man's head was crammed full of all manner of wonders, collected over a long and varied life, yet they were all seeping away with the blood. What was being lost? John had been taught some of it, but there must be so much more.

"What did he say?" someone asked. The question brought John back from his musings.

"We must get him up to the Good Christian's house." John put one arm under Umar's shoulders and hooked the other under his knees. He stood. Umar was incredibly light, much easier to carry than two full water buckets. John noticed a young man standing beside him. He was wearing a coarse wool scarf around his head.

"What's your name?"

"Stephen," the man said.

"Hold your scarf against the wound in the Perfect's head, Stephen," John ordered. "We will take him up the stairs." The young man obeyed and they started the long climb.

As John struggled up the stairs, his confusion and anger grew. Was Peter in Minerve to spy for de Montfort and Aumery? The way he'd run suggested that he was, but did it make any real difference? There were so many people coming and going through Minerve these days that any number of them could be spies, but what was there to spy on? There was no horde of gold here or library of forbidden books to discover. Once more, John was reminded of the benefit of holding books in the memory cloister.

But somehow, Peter spying seemed more of a betrayal than had it been some stranger from the crusader army. And there was the disturbing fact that, wherever his old friend showed up, someone died—Pierre of Castelnau at St. Gilles, Roger Trenceval at Carcassonne, and Peter had even been present at the hideous mutilation of the knights of Bram. But Umar wasn't dead. John looked down at the old man's head. He was unconscious and the scarf that Stephen was holding against his head was soaked in blood. It wouldn't be long. John felt tears well up. He had grown to love Umar and his books and stories.

John realized that Peter probably hadn't meant to hurt Umar, but still. Why did Peter have to take the side of the crusaders? Even if they weren't the Devil incarnate, as the Cathars believed, they were still so obviously wrong! Wrong to invade John's homeland, wrong to slaughter and mutilate the inhabitants, and wrong to force an unpopular religion on the people. How could Peter not see that?

As John moved out of the tunnel and into the streets of Minerve, people began to gather. Word of Umar's injury spread quickly through the small, crowded town and everyone wanted to see what had happened. Even though Umar was light, John was tiring, and now he had to push through the curious crowds.

"Come on! Make room!"

John couldn't help but smile to see Adso bustling through the crowd toward him. Without hesitation, he took Umar from John's arms.

"You, keep that cloth against the Perfect's 'ead," he ordered Stephen. Then, looking at John, "Can't let you out of my sight without you getting in trouble. What 'appened?"

"I don't know," John said, both out of honesty and a desire not to get into details about Peter. "We were at the spring and there was a scuffle. Umar fell and hit his head. He said something about a spy."

"Wouldn't surprise me. De Montfort'll 'ave men all over checking out our defences. But we can't do anything about that now. Let's get Umar back to the 'ouse. 'E don't look too good."

John nodded and stretched his aching limbs. The small, sad group pushed through the curious onlookers.

The Bad Neighbour

Minerve

JUNE 1210

A group of five men stood on the vineyard-covered slopes above the River Briant and gazed across the gorge at the grey walls and red-tiled roofs of Minerve. Peter knew three of the other four—Arnaud Aumery, Simon de Montfort and Oddo—but the fifth, a stocky, tough-looking man dressed in stained leather, was a stranger.

In the month since Alairac, a hard spring had given way to a hot summer and the June sun shone from a washed-out blue sky. It had been a long circuitous trek north, but the crusader army had grown as it travelled and now a force of some seven thousand men was gathering around the major heretic stronghold.

"It will be a tough nut to crack," de Montfort remarked.

"God will find a way," Aumery answered.

Oddo snorted.

The stone houses of Minerve, clinging to the slopes of the promontory, seemed impossibly far away across the deep gorge. Simon de Montfort stared to his right, to where the tower of the castle dominated the narrow neck of land.

"The only point where we can attack, unless we learn to fly like falcons," de Montfort mused, "is from the north along the causeway, and I doubt even you, Oddo, could get through those fortifications."

"That is true," Oddo replied. "The castle will not allow engineers to get close enough to undermine the walls and, in any case, those walls are too thick even for the largest siege engine. It will be a bloody business."

"You say they are well supplied with food and water?" De Montfort turned to Peter.

"They are," Peter replied. "It is difficult to find a room in which to lay your head for piled sacks of grain, and impossible to walk the streets without tripping over livestock. Every water cistern is full to overflowing."

After his escape, Peter had followed the Cesse for almost a mile, along the gorge and beneath arches and through tunnels of limestone before he had found a place where he could scramble up onto the plateau. There had been no pursuit, and Peter had had no trouble heading south and finding the crusader army only four days' march away.

"There." Peter pointed at the line of heavy masonry snaking down the side of the gorge from the southeast corner of the town. It was barely distinguishable from the surrounding rock. "That is the tunnel covering the steps down to the spring."

"And you say, boy," Oddo said gruffly, "that there is a door by the spring that leads to the gorge bottom?"

"There is," Peter said, guessing where Oddo's thoughts were heading, "but it would be difficult to get through it and fight up those stairs."

Oddo ignored Peter's comment and turned to de Montfort. "If you can get someone into the town to ensure that the door is open, my Falcons and I will travel along the gorge and, despite what our military expert here says," Oddo sneered at Peter, "fight our way up and into the town."

"God shall bless your endeavour," Aumery said.

De Montfort stood silent, looking across the gorge. Eventually he said, "I think, Oddo, that our young monk might be right this time. *If* you can travel undetected along the gorge beneath the town walls. *If* we can ensure that the gate at the spring is left open. *If* you can fight your way up the stairs. All the defenders need do is close and lock the iron gate at the top and you will be trapped like rats. And the stairs are long. They will have plenty of warning."

Oddo grunted in annoyance.

"But the spring may be the key, nonetheless," de Montfort went on. "This is Albrecht." He indicated the stocky stranger by his side. "He hails originally from some savage forest on the fringes of the world, but he travels so much in order to sell his skills that he no longer has a home. Most recently, he has been working in Brittany."

"What can he do that we cannot?" Oddo asked.

"Albrecht is most adept at building machines," de Montfort said with a smile.

"We have machines. Our trebuchets shattered the walls of Bram in three days. Minerve is not so far off that we cannot send rocks into the town. What is so special about his machines?"

"At Bram we could get close and we had a complete wall to aim at," de Montfort explained. "Here we cannot get close because of the ravines, and our target is very small."

Oddo looked puzzled, but de Montfort ignored him and pointed at the covered stairs. "Albrecht, can you build a machine that is powerful enough and accurate enough to destroy that line of masonry running down the edge of the gorge?"

De Montfort's logic was becoming clear. Peter watched as Albrecht, stroking his beard, studied the gorge.

"I think, yes," he said at last. "It will be a long business and much money, but it can be done. I shall build for you a trebuchet such as has never been seen. For them"—Albrecht swept his arm wide to indicate Minerve—"it will be a *Mala Vezina*—a Bad Neighbour."

"All very well," Oddo said. "You may be able, in enough time, to destroy the way down to the spring and, assuming it is their only source of water, cut it off. But we have heard that every cistern in the town is filled. If they are careful, they will have enough to last until the rains come at summer's end."

"You have solved that problem yourself, Oddo," de Montfort said. "We have other trebuchets and mangonels that are eminently capable of hurling rocks into the town. They may not be as accurate, or as powerful, as Albrecht's Bad Neighbour, but I am certain that, over the next few weeks, they will destroy or damage many of the rooftop cisterns. *Mala Vezina* and the hot dry weeks of summer will do the rest."

Attacking not the town itself but its water supply would be a lengthy process, Peter thought, but it should work.

"And we have young Peter to thank." De Montfort smiled and patted Peter on the back. "Without his spying, we would not have solved this puzzle nearly so quickly. But come, Albrecht must begin and, Oddo, we must see if we can find some work for your Falcons in the surrounding country."

The three men walked back toward the camp, leaving Peter with Aumery.

"You have done well," Aumery said. "De Montfort is in your debt and he is a powerful ally."

"Thank you," Peter said.

"And the information you brought me was of use as well," Aumery continued. "I had not realized there was such a cluster of the Devil's host in Minerve. We shall have a wonderful pyre when the town falls."

Peter was disturbed by the gleam in Aumery's eyes as he spoke about burning the heretics—Peter could reconcile killing as a necessity in God's name, but not enjoying it. He said nothing and let Aumery talk on.

"And I think you might be correct in assuming that the old man you met, Umar, held secrets in his head. I have heard others mention that name. He is an important heretic. Do you think you killed him?"

"I didn't mean to hurt him," Peter said. "I bumped him by accident, and he fell and hit his head."

"No matter. You did God's work, however He arranged it. The pity is that I should have liked to talk to this man, although our methods of persuasion do not work well with these fanatics. I think I shall go and pray."

Peter watched Aumery follow the others back to the camp. He felt pride in what he had achieved and pleasure at the compliments he was receiving, but he hoped he hadn't killed the old man and lost the secrets in his head.

Then there was John. Peter thought about him often and wondered if he had become a heretic. Seeing him with Umar suggested so. Did that mean John was evil? He was probably still in Minerve, trapped by the surrounding army, and Peter had helped find a way to destroy the town. Was Peter, then, causing his own friend's death? Why did God make it so difficult to tell the difference between good and evil? Not for the first time, Peter found himself wishing for Aumery's certainty.

"Stand clear!"

A man swung a large hammer, knocked out a holding pin and released the long arm of the mangonel. The arm of the siege engine shot up and came to rest with a shuddering crash against a cross beam of solid oak. Peter and Aumery stopped walking to watch a large rock arc through the air and crash into the centre of town, sending up a thin column of grey dust. Moments later, the dull sound of falling masonry reached their ears.

The mangonel crew set to work rewinding the arm of the catapult. It was back-breaking work, hauling the arm down against the tension of the twisted ropes attached to the arms of the crossbeam, but all the men were large and well muscled. Four others were busy manhandling a rock from the pile behind the mangonel so they would be ready to load when the priming process was complete.

"Leave the rock," the foreman of the crew shouted.

"We'll give 'em the donkey this time."

The men groaned and left the stone where it was. They disappeared behind a nearby limestone outcrop and returned dragging a rope net on which lay the rotting carcass of a donkey. A thick cloud of flies hovered above the body. Even from where he stood, several yards away, Peter could smell the sickly odour of decay.

"Why do they throw dead animals?" Peter asked Aumery.

"Three reasons," Aumery said casually. "First, there is little more disheartening for a defender than to have rotting animals fall from the heavens. Of course, it would be better to send some prisoners over the wall, but we haven't taken any yet.

"Second, there are a lot of people crammed inside Minerve. A few dead donkeys will spread a fine smell and, if we're lucky, some disease."

Aumery stopped as the foreman shouted at his crew, "Come on, you lazy lot. Put your backs into it. The sooner we get this donkey loaded, the sooner the smell'll be someone else's problem."

"You said there were three reasons," Peter prompted.

"Indeed there are," Aumery said with a smile. "Can you think of a better way to get rid of our waste?"

Peter and Aumery continued on their way. Peter never tired of watching the siege engines at work and often came to observe them hurl their missiles against the town. There were four engines spread around the town—a trebuchet to the north that could fire rocks along the neck at the main gate, and mangonels to the west, east and southwest. Peter and Aumery had been watching the eastern mangonel. They had all been busy lobbing rocks onto the unfortunate inhabitants and, Peter hoped, their water cisterns, for three weeks now. There was little obvious sign of the damage done, but Peter knew that the rocks landing in Minerve were probably injuring and killing people. The effects of the siege engines didn't bother him; watching them was far less personal than watching soldiers hack away at each other with swords. Safely out of crossbow range, Peter could admire the workmanship of the machines and the skill of their operators.

But Peter hadn't accompanied Arnaud Aumery this sunny morning just to watch another mangonel at work. Today was special—*Mala Vezina* was ready for her first shots at the covered stair.

The giant trebuchet was set up in the midst of the vineyard where Peter and the others had first observed Minerve. Under Albrecht's direction, it had taken twenty-five days to build *Mala Vezina*, and the finished product was awe-inspiring. If the mangonel was a catapult, the trebuchet was a slingshot. Where the mangonels were squat and powerful, relying on tension and brute force to hurl objects at their targets, the trebuchet was slender and elegant, like some immense, exotic animal.

Mala Vezina consisted of a long arm, set on a pivot supported more than thirty feet in the air by a spider web of beams thicker than Peter's body. The arm was not pivoted in its centre. The short piece was the length of a tall man, and the long portion was thirty feet from pivot to tip. A vast, enclosed box filled with tons of rubble and sand hung from a second pivot on the end of the short arm. A complex weave of ropes ran from the long arm to winches on the ground, which were being worked by pairs of sweating men under Albrecht's supervision. With painful slowness, the long arm was being winched down and the heavy box was rising in the air.

"Behold," Aumery said with a theatrical wave of his hand, "God's arm, ready to send destruction to the heretics."

"And show them the error of their ways," Peter added.

"Certainly," Aumery said silkily. "And all in Minerve, however misled and misdirected, shall be given a chance to see the true light. But these devils will not take it. They are mired too deep in sin and would rather face the flames than renounce Satan. Well, let them." Aumery's eyes gleamed at the thought. "The fire will cleanse their evil."

The tip of the trebuchet's long arm had been winched down until it was almost at the ground. Men were busy attaching a twenty-five-foot-long rope sling to the end. Others were rolling a massive rock toward it. They placed the rock, which weighed several hundred pounds, Peter guessed, in the sling and hooked it onto the end of the arm.

"Stand clear!" Albrecht shouted.

Men scurried in all directions. Peter and Aumery were far enough away to be safe, but the looming size of the machine made them step back farther.

Albrecht stepped forward and raised a huge hammer. With one swing, he knocked out the pin holding the winch ropes to the long arm. With a mighty groan, the weight on the short arm fell. The long arm shot into the air, whipping the sling after it.

Above the creaks of the shuddering machine, Peter could hear the whistling of the sling. At the top of its arc, Peter estimated the rock in the end of the sling must have been almost a hundred feet above his head.

When the weight reached its lowest point, the upper end of the arm slowed, but the sling kept going. It whipped past the vertical, releasing one end from its hook and sending the rock on its way. Peter watched in fascination as the boulder arced across the gorge and shattered against the far wall, some thirty feet to the right of the covered stairs. Large blocks of limestone and fragments of the boulder crashed into the riverbed below.

"It missed," Peter said, disappointed that the stairs had not been destroyed at the first attempt.

"It did," Aumery agreed, "but that is not the main problem. Albrecht will make adjustments and with a rate of throw of two rocks an hour, he will expect to hit the stairs several times a day. What is more worrying is the way the rock shattered on impact. Such a blow will not easily destroy the masonry covering the stairs. We may need to bring in firmer stones from some distance away. It all takes too long!"

Even though the counter weight was still swinging, a man was already scrambling up the structure. Timing his jump perfectly, he leaped onto the long arm and began climbing. He had a rope wound around his waist and, when he was halfway along and despite the fact that the arm was swaying frighteningly, he attached the rope to the arm and signalled to his companions on the ground. Gradually, they brought the swing under control and started the long process of winching the weight back up in the air.

Peter looked over to see Albrecht standing among a pile of rocks, hitting them with his hammer to select the best one for his next shot.

"Well," Aumery said, turning and starting off back to the camp, "it will be a long campaign, but the end will be worthwhile."

Peter hoped so.

Besieged

Minerve

JULY 1210

John and Adso walked down the narrow cobbled street, carefully stepping around the occasional piles of rubble. Their water buckets hung empty on either side of them, but it was not a problem. There were few people about these days. Three weeks into the siege, most preferred to stay indoors. Partly it was fear of the bombardment, but partly it was simply that it was cooler behind the thick stone walls now that the summer heat of July had arrived.

The two friends were making their daily trip to the spring to refill the cistern on top of the Perfect house. Most cisterns were still intact, being situated in the centre of houses, but people had become sloppy about keeping them topped up. It was a chore to fetch water from the spring every day, and most preferred to wait until they ran low and then spend a morning filling up. John made the daily trek because he wanted to do something in return for his keep, and most days he persuaded Adso to accompany him.

"That's one on our side," Adso said, pushing John against a house wall. The thud of the mangonel's arm hitting the crossbeam was clearly audible all over town. Adso had learned to distinguish each machine and knew where they were located. The ones on the far side of town were not a problem, they couldn't reach this far, but the one on the east bank could.

John didn't see the rock, but he heard it crash into a building behind him.

"Missed," Adso said cheerfully as they set off again.

"It hit something," John said.

Adso shrugged. "They make a lot of noise, but the 'ouses are sturdy enough to withstand anything but a direct 'it on the roof. Look, they've been 'urling everything they can find at us for days, and what's the result? A couple of dead, some broken bones and piles of rubble in the streets. People'r frightened, but there's little real 'arm being done."

"I suppose so. I just wish there was something to do. It's so boring just sitting waiting! Won't they attack?"

"Listen to you," Adso laughed. "You learn a couple of moves with an old blunt sword and you want to take on the 'ole crusader army. Patience! Remember, they're just as bored as us, an' if they get bored enough they'll do something stupid like attack us, else they'll go 'ome. We can 'old out 'til doomsday."

The crash of the mangonel sounded again.

"Busy this morning," Adso said as he moved to the shelter of another wall.

John looked up to see if he could catch the flight of the rock. What he saw was a shock. Arcing down toward him was some sort of creature, legs and head wobbling stupidly as it spun through the air. The grotesque thing landed with a sickening thud on the street just up the hill from John and Adso. The bloated stomach split open with the force, spilling glistening entrails over the cobbles.

"What was that?" John asked in horror.

"Looked like a donkey to me," Adso replied.

An evil smell wafted in on the morning breeze.

"And it's been dead for some time," Adso said, wrinkling his nose. "We'd best get on. Perhaps we might take a different route back."

John followed Adso as they continued on to the stairs.

"Why on earth are they throwing dead donkeys at us?" John asked.

"Showing their contempt, maybe, or trying to spread disease. I've 'eard of that being done."

"It's disgusting."

"It's unpleasant, certainly, but every donkey they send over is one less rock. I'd rather dodge dead donkeys!"

The pair reached the gates at the top of the stairs and began the long climb down. Every time John reached this spot, he remembered the trip with Umar.

The old man had lingered for two days after John and Adso had carried him back to the house, but he had never regained consciousness. The Perfects had celebrated when he died since, having taken the *consolamentum*, Umar was guaranteed a place in paradise. They had no interest in Umar's body because it was of the material world and was, therefore, merely a trap within which the old man's soul had been enslaved. Now that his spirit was free, the body was simply waste. John was not comfortable with just leaving Umar's body out in the open for the vultures and wolves, so he enlisted Adso and persuaded the Perfects to allow him to take the body outside the walls and bury it.

They shrugged and let him do as he wished.

John and Adso had buried Umar beneath a stunted tree on the edge of the gorge. There was not much soil, but John hoped they had piled enough rocks on top of the body to discourage wild animals. John had not said anything at the graveside, Umar would not have wanted that, but he did mumble goodbye as he left. The next day de Montfort and his army arrived and Minerve was under siege.

It was dark at the spring these days, since the door that led out to the riverbed was always kept closed and bolted. Two men in chain mail stood guard at all times. John nodded to them.

"Coolest place in town down 'ere," Adso commented.

The two men were silent. John and Adso filled their buckets and started back up the stairs.

"Good talking to you," Adso called back over his shoulder. As if in reply, the whole tunnel shook. Vibrations thrust up through the rock steps, making John stumble and drop his buckets. Dirt and small pieces of masonry fell from the roof.

"What was that?" John asked.

"My guess," Adso said, "is that our visitors across the gorge 'ave finished their little construction project. That, my friend, is what a trebuchet can do. Let's go and take a look."

John refilled his buckets and followed Adso up the stairs. Back in full daylight, they carefully placed the buckets by the wall and climbed the nearest tower.

The sun was still low and they had to squint to see the trebuchet clearly, but it was obviously preparing for another shot.

"Let's 'ope it's a donkey," Adso said wryly.

Several people had come to the wall to see what was happening. One had a crossbow and fired it speculatively in the direction of the crew resetting the trebuchet. The bolt made it over the gorge but fell short of the men.

"Waste of a good bolt," Adso said. He was leaning out as far as he could over the edge of the wall. "That's where the last one 'it, to the left of the stair."

John stared where Adso was pointing. He could just make out a scar on the rock wall of the gorge.

"They're way too low," John said. "The mangonels are doing more damage in the town."

"They're not aiming for the town," Adso said thoughtfully.

"What?" John asked, but Adso had leaned back and was watching the trebuchet.

The machine, looking like some huge animal grazing amidst the vines, was almost ready. John watched as the rock, as big as the men who were manhandling it, was placed in the sling. John heard the metallic clang as the pin was knocked out and the trebuchet's arm began its long swing up. It seemed slow and almost stately from this distance. The sling whipped over the top of the arm and the rock arced toward them. Instinctively, everyone ducked, but Adso kept upright, watching.

With reverberations that John could feel even this far away, the rock shattered against the cliff some fifty feet below the battlements and twenty to the right of the stairs.

Some of the people on the battlements laughed nervously and began shouting taunts at the trebuchet crew.

"Is that the best you can do?"

"We're up here."

"Are you trying to wear down the cliff?"

Adso looked pensive. "That one was closer."

"It was no higher than the last," John said.

"They're not trying for height. That thing could send a rock the size of a house over our heads and into the town with ease. They know what they're doing. It's adjusted to shoot low. They're not aiming for us, they're aiming for the stairs—and I reckon it'll only take another three or four attempts before they hit them."

"The stairs!" John said. Suddenly, Peter's presence at the spring and Umar calling him a spy made sense. Peter had been in town to spy out the water supply! It was because of the information he had escaped with that the trebuchet was targeting the stairs. If the crusaders could destroy the route to Minerve's only source of water, the town was doomed.

John kept his thoughts to himself and stared out across the distance, listening to Adso's musings.

"The tunnel is strong and those rocks they're throwing break too easy. But if they bring in some better rock, sooner or later the tunnel will be so collapsed that it'll be the devil's own job to get to the spring. And anyone clambering back up in the open with two 'eavy buckets'll be a sitting duck for crossbowmen on the far rim."

"What can we do?"

"Well, there's some things we might do. Even with that beast, it'll take a good long time to collapse the tunnel completely. The first thing we need to do is make sure all the cisterns are filled, and kept full. Come on."

Adso climbed down from the wall and retrieved his buckets. John followed, deep in thought. This changed things. Now they couldn't just sit and wait the siege out. They would have to do something, but what?

The group of twenty men gathered in the dark by the iron gate at the top of the stairs. All were dressed in dark clothing and were lightly armed, mostly with swords and daggers, although one man carried a crossbow slung across his back. Most had bundles of tar-soaked sticks and straw strapped to their bodies, and two had earthen pots filled with glowing coals. John wore the old sword he had been practising with, honed now to a razor-sharp edge. Adso carried a pot of coals and had his dagger tucked into his belt. It was ten days since the trebuchet had opened fire on the stairs and the group was setting off to destroy it.

"We travel in silence," Adso said in a low voice. "Stephen," he said, nodding at the young man who had helped with Umar and now hovered by the group's edge, "will lead us up the other wall of the gorge. With luck, the infernal machine will be unguarded and we will be able to set the fire unmolested. If we are discovered we retreat as quickly as possible. Do not get into a fight. We will lose. Travel as quietly as you can and good luck."

Stephen led the way through the gate and onto the stairs. At first the going was easy, but about a third of the way down, they came to the first place where the roof had collapsed. They had to scramble into the open and find a way over the steep pile of rubble. The night sky was clear, but the moon was new, so the darkness in the gorge was impenetrable. John had to feel his way along, following the heavy breathing of the man in front. Soon his shins and hands were scraped and bruised. He just hoped he wouldn't catch an ankle in a crevice between two boulders and break something.

Even with the poor-quality rocks the crusaders had been using, the trebuchet had scored so many hits that the tunnel was badly damaged in several places and completely collapsed in two. It was still possible to get to the spring and back, but it was much harder work and the open spaces were dangerous. Few people were inclined to make the journey often and the cisterns in the town were low.

Even more worrying, the day before yesterday had seen the arrival of a train of heavy carts from the north. Each cart was pulled by a team of four huge oxen and was loaded with boulders of hard, black volcanic rock. The first of these to be fired had shattered the tunnel roof and enlarged one of the collapses. In a day or two more, the stairs to the spring would no longer exist.

The night raid to destroy the trebuchet—their one chance, John thought—had been Adso's idea, but it had not been difficult to recruit men. No one wanted to surrender to the crusaders. Since there had been no raids on the crusader camp, the hope was that the guards might be complacent and give Adso's group a chance to set a large enough fire to destroy the machine.

Slowly, the group made its way down to the gorge floor.

Stephen, who had lived in Minerve all his life and spent his childhood scrambling up and down the gorge walls, knew every rock for miles around. He led them through the shallow water of the Briant to the foot of the gorge wall. To John's surprise and relief, the climb was not too steep or dangerous. The route followed a wide crack in the limestone, and the rock was rough and provided plenty of handholds. There were even a few stunted bushes that were well enough anchored to bear a man's weight.

At the top, the men crouched and gathered their breath. In the distance, a few patches of orange showed where cooking fires had been allowed to burn low, but there was no sign of life. The trebuchet was easy to see, even in the near blackness. Its looming bulk blacked out the stars near the horizon, and its soaring arm caused others to blink in and out as John moved his head.

"Stay here," Adso whispered.

Dropping his pot of coals, Adso disappeared through the wrecked vineyards. John followed a short way and listened. He could hear the soft rustle of Adso moving, but it was little more than the sound of a breeze in the dead leaves. Eventually, even the rustling stopped.

John cocked his head and stayed motionless. He was rewarded with a grunt, followed by a thump. After a few minutes, Adso returned. He held his dagger in one hand.

"Only one guard," he said. John could see the white of Adso's teeth as he smiled. "Let's go."

Working as quietly and quickly as possible, the men stacked their bundles around the base of the trebuchet. Up close, even in the dark, John was awed by the size of the thing and by the effort that had gone into its construction and operation. For the first time, he understood Beatrice's belief that the crusaders would never give up.

Adso and the other man carrying the coals were busy igniting the bundles that were in place. Already the tar in several had caught and bright flames were dancing up. The closest tents were about thirty feet away, but there was still no sign of life apart from a dying fire outside one. If only they were given enough time for the fires to join, the heat would be so intense that no one would be able to put out the flames, and the trebuchet would be doomed.

John's own bundle was burning fiercely now, and the flames were catching on the wood of the trebuchet's frame.

"To arms! To arms!"

The shout was almost deafening after the enforced silence. John looked toward the tents. By the light of the spreading fires, he could see a man, dressed only in a long linen nightshirt. He was yelling and waving his arms frantically.

There was a thud and a crossbow bolt whistled past John. The shouting man staggered and held a hand to his throat. His whole body shuddered and he slipped to the ground. But it was too late. The man's cries had woken others, and several armed men were coming out of nearby tents to see what the commotion was about. They were confused and rubbing sleep from their eyes, but one large figure was already heading for the trebuchet. The sight of the axe in the man's left hand made John's heart miss a beat.

"Get back," Adso yelled, "back down the gorge."

The men began to retreat as more crusaders appeared.

Stephen and Adso stayed by the trebuchet, frantically stuffing coals into bundles that had not yet ignited. Oddo was running now, his axe raised.

"Adso!" John shouted. "Come on." His friend ignored him.

John unsheathed his sword and moved forward. The pile of sticks Adso was working on burst into sudden bright flame, and John could see Adso smile as he stepped away. But Oddo was at Adso's back.

"Behind you!" John yelled. The axe was almost over Adso's head and beginning its descent. At the last minute, Stephen flung himself to his right, shoving Adso out of the way. Adso cursed and John saw the blade of his dagger glint in the firelight as he fell.

The axe swept down, almost disappearing in Stephen's side and embedding itself in the trebuchet's wooden frame. John screamed and leaped forward over the burning pile of sticks. Blinded by rage, he forgot everything Adso had taught him and simply lunged at the big man.

Oddo punched hard with his right hand, catching John on the jaw, knocking him backwards and scattering coals and burning sticks. By the flickering light, John watched as the big man struggled to release his axe. Stephen's body, almost cut in half, lolled stupidly with each tug.

Out of the corner of his eye, John saw Adso struggle to his knees. The axe jerked free and Stephen's body slumped to the ground. Oddo turned toward Adso, the deadly axe poised for a swing. Without thinking, John grabbed a handful of red hot coals in his left hand and flung them at the knight's face. Two pieces caught him on the cheek below his left eye and another hit his forehead. Oddo roared in pain and staggered back. Adso reached up and plunged his dagger deep into the man's thigh.

John reached over and grabbed Adso's tunic. "Adso, come on, we've got to get out of here." Already men from the tents were working to extinguish the fires on the other side of the trebuchet and other figures were rushing toward them. Several wore coats emblazoned with a falcon.

John's left hand was a mass of pain and he could smell his own burned flesh. Oddo clutched his thigh, dark blood welling up between his fingers. In the firelight, his face was a mask of hate, made more horrible by the patches of red, blistering flesh where the coals had struck him. He raised his axe and attempted to stand, but his wounded leg gave out and he slumped down. He stared at John.

"Do not think I will forget you, boy," he snarled. "The next time we meet will be your last moment on this earth."

In a stumbling run, Adso and John made it back to the gorge edge and slithered down into the relative safety of the river bed. A couple of Falcons attempted to follow, but a crossbow bolt thudding into a tree by their heads discouraged the effort. The nineteen survivors made it across the gorge and up the stairs without hindrance. John remembered almost nothing of the journey except the pain in his hand.

For five days, John lay in the Perfect house by the town gates as the rocks from the mangonels crashed around him. The Good Christians put salves on his hand, bandaged it as best they could and gave him what little water and food he wanted. The pain in his hand was intense, as if it were still on fire, and the sight of the red, blistered, suppurating flesh was frightening, but gradually he improved. Adso visited frequently.

"Thank you for saving my life," he said on several occasions. "That was quick thinking."

"It was no thinking at all," John said with an attempt at a smile. "After all the tricks you taught me, all I managed to do was burn my own hand."

"There's always new tricks. It's a shame we didn't manage to kill that brute, Oddo. At least 'e'll be limping for a while."

John nodded.

"Our efforts were all in vain," Adso told John on another one of his visits. "The fires never had a chance to join, and the trebuchet was back in action that very day. I fear we have but little time left."

"So, Minerve will fall." It was more a statement than a question.

"It's certain, and in not too many days."

John wondered aloud whether the citizens of Minerve would be massacred like their counterparts in Béziers.

"I think not." Adso shook his head. "Count William is trying to arrange a truce to talk terms. I fear the Perfects are doomed though."

The thought of all his Cathar friends being burned at the stake pushed John into a pit of misery. He was lying down, on the afternoon of the fifth day, thinking of that and feeling sorry for himself, when he heard the door open.

"Self-pity is one of the Devil's emotions."

The familiar voice startled John into sitting up.

"What are you doing here?" he asked.

Beatrice smiled gently. "I came to see how much trouble you had got into."

"But how did you get in?"

"Along the dry riverbed and up what is left of the stairs. No one is looking for people trying to get into Minerve. The trick is getting out."

"But now you're trapped here."

"Being trapped or not is a matter of outlook. I know men who have the freedom of entire kingdoms, and yet they are trapped more certainly than we are. For myself, I have been trapped in this body since I first came screaming into the world."

"But Minerve will fall any day now! You must escape. You said yourself that Aumery will not rest until all the Elect are burned."

"Then there is not much point in running, is there?" Beatrice's smile widened. "Do not worry about me. I heard about your adventure. How is your hand?"

"It hurts fiercely, but it is getting better. What worries me most is that the fingers are curling in and I cannot straighten them. I fear I may have to live with a claw."

"The Devil's work," Beatrice said. "I hear that Umar's soul has gone to a better place."

"Yes, he fell and hit his head. It was a tragedy."

"Not for him, so we should not think of it as such."

"But all the wisdom in his head! It is lost now," John said.

"To us. Do you not think it selfish and arrogant to

wallow in regret for our own loss, when we should be happy for Umar's soul?"

John felt a pang of guilt.

"He was not alone in knowing secrets," Beatrice went on. "His work was done. It was time for him to rest. He passed on much." Beatrice delved into her habit and produced a small parchment volume. "I have brought you three presents, material things and the Devil's work, but you may find something in each to aid the spirit."

"Another book for me to learn?" John asked.

"If you wish. I found it in the library at Montségur and thought it might interest you."

John accepted the book as graciously as he could. The cover was of faded leather with a one-word title picked out in barely legible gold letters: *Scultura*. John opened the book and let his eyes scan the first words. They were written in Latin. "*My name is Lucius of the Macrinus family and I respectfully write this modest volume as a companion to my treatise on the art of drawing. The drawing system I presented in my other work, if studied and applied with rigour, allows the recreation of the real world around us on a manuscript page, wall or board with a fidelity that few can imagine. I aim here to show how this can also be achieved with a statue hewn from a rough block of stone.*"

With a thrill, John realized what he was holding. "It's a book on sculpture by the same Roman who wrote the lost book on drawing!"

Beatrice nodded. "I am sorry I could not find the drawing book, but perhaps this will aid you in your quest for beauty and its representation. If I am honest, I must admit that I think it a waste of time, but I do find some of the pictures within pleasing."

John carefully thumbed through the fragile pages. Several contained illustrations of statues and they certainly did look much more lifelike than the ones he was used to seeing flanking cathedral doorways.

"Thank you," he said. "I shall work at copying these pictures."

"And this will help." Beatrice said, handing John a second book. This one was about the same size as *Scultura*, but it was roughly bound and made of paper instead of parchment. The pages were blank.

"It is from the Moors in Al-Andalus, where they use this paper instead of the animal skins we write on. Umar used to say that paper holds the ink much better and does not allow it to run. I thought it might be good for you to practice with, if you are set on this drawing."

"It must be very valuable," John said, feeling the smoothness of the pages.

"Money is the Devil's tool."

"Thank you, again," John said.

"You are welcome. Perhaps when you have satisfied this passing phase, you will return to the memory cloister and what is truly important."

"Perhaps," John said with a smile. It was the first time he had felt like smiling since the raid on the trebuchet. He swung his legs out of the alcove where he had been lying. He had to admit it felt good to be on his feet again.

"I will practise my drawing with great care," he said.

"That is good, but I suspect you will have to wait. This

afternoon a delegation will meet with de Montfort to discuss surrender."

John nodded. It was inevitable. The sooner the surrender was worked out, the greater the chance that the population would be spared.

"You must escape tonight," John said.

"Must I?"

"Yes! You told me yourself that they will burn every member of the Elect they can find."

"And I have also said that leaving this world is to be welcomed. But there is another reason I cannot leave. There are a number of Credents who wish to take the *consolamentum* before the surrender and I must perform that this evening."

"Couldn't someone else?"

"Yes, but should I pass that responsibility to others while I flee to safety?"

John didn't answer. It was obvious that nothing he could say would change Beatrice's mind.

"Will you come to the ceremony?" she asked.

"I thought outsiders weren't allowed."

"Their presence is not encouraged, but no one is banned from our activities. In any case, it would be one more thing for you to remember. I fear there will be fewer and fewer *consolamentum* ceremonies in the coming years."

"I should be honoured."

"Good. And there is one more thing I would ask. As a member of the Elect, it would not be wise for me to attend the negotiations. My presence might set the priests off on a tirade. Would you attend and tell me what transpires?"

"Will I be allowed?"

"I shall clear it with Count William."

"Then yes." John could think of no reason to refuse.

"Thank you."

John remembered something. "You said you had brought three things."

"Indeed I did, although the last one is not a thing." Beatrice smiled and left the room. Puzzled, John watched the door. The stone floor shuddered as a rock landed nearby, and an earthenware pot crashed off the mantle above the fireplace. John bent to pick up the pieces.

"A tidy mind is a good thing."

John looked up to see Isabella standing in the doorway. Her dark hair cascaded over her shoulders, and her almost black eyes stared at John while a half smile played on her lips.

"Isabella!" he exclaimed, standing up and catching his head a painful glancing blow on the mantle.

Isabella laughed lightly, a sound that even through his embarrassed pain sounded to John like golden bells in the wind.

"Are you all right?" she asked.

"I'm fine, but feeling stupid," he said rubbing his head with his healthy hand. "You look good."

Isabella's smile broadened in acknowledgement. "How is your hand?"

John looked down at his bandaged claw. "It hurts less now. But why are you here?"

"You don't want to see me?"

"No! I didn't mean that."

"Let's sit down." Isabella moved into the room and sat at the table. John sat opposite. "I came to see you."

"Me? Why?" John was thoroughly confused. He was happy to see Isabella, happier than he thought he could be, but they'd had no contact for years. Why had she suddenly shown up?

"John, you are the most foolish clever person I have ever known!" Isabella smiled, and John's knees felt so weak he was glad he was sitting down.

"In all our years as friends in Toulouse, did you never notice that I sought you out and sat next to you whenever possible? Did you never wonder why I continually asked you about the books you were reading? Did it never once cross your mind that I had feelings for you?"

"Peter was your close friend."

"No. He was the one who sat beside me and sought me out to engage in conversation. Oh, I liked Peter, but he was too intense and lacked your inquiring mind. I talked with all our friends equally but, I fear, Peter misread me."

"What do you mean?"

A frown replaced Isabella's smile. "On that last night in Toulouse, Peter declared his feelings for me. I could not return them and before he could ask me to be his betrothed, I told him so in the gentlest way I could. I was also going to explain my feelings for you, but he was taken by his terrifying fit of visions. I thought for the longest time that I was to blame in some way, but Peter thinks not."

"You have seen him?"

"He was in Toulouse some months ago with that monster Aumery. In any case, after the visions, everything happened

317

so fast. The next day Peter was becoming a monk, and you had vanished with that troubadour."

Isabella fell silent and John pondered what she had said. It made sense. He remembered the way she had always sought him out to ask about books. He had been happy to tell her and pleased to be in her company, but she had been just a friend.

"I never realized."

Isabella's smile returned. "I know. That's why I came to look for you. It took me a long time to decide this is what I must do and, for much of that time, I had no idea where you were. But these are troubled times, and I fear if we do not seize what we wish, it will be lost."

"How did you know where to find me?"

"Peter told me you were with Beatrice, and William the troubadour said he had heard that Beatrice was in Minerve. I was planning on coming here on my way to Aragon, and perhaps Al-Andalus, when I heard that de Montfort was besieging the town. Then Beatrice arrived in Toulouse. Apparently William had stopped in Minerve and told her where I was and how he surmised I felt about you. When she said she was coming back to Minerve, I decided to come too. The journey was fun. Mostly we had to travel by night."

"You have just passed through an enemy army with a Perfect that they would burn on sight, and you say it was fun?"

Isabella laughed. "It was."

"On your way to Al-Andalus?" Something Isabella said suddenly struck John.

"Yes," Isabella's face darkened. "I left when I was an

infant and an orphan like you. But it is where my family is from, and I would like to . . ." Isabella hesitated as if deciding what to say next. "See the land," she finished weakly. John was about to ask if there was anything else she meant, but she hurried on. "Besides, I hear that King Pedro is sympathetic to Good Christians. From Aragon it is but a short step to Al-Andalus, and I should like to see the world our Moorish neighbours have created there."

"You're a Cathar?" John asked.

"I am, and one day I hope to take the *consolamentum,* but for now I wish to learn what good this corrupt world can teach me."

"I want to go to Al-Andalus too," John said, thinking of the drawing book that might be in Cordova. "Umar, an old Perfect who was here, mentioned a book I should very much like to see in the library at Madinat al-Zahra, outside Cordova. The old librarian, Nasir al-Din, was Umar's teacher and there is a black man, Shabaka, who helps him." John found the details he stored automatically in his memory useful but, sometimes, he couldn't help letting everything pour out.

"Then we should travel together," Isabella said. "I wish to spend time in Aragon, but I would be happy to go south after that. We could—"

The door flew open and crashed back against the wall. "Satan's spawn are coming under a flag of truce," Adso said. He stopped and stared at Isabella. "Beatrice said she had brought a lady from Toulouse, but she did not say you were beautiful." Adso bowed theatrically. "And you came all this way to see 'im," he jerked a thumb at John. "When there are plenty noble and 'andsome knights about to choose from?" He stepped forward and kissed Isabella's hand. "I daresay there is no accounting for taste.

"But, before you two lovebirds sneak away to sit in a bower and recite courtly poems to one another, there is work to be done. As I said, the Devil is at the gate. It is time to go and meet the enemy."

Who Lives, Who Dies

Minerve

JULY 21, 1210

Peter watched the small procession approach along the causeway from Minerve. It was led by William, Count of Minerve, who was attended by a scribe and two pages. All were brightly dressed in tunics that bore the count's coat of arms. A step behind them, Peter was surprised to see a fifth figure: John.

Peter had not seen John since the night of the attack on the trebuchet. He'd awakened and gone out to see what the commotion was about, arriving just in time to witness four figures fighting in the firelight. He had seen one man struck down and a second, whom he recognized as Oddo, wounded and driven back. As the two attackers turned to go, Peter realized that one of them was John.

Peter had stood back and watched as the fires on the trebuchet had been brought under control and extinguished. He had heard Oddo roar out his anger and hoped that the man who had humiliated him in Béziers, and whose power he still envied, was dying. He wasn't. Several Falcons half carried, half led their leader away. Oddo's face was badly burned, and the wound in his thigh was deep, but the bleeding had stopped and, if no infections set in, he would survive to fight again in de Montfort's crusade.

Now Peter stood between Arnaud Aumery and Simon de Montfort, a step or two behind them. Both were dressed simply, and the only bright colour other than the red cross on de Montfort's tunic was the red ecclesiastical cloak worn by Bishop Foulques, who stood on Aumery's other side.

William stopped several paces in front of de Montfort and nodded slightly. Peter stared at the count so as to avoid catching John's eye.

"I have come," Count William said formally, "to offer the surrender of my town and all my lands in keeping with the rules of warfare."

"I accept your surrender," de Montfort replied, "and will abide by the rules governing the submission of a brave enemy."

"Very well," William said, his face a stern, unreadable mask. "At dawn on the morrow, I shall throw open the gates of Minerve and welcome you to the best of my abilities. You shall be known as Count of Minerve, and all those who owe fealty to me will do so to you. At the same time, all those presently within the walls will be allowed, should they so choose, to leave unhindered to go about their business."

"I thank you," de Montfort said with a faint smile, "but I cannot accept your final condition. There are, within your walls, a number of heretics we know as Cathars."

"Filthy vermin," Foulques spat.

"We come in the name of Christ," de Montfort continued, ignoring the interruption, "and with the blessings of His Holiness Pope Innocent III, to rid this land of foul heresy. We cannot allow these people to leave and spread their lies. They must be handed over to Father Aumery for investigation."

"I cannot agree to that." Count William's voice hardened. "Heretics or not, these are my people and I have a sworn duty to protect them. I shall honour that duty."

"Then I suggest you return to your town and prepare to defend it as best you can," de Montfort said.

"I came here in good faith, to stop suffering, but I am not defeated yet. There are still a wealth of crossbow bolts in Minerve to pierce many crusaders' hearts."

"Gentlemen. Gentlemen." Aumery stepped forward and spoke in his silkiest voice. "There is no need for all this unpleasantness over such a trivial matter. I am the voice here of Pope Innocent, and I see no difficulty with William's request."

Everyone stared at Aumery. The most avowed heretic hater in the land, the man who had launched the massacre at Béziers, was offering to let the heretics go.

De Montfort stared hard at Aumery. "Go on."

"I have no objection," Aumery said with a smile, "to letting everyone go about their business freely. It is not my wish to cause undue suffering and pain to honest Christian folk. Let all live—"

"This is preposterous," Bishop Foulques interrupted, his face scarlet with anger. "One hundred and fifty of the worst sort of vermin, in our grasp, and you propose to let them go! It is a disgrace!"

"Let all live," Aumery repeated calmly, "who will be reconciled with and obey the orders of the Church. If any hold contrary opinions, they need only convert to the Catholic faith."

"So the spawn of the Devil need only bend a lying knee to go free?" Foulques asked angrily.

"Indeed. But I think, my dear Bishop, that you do not know your enemy as well as you should. You will search long before you find a Perfect heretic who will 'bend a lying knee.'"

De Montfort was smiling broadly. "Are these terms acceptable, Count William?"

"They are." The count let out a sigh, and his features relaxed. He looked suddenly exhausted and his eyes carried a look of terrible sadness. There was nothing more he could do. He had secured for all his subjects a way to survive. He could not do more to protect the unrepentant heretics without drawing suspicion himself.

"Very well, then. At first light tomorrow, we shall approach the gates and expect them open." De Montfort turned and strode back toward his camp.

Peter was smiling at the clever way Aumery had resolved the difficulty. He glanced up before William and his delegation turned to leave and briefly met John's eyes. He shuddered at the look of hatred he saw there.

"Come," Aumery said. "There is much to do. We will need a large fire to accomplish God's work tomorrow."

Consolamentum
Minerve
JULY 22, 1210

John stood on the battlements above the town gates, staring morosely over the causeway at the victorious enemy camp. It was past midnight, but fires still sparkled among tents. On the cool breeze, he could hear the sound of music and singing and smell the odour of roasting pigs and goats. The crusaders were celebrating. And why not? The greatest heretic stronghold had fallen in a matter of weeks with barely any casualties. De Montfort was established now and there was no chance that these foreign knights would simply go home.

John's eyes drifted to a flat area of ground lit by a ring of torches. In the centre of the ring, several priests were busy adding the finishing touches to a huge mound of wood and straw. It seemed Aumery was certain that Minerve's Elect would not even attempt to escape the flames. He was right. None was prepared to lie about his or her faith, and John had noticed that several seemed almost eager for the next day. A few were even preparing to take the *consolamentum* this night so that they could walk into the fire in a few hours. John shivered at the thought of flames blistering skin and heat searing lungs. His hand still ached from his own encounter with fire, and he tried to imagine the pain of that wound spread over his entire body. He couldn't conceive of having the strength to walk voluntarily into the flames.

As figures moved in and out of patches of light, John strained to see if Peter was working on the pyre. He caught a glimpse of one tall, gangly figure, but the distance was too great to be sure. John had been surprised at the surge of hatred he'd felt toward Peter when he saw him standing smugly beside Aumery as Count William had been forced to give up Minerve's Perfects. Ever since his vision, John realized Death *had* been at Peter's shoulder—striking down those around him.

Anger boiled up inside John. If the Devil was abroad in this land, he was out there with the crusaders. Reflexively, John's good hand clenched around his sword's hilt. If Aumery were magically to appear before him now, John would have no trouble cutting the evil man down. And Peter? Would he kill Peter, too?

John sighed and slumped against the battlements, his anger gone as fast as it had arisen. What was he to do? It seemed only yesterday he was a naive boy thrilled at a world overloaded with wonderful possibilities. Now what was he: a soldier wishing for a chance to kill his best friend?

"They look like devils walking through the fires of hell." The soft voice startled John. He turned away from the battlements to see Isabella standing behind him. She looked peaceful in the light from the nearby torch. John swept his arm wide to encompass the camp and the pyre.

"How can they be so cruel?" he asked, desolately.

"It's the Devil in them that creates cruelty. Is Peter cruel?"

"What he's doing is cruel, and I am beginning to hate him for that."

"He was never cruel when we were all friends in Toulouse," Isabella said gently. "Maybe he isn't now. Beatrice would say he is misled and that it is the Devil seducing him into the arms of a corrupt Church."

"Is that what you would say?" John asked.

"Beatrice could forgive the Devil himself." Isabella smiled sadly. "I do not have her mercy." She fell silent for a moment, then said, "I was tempted in Toulouse to take the *consolamentum.*"

"Why didn't you?"

"I do not have Beatrice's certainty either. I admire the Perfects, and I *am* certain that they are closer to the truth than Aumery and Foulques, but I am not ready to renounce the world, even if it is the work of Satan. There is too much to discover."

John nodded. "That's how I feel, but sometimes, I wish for certainty. I envy Beatrice"—John hesitated—"and even Peter. They both know they are right. It must be simple for them. I always doubt."

"Maybe we are meant to doubt," Isabella said with a shrug. "Look where certainty has led Peter and Beatrice, one builds a pyre and the other must climb it. In any case, this land is corrupted now and, if we do not wish to take the *consolamentum* and die with the Perfects, our choices have narrowed—accept what the crusaders are doing and all the hatred that goes with it, or fight. Either way, the result is death and destruction. That's why I am going to Al-Andalus. I want to go somewhere where learning is still possible. Did you mean it when you said you wanted to go, too?"

"I did," John said firmly. "I have to escape before I become as cruel as them." He pointed at the funeral pyre. "And there are also things I want to learn. Cordova might be a good place to begin."

"Then we should travel together. I should like to show you Aragon, and see it for myself." Isabella lowered her gaze and, for a moment, looked terribly sad. "No one will know me," she said.

John was about to ask what she meant, but she looked up and continued. "Anyway, the Perfects say one should never travel alone. The bond of companionship is a consolation and a strong protection against Satan whispering in an ear." Isabella's smile returned, overwhelming any questions John had.

"I would like that." John spoke calmly, but inside he was wildly excited. Isabella's sudden appearance in Minerve and the revelation that she had always had feelings for him had been a complete shock. But the more he thought about it, the more he realized that he had also had feelings for Isabella; he had simply ignored them or pushed them into the background because of Peter. But now Peter was on the other side in a war and Isabella was suggesting that they travel together to a place he desperately wanted to go. A dream John had barely realized he had was coming true.

"Will your friend Adso come with us?" Isabella interrupted John's thoughts.

"I don't think so. He is set on continuing the fight against de Montfort and the crusaders. But I can protect us."

"We shall protect each other," Isabella said with a slight laugh. "And I have a small bag of coins saved. That will protect us when we are hungry or cannot find a pilgrim's roof in a monastery."

"It is good to hear laughter this night." The pair turned to see Beatrice standing nearby. "It is something they have forgotten." She gestured toward the crusader camp. "I think it might be our strongest weapon yet."

For a long moment, Beatrice stared out at the growing pile of wood across the causeway. "We are ready for the *consolamentum*," she said, turning back to John. "Do you still wish to observe?"

"I do," John replied.

"And you?"

"If I may," Isabella answered.

Beatrice nodded. "Then let us go."

"Don't you ever doubt?" John blurted out.

Beatrice smiled and shook her head. "There is no need. I believe the Good Christian way is the true way. All else follows from that."

"But the crusaders don't doubt either," John said.

"Some are certain they are right, that's true, but look at the consequences of their certainty—death, suffering and destruction. The trick is being able to recognize the Devil's seductions."

"But I doubt all the time," John said helplessly.

"Perhaps one day you will find certainty," Beatrice said gently.

"And if I don't?" John asked.

"Then you will do what the rest of humanity does—the best you can."

"How will you have the courage to face the flames to-morrow?" Isabella asked, all laughter vanished and her voice choked with emotion.

"I do not need much courage," Beatrice said, placing a hand on Isabella's shoulder. "My courage is only a small part of the bravery of all those who will walk out there when the sun rises. Nothing need be withstood alone. We are all of a like mind, and in our certainty there is great strength. I shall be fine tomorrow. I am old and tired and I look forward to the release. But what will you do? Where will you go?"

"John and I will go to Aragon to see my homeland and then to Al-Andalus," Isabella answered.

"I am glad that you've found each other and that you're leaving this sad land. When you are tired of searching in this world, think of the next."

Beatrice faced John. "Will you continue to fill the memory cloister?"

"I will," John said. "We plan to go to the great library at Madinat al-Zahra, and I shall fill many empty alcoves there. Perhaps I will teach Isabella."

"That would be good." Beatrice's face became serious in the torchlight. "You have a gift and I am glad you will not waste it. You're the best student I have ever taught and you've learned much very fast. But remember, with a gift comes responsibility. You have things in your mind that are important and very dangerous, not only to you but to many others as well.

"Tomorrow, you will walk out through the crusader camp, free to go where you wish. But be aware that there will be many around you who would kill you without a second thought for simply having the Gospel of Christ in your head. Keep it, and the other books you have and will learn, safe. When you meet someone who you think will understand, pass on the wisdom you have accumulated. That is the responsibility you carry with you."

John nodded, slightly overwhelmed at the seriousness of Beatrice's words. Since Adso had begun to teach him soldiering, he hadn't given much thought to the memory cloister, but Beatrice had been right when she'd first explained the cloister—he couldn't forget anything that was stored within.

"I'll do my best," John said.

"Good." Beatrice's face relaxed. "So, travel, learn, teach and beware the Devil's seductions. Perhaps you are right to believe that God has placed beauty in the world to help us on our journey through the Devil's domain. If so, I wish you luck with your dream of portraying that beauty. I hope you find the book you seek."

"Thank you," John said.

Beatrice placed a hand each on John and Isabella's foreheads. "Be consoled as you journey through this corrupt world by wisdom, each other and the Holy Spirit."

John felt oddly calm at this strange woman's words and touch.

Beatrice lowered her hands and smiled. "And now we must go to the *consolamentum*."

John and Isabella followed Beatrice off the battlements, through Minerve's streets and into the main hall of Count William's castle. The hall showed signs of the siege—everything was covered in a thick layer of dust, the walls were bare stone where the tapestries had been removed, and one corner of the roof was open to the night sky where a rock from a mangonel had crashed through. It was full of Elect standing in their hoodless black robes. A small group of five Credents stood at the front by the huge ceiling-high fireplace. They looked nervous at being the centre of attention.

Beatrice ushered John and Isabella to a bench carved out of the side wall where they would be out of the way but could still watch what was going on. Then she walked to the front. The hall fell silent. Without preliminaries, Beatrice raised her hands and began. Her voice was soft, yet it carried to every corner of the room.

"Christ says in the Gospel according to St. Matthew, 'Wheresoever two or three are gathered together in my name, there I am in the midst of them.'"

John counted those in the hall. In addition to the five Credents, there were one hundred and forty-five Elect. Would they all die willingly in a few hours?

Two of the Credents were women, wives of men killed in the siege; two others, one so seriously wounded that he had to be supported by his companion, were knights; and one was a local baker. All wore simple clothes—tunics, shirts, leggings—and all were barefoot on the cold stone tiles. Four appeared calm, but the baker fidgeted continuously and looked around the hall nervously.

"'Seek ye the proof of Christ who speaketh in me.'"

They are going to become living saints, John thought in wonder. Would I ever have the certainty to do this? To die for my beliefs?

"Lo, I am with you always, even unto the end of the world."

After each recitation the congregation affirmed by nodding. John was fascinated to see this ritual, the holiest of the heretics', but his mind kept wandering to the pyre on the plain. Is that what the baker was thinking? He was a fat man and John could see his chins quivering with fright.

"'If ye forgive not men their trespasses, neither will your Heavenly Father forgive your trespasses.'"

Beatrice beckoned the Credents forward. As they stepped up, she recited the only prayer that the Elect were allowed to say.

Pater noster qui es in caelis,
sanctificetur nomen tuum.

Our Father who art in Heaven,
Hallowed be Thy name.

Her voice was gentle, almost mesmerizing.

Adveniat regnum tuum.
Fiat voluntas tua sicut in caelo et in terra.

Thy kingdom come
Thy will be done on earth as it is in Heaven

John focused on the words. He could hear Isabella softly repeating each line under her breath.

Panem nostrum supersubstancialem da nobis hodie.
Et dimitte nobis debita nostra sicut et nos dimittimus
debitoribus nostris.

Give us this day our supplementary bread,
and remit our debts as we forgive our debtors.

Did the Credents realize what each step took them toward?

Et ne nos inducas in temptationem

And keep us from temptation

Step. The baker hesitated, but moved forward.

sed libera nos a malo.

and free us from evil.

Step. The baker stumbled.

Quoniam tuum est regnum

Thine is the kingdom,

Step. One of the women took the baker's arm and steadied him.

et virtus et gloria

the power and glory

Step. The baker turned and smiled at the woman.

in secula.

for ever and ever.

Amen.

When the Credents reached the front, Beatrice told them, "We deliver you this holy prayer and the power to say it all your life, day or night alone or in company. You must never eat or drink without first reciting it. If you omit to do so, you must do penance."

Together the Credents replied, "I receive it of you and of the Church." The baker's voice was thin and reedy, and his replies came a split second after everyone else's.

One by one the Credents bowed at Beatrice's feet. One by one, she asked them, "My brother, do you desire to give yourself to our faith?" Each answered, "Yes." The baker hesitated a long time before he spoke.

"Then God bless you," Beatrice said to them all, "and bring you to the good end."

At the mention of tomorrow's inevitable conclusion, the baker visibly shivered.

"All is vanity. Hate the solid garment of flesh."

John had a sudden vivid image of the baker's ample flesh, blackening and falling off his bones. Why was he forcing himself to do this? He could just walk out of Minerve tomorrow. In his mind, John knew that the soul was what mattered and that it was immortal, imprisoned for only a brief moment in this world, but he could not understand either the cruelty of the Inquisition or the level of belief that impelled the baker to undergo such self-imposed torture.

"Do you promise that henceforth, you will eat neither meat, nor eggs, nor cheese, nor fat, that you will not lie, that you will not curse, that you will swear no oath, that you will not kill, that you will forsake luxury, that you will forgive whoever wrongs you, and that you will hate this world and all things in it and never abandon your faith for fear of water, fire or any other manner of death?"

"Yes," the Credents answered

"Love not this world. It is corrupt and lustful. The world passeth away and the lust thereof, but he that doeth the will of God abideth forever."

Beatrice stepped forward and placed her hand on each Credent's head in turn. This was the heart of the ceremony, the passing of the Holy Ghost from an Elect to a Credent through the laying on of hands. As she touched each head, Beatrice said, "He that believeth and is baptized shall be saved, but he that believeth not shall be damned. Receive ye the Holy Ghost."

As she reached the baker, John thought the poor man was about to pass out. Oddly, as Beatrice placed her hand on his head, he quieted. His shaking and his nervous glances stopped. As she recited the words, he looked up at her. It was as if his fear was draining out of him, being pulled away by Beatrice's blessing. Suddenly John understood. The baker was no longer alone. Now he was supported by all the others in the room. He was no longer one person, but a tiny part of something much larger. That was what *consolamentum* meant. It was a consoling—a comfort to the spirit trapped and alone in a corrupt body. The baker need never be alone again. John remembered the strange feeling of calm when Beatrice had blessed him and Isabella on the battlements.

"For all the sins I have ever done in thought, word and deed," the Credents recited together, turning to look on the Elect, "I ask pardon of God, of the Church, and of you all."

"By God, and by us, and by the Church, may your sins be forgiven, and we pray God to forgive you them," the Elect answered as one.

"*Adoremus, Patrem, et Filium et Spiritum Sanctum.*"

The Elect surged forward to congratulate the five. Even the baker was smiling from ear to ear.

Beatrice made her way over to John and Isabella.

"I was watching the baker," John said. "He was terrified, but when you laid on your hands, he grew calm and suddenly became happy."

"That is the power of the *consolamentum*. That is what

the Pope and his minions fear and hate so much."

"But tomorrow all will die a hideous death."

"All die," Beatrice said. "Life is but a flicker in eternity. Is one brief death better or worse than another?"

John shrugged. He didn't have an answer.

"Now I must say farewell," Beatrice said. "I would go to meditate in the few hours before dawn."

Isabella stood and embraced Beatrice.

"We *will* meet again," John said desperately, tears welling up in his eyes.

"Certainly," Beatrice responded, "but I doubt in this world. Find your own way. I wish you both luck on your journey."

"Thank you," John managed to croak out.

"Goodbye." Beatrice turned and walked out of the room, her staff clacking hollowly on the stone floor.

"Goodbye," John said after her. "And thank you." For a moment, he was utterly alone and confused. Then he felt Isabella's arm around his shoulder. He looked up at her through his tears. Her dark eyes were clear.

"It is her choice and her way," she said. "We should feel happy."

John supposed so, but even with Isabella's arm around him, he couldn't feel happy about Beatrice's coming death.

"We should go and prepare for the morning," Isabella said. "It's a long walk over the mountains to Aragon."

Rome and Al-Andalus

Minerve

JULY 22, 1210

Peter shivered in the pre-dawn chill. It reminded him of the cold morning years before when he had stood waiting for the ferry to take him, Arnaud Aumery, Pierre of Castelnau and John across the Rhône to Arles. Much had changed since then: John was lost to the heretics, Pierre was murdered and Peter was an ordained monk with considerable power. Aumery, who was standing beside Peter on the low hill outside Minerve looking down on the monks putting the finishing touches on the pyre, had had a part in all of those events.

"This is one of the things I came for," Aumery said. He was rubbing his hands together in front of him. Peter could not tell if it was in gleeful anticipation of the bonfire or because of the cold. "One of my tasks is done. The Holy Crusade is finally established and the first batch of heretics will burn before the sun is risen an hour. It will be a long, hard struggle and I may not live to see the end of it, but it is well begun."

Peter was not looking forward to the mass burning with the same enthusiasm. Secretly, he hoped that the Perfects of Minerve would accept Aumery's offer, convert and live, but he knew that hope was slim. At least John would survive.

"What is the other thing you came for?" Peter asked.

"You know." Aumery turned his head and the first rays of the sun glinted off his peculiar, staring eyes. "The Cathar Treasure, the heretic's secret, the Holy Grail that touched Christ's lips at the Last Supper. The cup that, in the hands of the righteous, will transform our sorry world and usher in the Last Days. The Judgment is coming, Peter. Are you ready?"

"I am," Peter replied, although he was far from convinced that he was. "You're still certain that the Treasure is the Grail?"

"It can be nothing else. It is a well-kept secret, but I shall discover it. These heretical vermin have had a long time to conceal it and it is better hidden than I had anticipated. That is why you must go to Cîteaux."

"Cîteaux?"

"Of course! You have progressed rapidly and performed well, but you have much to learn. Our struggle against the heretics and our quest are long. There is time for you to learn all that is required of a full monk in the Cistercian brotherhood. A year at Cîteaux, my home abbey and monastery, under the guidance of Brother Armand Gauthier. You will be of more use to me once you are fully trained. Perhaps then I shall send you to Rome."

Peter's heart leapt at the mention of Rome. That was where he wanted to go, the seat of Catholic power, and Aumery was talking of sending him there in only a year.

"The crusade will carry on here," Aumery continued. "Oddo and his Falcons and de Montfort will capture more castles and burn more heretics, and I shall make sure it is all done in accordance with God's will. But I do not have enough lifetimes to await the capture of every castle and search every hidden nook and cranny. I underestimated these heretics. To combat them I must find out more about them and their ways.

"The heretics accuse us of burning books, and they are right, but we only burn the books so that they may not fall into the hands of those who cannot understand them and would be misled. Many are preserved in Rome for the eyes of only those who can understand them through true belief. Perhaps you will find clues as to the location of the Grail in those books."

"I should be honoured," Peter said.

Aumery grunted an acknowledgement and returned his gaze to the pyre.

"When do I leave?" Peter asked.

"Tomorrow," Aumery said. "I shall prepare a letter for you to take to brother Gauthier. But now"—he turned and looked down the other side of the hill where knights were congregating beneath the unfurled banners of the crusade—"we must go and see to the fire."

Despite the sun only just having risen over the eastern hills, most of Minerve's population was awake to see the victors enter the town. They lined the battlements or leaned from windows and watched in silence as Arnaud Aumery and Bishop Foulques led the way through the narrow streets.

They were followed by a group of priests and lay brothers carrying a large wooden cross and lustily singing the *Te Deum*. Behind them, below their colourful battle standards, came Simon de Montfort and the lords of the crusade dressed in their war finery.

John, in his travelling cloak and with his satchel slung over his shoulder, watched despondently as the group crossed the main square and entered the church of St. Etienne. The Elect, including the baker and his four companions, were already there, standing silently in the nave. John pushed through the sullen crowd into the church, where he stood at the back. Aumery and de Montfort stood side by side in front of the altar. John noticed Peter with the other monks off to one side.

"God is merciful," Aumery said in his high-pitched voice. "I come with the authority of His Holiness, Pope Innocent III, to offer you all salvation. Even though you have transgressed these many years past and sunk deep into the ways of Satan, the Church will still welcome you back with open arms if you only renounce your errors. All you need do is convert to the Holy Catholic faith, the one true faith, and you will be blessed on the Day of Judgment. Otherwise, the pyre is ready beyond your walls."

Several Perfects shouted out replies: "Why do you preach your filth to us?" "We want nothing of your corrupt Roman faith." "We renounce your evil ways." "You labour in Satan's name in vain." "Neither death nor life can separate us from the beliefs we hold."

Beatrice stepped forward and the crowd fell silent. "You know so little," she said, almost sadly. "You have fallen so far from the Word of God and corrupted so much with your arrogance and debauchery that you have condemned count-less thousands to eternal damnation.

"You offer us conversion to the Devil's work or the mo-mentary pain of the flames. I offer you a chance to save your eternal souls from the torments of this degenerate and depraved world. Renounce the sins of this world and join us as Good Christians."

"How dare you," Bishop Foulques shouted, spraying spit-tle over the nearest listeners. "You are nothing but filthy swine who pervert the natural order by denying the divinity of Christ and undertaking all manner of disgusting and de-viant behaviour. You deserve to rot in hell in eternal torment."

"And eternal torment they shall undoubtedly have," Aumery added, cutting off Foulques's tirade. "But their fate is no longer in our hands. We have offered them the infinite mercy of the Mother Church and they have spurned it. It is for the secular authorities to determine their fate."

Aumery glanced at de Montfort, who stepped forward. "You will not admit the error of your ways and return to the fold of the Church?"

"Had we committed an error," Beatrice said, "we would gladly admit it, but we have not. We renounce your Pope, your Church and all its works."

"Then I have no choice. I condemn you in the name of the Holy Crusade to suffer death by burning. May the fire cleanse your souls."

An almost imperceptible shudder passed through the crowd, but no one said a word. In silence, every member of the Elect followed de Montfort out of the church and down the hill to the gates. John followed behind, as did many of the townsfolk. Several wept silently.

"Are you a heretic now?"

John looked to his right to see Peter in his priest's habit walking beside him. His eyes met Peter's for a brief moment, but he looked away before answering.

"If hating those who would kill so many good and gentle people means I am a heretic, then yes I am."

"That is not what I meant. Do you hold with their beliefs and worship the Devil as they do?"

Anger swept over John. "What do you know of the Devil or these people's beliefs? All you do is follow that rat Aumery and wallow in his hatred. Do you really think God judges people simply by what prayer they mouth or which arrogant bishop they fawn over? Does being good and doing good count for nothing if you bend your knee to the wrong idol? I want no part of that God."

"I could have you thrown on the pyre with your friends for saying that," Peter said quietly.

"Go ahead. That's all your precious crusade can do, destroy what it cannot understand."

The pair walked in silence for a while. Eventually, Peter said, "How have you grown so far from what we were both taught as children by the sisters?"

"Because I have kept my mind open. I am grateful to the sisters for what they taught me, but it was not everything. The world is a much larger place than even your Church. I intend to discover what I can of it."

"Even if that search leads to heresy and the condemnation of your soul?"

"If, as the Good Christians believe, the Devil created the material world, then what I do in it makes no difference. If, as you believe, God created the world and all the infinite wonder in it, how can He condemn me for wanting to discover the beauty of His work? He gave us free will. How can He then condemn us for using it?"

As he passed through the gate, John unbuckled his sword and threw it on the pile of weapons being collected by a group of Falcons; no one was allowed to leave the city with a weapon. The crowd walked over the causeway toward the pile of wood and straw. The route was lined with armed men, and others, several holding lighted torches, surrounded the pyre.

"Does that not trouble your soul?" John asked, pointing to the pyre.

"The land must be cleansed," Peter said. "That is the only way we can reach the kingdom of God."

"Even if it means climbing over mountains of charred bodies?"

Peter didn't answer.

"You have become trapped in a system that allows no thought," John said. "You are doing well and have risen fast. If that is what you want, you will continue to prosper and I wish you well, but it is not for me."

"What will you do?"

"I am going to Al-Andalus."

"The land of the Moorish heathen?"

"A different land where there is much to learn." John ignored the sneer in Peter's voice. "And you?"

"I am going to Cîteaux, to gather true learning, and then to Rome," Peter said proudly.

"So we are both leaving our homeland in opposite directions," John said sadly. "These are indeed strange times. We are not the children we were. This war has changed us, and I suspect it will change much more before it is done. I wish you well."

"And I you," Peter replied. "I shall pray that you come to see the true light."

"Hello, Peter."

The pair turned to see Isabella and Adso standing nearby, both dressed in travelling cloaks. Isabella had cut her black hair short for the journey and carried Beatrice's knotted staff. In different circumstances, the look of horrified recognition that crossed Peter's face would have been comical.

"Your visions of death are coming true," she added coldly, glancing at the pyre.

"Why are you here?" Peter asked, struggling to keep the emotion from his voice.

"I came to seek out John," Isabella replied.

"John?" Peter looked back and forth between his two childhood friends.

"Yes," Isabella said. There was not the slightest trace of a smile on her lips. "He seeks answers through enquiry and learning, not through the thoughtless repetition of a corrupt belief."

Isabella's words hit Peter like hammer blows. Tears ran down his cheeks and he appeared to shrink into himself. "I—" he began, but he choked on the next word and, turning away, stumbled roughly through the crowd.

"That was cruel," John said. "He was very fond of you once."

"No," Isabella said, moving to John's side. "What I said was true. That"—she pointed at the pyre and the line of black-clad Perfects walking silently toward it—"that is cruel. Peter cries for me and an impossible dream he had years ago. He should be weeping for what is happening this day."

"There'll be no shortage of weeping today," Adso said, moving up beside his friends, "and in many days to come."

"We cannot persuade you to come with us?" Isabella asked.

Adso shook his head. "This is my land these people are raping and my friends they are burning. I must fight them as best I can."

"They will not give up and go home as you once believed," John said.

"I must fight nonetheless. You and Isabella go to the land of the Moors and find your learning. Come back with knowledge, although I would prefer you came back with an army."

"Be careful," John said.

"Always," Adso said, "and you watch out, too. It's a long way you go. But I must leave now—I 'ave no wish to see this fire."

The three embraced for the last time before Adso slipped away through the crowd.

John looked toward the pyre. It was in the form of a large raised square, more than twenty feet on each side and higher than a man. Crude stairs had been built on one side and, already, Perfects were clambering up. The soldiers stood by threateningly, but they were not required. The Perfects went voluntarily to their fate.

Beatrice stood at the foot of the steps, helping those who stumbled. She offered a hand to the baker but he shrugged it off with a smile.

John counted. There were one hundred and fifty men and women on the pyre. Many were holding hands both for comfort and to help keep balanced on the uneven bed of logs and sticks. A few embraced.

Beatrice was the last to ascend. At the top, she turned and looked over the crowd. John thought for a moment she was going to address the assembled townsfolk and soldiers, but she said nothing. At last, her eyes came to rest on John and Isabella. She smiled.

Tears flooded John's eyes, blurring the scene, but he could still see the shapes of soldiers stepping forward and thrusting their torches into the pile. Sharp hearts of bright flame caught eagerly at the dry sticks and straw and a low moan rose from the crowd.

Aumery was chanting something but John ignored him. He rubbed his eyes and watched as the flames grew and co-alesced. Smoke rose and thickened, swirling across the view of the Perfects standing still and silent. Beatrice was looking at John and smiling. Slowly she raised her hand and waved. John returned the gesture as a cloud of smoke obscured her.

Bowing his head, John took Isabella's arm and pushed through the crowd. The pair found the road and turned south without looking back. Behind them, the crackling of the flames drowned out Aumery's voice.